CONFESSIONS OF A SUICIDAL POLICEWOMAN

THOMAS FITZSIMMONS

Although inspired by real life characters and actual events, Confessions of a Suicidal Policewoman is a work of fiction. Names, characters, places, and incidents are either the products of the author's imagination or are used fictitiously. Any resemblance to actual persons, living or dead, events, or locales are entirely coincidental.

Confessions of a Suicidal Policewoman

Copyright © 2011 Thomas Fitzsimmons

All rights reserved

ISBN-10 0978976258

ISBN-13 9780978976255

Manufactured in the United States of America

www.thomasfitzsimmons.com

ALSO BY
THOMAS FITZSIMMONS

Fiction

Confessions of a Catholic Cop

Confessions of a Celebrity Bodyguard

For Wendy,
again-

PROLOGUE

His eyes were gray, lifeless, like bullet tips. And they were trained on a yellow cab he'd followed from a Meatpacking District nightclub.

A slick, well-dressed hombre who'd been flashing cash, buying drinks, and handing out hits of coke to every big-titted woman in sight, was a passenger in that cab. And predicate felon, Paco—*El Loco*—Castalia planned to rob him.

The cab moved along snowy 109th Street in Spanish Harlem, stopped by a fire hydrant, and the cab's rooftop "available" light popped on; the hombre had arrived at his destination.

Paco steered his beat-up Hyundai to the curb fifty feet behind the cab, placed the car in park, killed the engine. He scanned the area for witnesses. Spotted a dreadlocked teenager—a lookout for one of those deadly Jamaican drug gangs—sheltered from the cold in a tenement doorway; he'd be no problem. Paco looked east, then west. But there was no one else on the pre-dawn streets, no traffic, no movement of any kind.

Paco racked a round into the chamber of an untraceable .45 automatic and stuck it into his waistband. Then he checked that his five-shot, .38 backup gun was fully loaded and easily accessible.

The hombre exited the taxi, stumbled drunkenly over the icy sidewalk, fought to keep his balance.

Paco stepped out of his car, pulled the .45.

Headlights.

Paco turned, saw a police car cruising in his direction.

"*Ala puta!*" Paco bolted back to the Hyundai, dove inside, dropped down low in his seat. His stomach did a three-sixty. Sweat broke through his skin. He thought about what to do with his two weapons: shove them under the seat, toss them out the window? A three-time loser, he could not afford another gun possession arrest.

The police car prowled by.

Whew.

Paco threw open the car door. Rushed out.

The hombre was nowhere in sight.

Paco ran to the corner. Peered into several tenement vestibules. Dashed across the street, his eyes everywhere. Ears cocked for sound. *Nada.* The hombre had vanished.

"*Puta!*" Paco threw his hands up in utter frustration. He kicked a small snowdrift, stomped it until the heel of his sneaker-clad foot hurt. Then he limped despondently back to his car.

Paco stepped into the Hyundai, lit a cigarette, and thought about where he could get his hands on some money—rob the White Castle he'd robbed twice before?—and tried to calm down. He cracked the driver's side window, let the smoke stream out and the winter air in. The interior of his car was suddenly illuminated from the rear by high beam headlights.

Now what?

Paco scrunched down low in his seat, squinted into the Hyundai's side-view mirror.

A battered, nondescript van cruised down the street and double-parked alongside Paco, effectively blocking him in. The van's headlights died and its engine shuddered to a stop.

What the fuck?

Paco was about to honk his horn, tell the *estúpido* driver to move, or else, when the van's four doors flew open and five large men wearing black ski masks and carrying shotguns alighted.

Paco ducked.

One of the masked men ran around to the back of a tenement. The others charged up the stoop and accosted the dreadlocked Jamaican drug lookout. They shoved him through the vestibule door and disappeared into the building.

Boom! A shotgun blast punctured the winter morning.

Up and down the block, apartment lights flicked on. Curtains parted. People looked down onto the street. But Paco knew that no one would call the police, or acknowledge that they'd seen or heard anything. In *el barrio,* staying healthy, remaining in the United States, meant minding your own business.

Paco kept his eyes on the tenement.

The front doors crashed open and the masked gang shoved and kicked six bloodied and battered dreadlocked men down the stoop onto the street. Paco saw that one of the masked men was hurt, having difficulty walking. He was bent over, holding his arm in obvious pain.

"You're outta here, evicted," the fattest of the masked men told the battered Jamaicans. "You ever come back, and I'll fucking kill you."

One of the Jamaicans said something Paco did not understand. The fat masked man cracked the guy on the bridge of his nose with the butt of his shotgun. He crumbled, blood gushing, to the slushy sidewalk.

"Now, get 'im the fuck outta here," the fat masked man said. The cowering men did as they were told. They picked up their companion and, with great difficulty, carted him away.

"His arm's broke." A skinny masked man crossed in front of Paco's Hyundai, opened the van's side door, and helped the injured man in. Skinny pulled off his mask—he had surfer-blond hair and blue eyes. "Whaddaya wanna do?"

A black and a Hispanic unmasked and looked at the fat guy.

"We'll take him to the hospital." The fat guy yanked off his own hood, turned in Paco's direction—Paco gaped, peered over the steering wheel in disbelief. He couldn't believe his eyes.

"Hey." The guy who'd gone around to the back of the building, now unmasked, was standing alongside the Hyundai. "We got a witness." He gestured at Paco.

"Great," the Hispanic said, glaring into the Hyundai. "Just fuckin' great. Now what?"

"The mook's seen our faces," the black said.

"Yeah," the fat guy said. "He has." The fat guy finger-combed a thick gray mustache, stepped over to the Hyundai, and used the butt of the shotgun to shatter the passenger side window. He leaned in and saw a .45 pointing at his face. He looked at the weapon, then the man holding it, and a look of recognition spread across his craggy face. "Hello, Paco."

"*Buenos días*, Officer Tesser." Paco's voice was steady, his gun hand unwavering. Until he noticed the blond guy with the shotgun pressed against the Hyundai driver's side window.

"Gimme the gun," Tesser reached into the car with a gloved hand. "C'mon, hand it over."

"*Lo siento*," Paco struggled with his face. "*No problemo*, Officer Tesser." He handed over the .45.

"You can call me Mark." Tesser's twisted smile revealed pointy, rodent small teeth. "I retired from the force."

"*Ay carumba*," Paco said.

"Outta the car," the blond guy said. "Now."

Paco felt the blood drain from his face. His breathing became labored. He looked at the five men's faces. If they were not cops, what were they planning to do? "Officer Tesser, I see nothing," Paco said convincingly. "Nothing. I swear." He used his right hand to make the sign of the cross. "I swear on the Virgin Mary."

"Sorry, Paco," Tesser said.

"Sorry?" Paco said. "Sorry for what?" But Paco knew what. If ever apprehended by the police, he could and would inform on Tesser and his gang, tell the DA what he had witnessed, use the information as leverage, make a deal for a reduced sentence.

And Tesser knew it.

"Out!" The blond guy repeated.

Paco shook his head, his hands tight on the steering wheel.

The blond guy yanked open the Hyundai door, made a grab for Paco.

"*Policía! Policía!*" a woman was leaning out of her apartment window, screaming into her cell phone.

The armed men looked toward the second floor, momentarily distracted. Paco slammed the car door into the blond guy. Dove out onto the slushy, potholed blacktop. He rolled under the van to the other side. Scampered to his feet. Bolted to the opposite side of the street. Ducked behind a parked car.

Bam!

A shotgun blast shattered the parked car's windows. The next one took out two tires. Paco pulled his backup gun, returned fire. Squeezed off three quick shots. Tesser's men scrambled for cover.

"Hold your fire," Tesser yelled to his men. "Hold it." The shooting stopped. "Give it up, Paco," Tesser said.

"Chupa mis huevos!" Paco said.

A Tesser man laughed. "I think he just told us to suck his balls."

"Oh, yeah?" Tesser said. "Spread out."

Paco saw that the gang was on the move. They'd catch him in a crossfire if he stayed where he was.

Paco jumped up. Squeezed off the last two rounds. Made a run for it. Beat feet toward Second Avenue, feet pounding, heart pumping, hoping for the first time in his criminal career to run into a patrolling police car. But there were no cops in sight; he had to get off the street.

Paco leapt over a pile of ravaged garbage bags. Darted up a

stoop. Kicked a tenement vestibule door open. Took five flights of steps two at a time.

He burst onto the roof. Stopped. Fought to catch his breath. Listened; the gunmen were not following.

He heard police sirens.

Finally!

Paco walked to the street-side of the roof and, using the ledge for cover, peered down. The nondescript van sped off and made a squealing left on Second Avenue. A moment later three police cars roared down the street and skidded to a stop. The cops alighted, guns drawn. They checked the area, searched inside a dozen tenement vestibules. But the complainant, the woman who'd screamed from the window and called 911, was nowhere to be seen. There was no van. No men with guns.

The cops got back into their cars and drove away.

Paco leaned against the ledge, his legs so adrenaline-drained he could barely stand. He took a moment to light a cigarette— his lungs burned—one eye on the street just in case Tesser circled back. After a few minutes, he flicked the butt off the roof. Watched as it sailed, sparks flying, to the ground.

Paco moved cautiously but quickly across the dark roof, side-stepping all manner of big city debris—piles of bricks, old tires, discarded furniture. He leapt across a perilous four-foot-wide courtyard chasm onto the next roof that fronted East 108th Street. He opened the rickety roof door and, even though the gunmen had gone, took a moment to listen before he descended.

Silence.

Paco made his way down the stairs, thinking hard about whether he should take a chance and go back to his car, or make his way to the subway.

Paco stopped in the building vestibule, opened the front door, and looked out onto the street; first left, then right. There was no movement on the block, only the sound of a car alarm somewhere in the distance.

Paco hit the street, stuffed his hands in his pockets, tucked his head into the collar of his coat, and headed away from his car, toward the subway.

The ex-cop Mark Tesser stepped from the shadows, pointing Paco's own .45 at him.

"Sorry, Paco," Tesser said and pulled the trigger.

CHAPTER 1

"THAT WAS A dumb movie," Destiny Jones said as we walked out of the Loews Orpheum Theater at 86th Street and Third Avenue into a light, wet snow.

The sidewalk was clogged with hunkered-down, determined New Yorkers. Traffic was at a standstill. Several frustrated drivers had their vehicle windows rolled down and were cursing one another. One rage-faced taxi driver looked ready to commit homicide.

Off to our right I spotted two loitering gangsta types probing the movie theater crowd, picking through faces—a team of predators searching for a victim?

"What was dumb about it?" I said. "I mean, the acting was good." I considered telling Destiny to go ahead without me, follow the gangstas, tail them until they made their move, pulled guns, and tried to rob someone—all I needed was one good felony collar to rescue me from the Building Maintenance Division and propel me back to the streets. "And I related to the story."

"The setup was dumb." Destiny shrugged into her faux-fur coat, positioned her wool scarf high on her long, sleek neck, and flipped her fur-lined hood atop her elegantly cornrowed head. "You get fired in today's corporate world—". She ducked to avoid a passing eye-poking umbrella. "They don't let you 'finish out the week.' They have security escort you out of the building."

The gangstas moved down the street, turned into the Papaya King hotdog stand; so much for me making a felony arrest. "And you know this how?" I buttoned my dark blue overcoat, pulled on kidskin gloves, braced my six-foot one-inch, two hundred pound frame against the harsh, wet wind.

"Oh, I've been fired before," Destiny said.

Screeching brakes.

The sound of crunching metal.

The rage-faced taxi driver sprang from his vehicle and shook his fist at a driver who had just rear-ended him. That's when I spotted a man in a hooded black ski parka eyeballing me. The guy saw that I was looking back and averted his gaze—a little too quickly. Something about him was familiar.

I popped open my oversized umbrella, offered Destiny my arm. "A cocktail, me lady?"

"Yes, kind sir."

A sudden wind gust nearly turned my umbrella inside out. I held on with both hands as we negotiated our way across 87th Street, stopped for a red light at 88th. I turned and looked back toward Papaya King; the guy in the black ski parka, face now obscured by his hood, was walking slowly in our direction.

The light changed. We sloshed cautiously across Third Avenue. Took baby steps as we made our way down a slushy 88th Street hill, past rows of shambling tenements that commanded stratospheric rents, heading to Second Avenue.

"Let me get this straight," I said. "Are you telling me you've been fired in the past, and escorted from your place of employment by security?"

Destiny turned her high-voltage smile at me. "Sho 'nuff."

We squeezed by a group of middle-aged women heading in

the opposite direction. They were having a tough time picking their way up the hill.

"More than once?"

Destiny used her gloved fingers to count, lost count, shuffled her fingers, and counted again. "Once when I was teaching grammar school. Three times in retail sales. Twice when I was an executive assistant."

I glanced behind us. Spotted the guy in the hooded black ski parka, three quarters of a block back, close to the building line in the tenement shadows. *What was this about?*

I felt for my off-duty .38. "That must have been embarrassing," I said distractedly, my mind on Ski Parka. "Having security escort you out."

"Not in the least," Destiny said. We turned north on Second Avenue. "But I was really pissed off," she added. "Gave 'em a hard time whenever I was fired. Screwed with the security staff, took my time packing my personal belongings, really broke balls, caused major scenes."

"Why not go quietly?"

"Guess you could say—". She gave me a mock-hard nudge. "I've got problems with authority."

"Ah." I smiled warmly at my former partner. "Which is why you became a New York City cop."

"Precisely."

We paused just outside Elaine's Restaurant to allow several departing customers to exit and claim the sleek, chauffeur-driven limos that were idling curbside.

Ski Parka came rushing down 88th Street, skidded to a stop at the corner, glanced furtively in our direction, and then crossed over to the opposite side of Second Avenue.

"We're being followed," I said, annoyed.

"Duh?" Destiny said. "I spotted him at the theater."

"Recognize him?"

"Not with that hood."

A familiar, toothless panhandler lurched over. "Get that door for you?" He held the restaurant's outer door open. "Have a nice evening."

"Thank you." I handed the bum the usual $5 and squired Destiny through the double doors.

The bar area was occupied by mostly neighborhood regulars that evening. I shook a few hands and absorbed Elaine's classic salon atmosphere: the dark wood, the framed book jacket covers on the walls, the bentwood chairs, and checkered tablecloths. Sinatra played on the restaurant's sound system.

I glanced at the much sought-after tables, noticed two undercover narcotics cops hunched over a table in back with a couple of organized crime types; the undercovers would ignore me. I would ignore them. There was Kirk Douglas at a table speaking to Kathleen Turner. A few TV stars and network news anchors were scattered around the room. That's not to mention the usual assortment of brash bridge-and-tunnel types, celebrity gawkers, and the ever-present hangers-on and anxious wannabes.

"Beckett." Vernon, Elaine's bartender, waved to me. He pointed at a couple of businessmen who were paying their bill. The suits slipped off their bar stools, gathered up their coats, squeezed past Destiny and me. We hurried to claim our "reserved" seats at the cramped mahogany bar.

I helped Destiny off with her coat, hung it on a brass hook atop several sodden furs.

"Hey, gorgeous." Vernon stopped in front of Destiny, reached across the bar for her hand and kissed it. "How's the honkie treating you?"

"Like a plantation slave." Destiny squinted at me. "Nothing I can't handle."

"Of that," Vernon said, "I'm certain."

Vernon was a Catholic high school classmate of mine, and the only reason I frequented the lovingly seedy little Second Avenue saloon most Saturday nights.

"Gimme a beer," I said.

"Yassuh, masser." Vernon dug deep into the ice bin and handed me a frosty Coors Light, no glass. "What'll it be for you, my sistah?"

"Long as the masser's buying," Destiny said, "I'll have a glass of that divine sauvignon blanc."

"I'm buying your wine?" I said for management's ears. Fact was Vernon was well aware of just how low a police officer's salary was. And so he gave us special treatment, didn't charge for most of our drinks.

"Count your blessings, white boy," Destiny said. "I'm only having one."

"Don't tell me," I said. "Another headache?"

"No. My hubby's making dinner."

Vernon served her wine. "Frozen pizza, again?"

Destiny shot Vernon a look that could scorch blue steel. "How'd you like five fingers shoved up your fucking nose?"

"Michael," a voice off to my right said.

I saw a startlingly obese woman on her way out the door. "Hi, Julie." Julie Gunder was a five-night-a-week Elaine's regular, a former Naval Intelligence officer who had once hired me as a private investigator—although she never paid me.

"You get my message?" Gunder positioned a wool scarf around her turkey neck, buttoned her tent-sized coat, pulled on large mink mittens.

"Got it."

"We all set?" Gunder said.

I gave her the thumbs up sign. "I'll see you tomorrow afternoon. Plaza Hotel."

"Four P.M.," Gunder said as she waddled off.

"Hey," Destiny said. "Isn't that the one who owes you the money?"

"Yeah." I watched Gunder walk out. Spotted the guy in the hooded black ski parka loitering by the restaurant door. He stepped aside, allowing Gunder to exit.

He strode into the bar.

CHAPTER 2

"I SEE HIM," Destiny said. She adjusted the .22 Beretta that was hidden beneath her waistband. "Maybe he's not following us," she said. "He could've been coming here for dinner."

"Since when did you start believing in coincidence?" I felt Ski Parka standing behind me and braced myself.

"Michael Beckett," Ski Parka said.

I turned on my stool. "I know you?"

"We worked together, up in the 41 Precinct," Ski Parka said. "I was about fifty-pounds thinner then." He patted his ample belly. "Retirement's been good."

It took me a long moment to recognize the former cop.

"Mark Tesser?" I said.

"That's me."

Once a hard body, Tesser now looked like one of those cartoon characters who swallows an air hose and is blown up to four times his size. His North Face ski parka was a size too small. His unruly hair and thick mustache were now completely gray.

"How's it going?" I shook his calloused hand.

"Going good."

I said, "You remember Destiny."

"I sure do." Tesser shook her hand. "Thought that was you two coming out of the theater," he said. "You look like a couple of celebrities."

"So you followed us?" Destiny said.

"Well, yeah."

"Dumb-ass thing to do." Destiny squinted at Tesser.

"Uh hum—buy you a drink, Tesser?" I said.

"Twist my arm," Tesser said.

"You'll excuse me." Destiny popped off her stool and threaded through the crowd toward the ladies' room.

"What'll it be?" I said.

Tesser ordered a vodka, rocks. I worked on my beer.

"Look, I never got the chance to tell you at the time," Tesser said and sat on Destiny's stool, "but I was real sorry to hear about D'Amato." He was referring to my former partner and friend who'd committed suicide—a long story. "Terrible thing, that."

"Thanks," I said.

Tesser's vodka came. He lifted his glass, toasted. "To Police Officer Vinnie D'Amato; rest in peace." He threw back his drink.

"D'Amato." I lifted my bottle, took a sip.

Elaine's front door opened and a blast of cold air preceded a group of chattering, aging man-eaters. They paused to check out the pickings at the bar. Apparently didn't see anything they liked and moved on to a table.

"So, how're things?" Tesser said. "You still moonlighting as an actor?"

"No," I said. "Doing PI work. I ran an investigation a few months ago. Got stiffed for the fee. I do bodyguard work whenever I can get it. Why? You got something going?"

"I just might." Tesser lowered his voice. "How'd you like to make five hundred for an hour's work?"

"Yeah, right," I said. "Who do I have to shoot?"

Tesser glanced around to see that no one was close enough to overhear. "I'm a rocker."

As an Irish cop raised in a family of cops, I'd known about rockers since I was a boy—a secret society of cops and ex-cops who protect businesses and individuals from organized crime shake-downs, bar owners from local gangs, even evict drug dealers from residential buildings—for a price. Although many active duty cops deride rockers as common criminals, others feel that they perform a necessary service. "After all," my police lieutenant father once told me, "rockers only deal with scum the law can't touch, and," he winked, "they never hurt anyone who doesn't deserve to be hurt."

Tesser said he'd been working for a local landlord who had purchased distressed, foreclosed buildings up in Spanish Har-lem. The buildings were now infested with squatters. If the land-lord could manage to quickly evict those illegal tenants—the civil courts took too long—then rehabilitate the buildings, he could sell them for a handsome profit. Tesser said that's where he came in. It was his job to put together a team to go into the apartments and "rock" the squatters out. "One of my men broke his arm," Tesser said. "I need a replacement."

I told Tesser I had no problem with rocking thugs and crimi-nals. But I wasn't about to forcibly evict some down-and-out fam-ily from a cold-water dive that served as home. "Thanks for the offer." I drained my bottle. "Think I'll pass."

"No, you won't." Tesser said. "Not a Boy Scout like you."

I gave Tesser a sideways glance. I didn't know if it was the vodka talking, but I didn't like his tone. "You got something to say?"

"Gotta admit." Tesser threw back his next drink. "I wasn't sur-prised when Internal Affairs found heroin in your car."

"Really." All at once I was reminded that Tesser was never one of my favorite people. We'd been 41 Precinct co-workers but never actual friends. I mean, I'd never had a problem with him and Tes-ser had a reputation as a good cop. But he'd had his own crowd: a small group of slick, shifty elitists who, I now remembered, kept to themselves.

"Why's that?" I eye-strafed the former cop.

"Relax," Tesser said. "I'm on your side. Everyone knows you were framed. There's no way you'd filch drugs. That was your problem. You weren't a team player." Tesser gestured to Vernon. "Two more." He turned back to me. "Explain it to me: You arrest one of the biggest drug dealers in the city. The dealer offers you fifty-thousand *cash* to let him go. And what do you do? You charge him with attempted bribery on top of everything else—what is that? You should have taken the money. I mean, who would've known?"

"I would."

"See? That's the difference between you and me, Beckett. You always took policing personal, like you were better than the rest of us. Like you were some sort of white fucking knight."

Frankly, I was surprised. I didn't know that Tesser, or anyone else, felt that way about me.

Tesser rested his elbows on the bar. "Look, everyone knows about your baby sister, that she died from a drug overdose."

I bristled. "Leave my sister out of this."

"Fine. Point is, you made a lot of enemies when you tore up the city looking for her supplier."

"Tough shit."

"That's exactly the attitude that got you suspended, taken off the street—where you working now, huh? Headquarters, right? Building Maintenance? You're a fucking 'broom' for Christ's sake. What kind of job is that for an active street cop?"

"I did my job, Tesser."

"Yeah. And got fucked for it."

Vernon served the drinks.

"In the end, the drug dealers won." Tesser picked up his drink and toasted. "You and your integrity lost."

I placed my right hand on the bar, thinking I just might crack

Tesser on the mouth. "You seem to know an awful lot about me, for a retired guy."

"Hey, I still go to the PBA dinner dance every year. 10-13 Club meetings. People talk."

"Yeah. Well, this talk is over. Nice seeing you again, Tesser. You know the way out."

"Aw, c'mon. Don't be like that."

I turned my back.

"All right, look, I'm sorry. I get carried away sometimes. I'm an asshole. I'm sorry. Really."

"Apology accepted," I said. "See you around."

But Tesser didn't walk away. He just stood there.

"Look. I need you, man," Tesser finally said. "These squatters I'm gonna rock, they're not some poor, down and out immigrant family. They're a Mexican drug gang, part of the Sinaloa cartel. They scared off the building superintendent, beat the living hell out of the landlord. Threatened his kids—a two- and a five-year-old—if he went to the police. Question is, you gonna let them get away with it, or you gonna help me evict them?"

Drug dealers. Tesser was baiting me.

I took a thoughtful swallow of beer; I didn't care for Tesser's outspoken opinions, but $500 was a lot of money to me right then. "When?"

"Tomorrow morning, five A.M."

I considered the offer. I didn't have to be in purgatory until 1600 hours. The drug gang was located in Spanish Harlem. My dead sister Shannon had bought her drugs in Spanish Harlem.

"Well?" Tesser said.

"I don't know."

"C'mon, Beckett," Tesser said with a sudden, warm backslapping familiarity. "These gangbangers are real punks. We'll take 'em by surprise. The eviction will be a piece of cake."

I could see Destiny coming back from the ladies room. "Okay," I said. "Count me in. Don't say anything to Destiny."

"I won't." Tesser pulled a business card from his ski parka pocket and handed it over. "Call me later for the details." Tesser stepped back allowing Destiny to reclaim her stool.

"Well, I've got to run," Tesser said. "Got places to go, people to see, and things to do."

"Come again." Destiny leaned back and crossed her legs. "When you can't stay as long."

"Good one," Tesser laughed. "Beauty *and* a sense of humor."

"A laugh a minute," Destiny said. "That's me."

CHAPTER 3

"HE'S AN ASSHOLE." Destiny watched Tesser leave. "Ya think?"

Destiny settled onto her seat, glanced around and fielded the ever-present smiles and silent come-ons from every man, and some women, within sight. A truly distracting beauty, Destiny was dressed elegantly as always in a cashmere sweater, slacks, and heeled boot. Her dark cornrowed hair was pulled away from her mocha face. Her makeup was salon perfect—not that she needed makeup, or the stylish clothes. Destiny would look great wearing rags.

Vernon topped off Destiny's wine. Gave me another beer.

"How's Solana?" Vernon said, referring to my girlfriend Solana Ortiz, a writer on the TV show *Law & Order*.

I looked into my fresh beer for a beat. Good a friend as Vernon could be, I didn't care for the fact he was a loose-lipped gossip. "She's working."

"Again? She's always working."

A waiter called a drink order to Vernon who quick-stepped to the service area at the far end of the bar.

"Dickhead," I said, eyes on Vernon.

"Articulate," Destiny said.

I took my time, considering whether to trust my wholly unsympathetic ex-partner with my relationship troubles. I wasn't in the mood to be worked over. I started cautiously: "I've been thinking."

"How refreshing."

"Solana and I are having issues."

"A relationship with issues. How positively extraordinary." Destiny sipped her wine.

"Solana's depressed all the time."

"Living with you would depress me too."

"I'm serious."

"So am I."

"Everything was great until she moved in with me," I said. "We had great fun, laughed a lot. Now she spends most of her time at work. When she's home she mopes around."

"You ask her what's wrong?"

I nodded. "She says I wouldn't understand."

"She's probably right."

"We don't communicate anymore. We never make love. My gut tells me she's involved with someone else."

Destiny scowled at the idea. "You should be so lucky."

"You hate her," I said.

"She hates me."

"She... respects you."

"Great," Destiny smirked. "I'll die a happy woman."

"Forget it," I sulked. "Sorry I troubled you with my problems."

"OK. I apologize," Destiny said. "You wanna discuss your relationship? Fine. First you gotta admit that you attract neurotics."

"Like who, for instance?"

"Solana, for instance. And what about the Rogues Gallery of Looney Tunes you dated before her. Let's see: first there was the legal assistant who wouldn't have sex with you unless you held a loaded gun to her head."

"Here we go—".

"And then there was the makeup artist. She was so unstable that you hid all your steak knives whenever she came to your apartment. And let's not forget my all-time, personal favorite, the one who hustled you for thousands, then stole your credit cards and maxed them out: Enia the Romanian Slut."

Vernon stopped in front of us. "She's been in."

I looked at him. "Who?"

"Enia," Vernon said.

"I thought she hightailed it back to Romania," Destiny said.

"She did," I said.

"Well, she's back," Vernon said. "Been in with her husband."

"Husband?" I said, jarred.

"Well. Well," Destiny said. "Of all the gin joints, in all the towns, in all the world…."

I looked off into space, found myself trying to conjure up an image of my former lover's husband. I couldn't.

"What's he like?" I said, doing my best to hide the embarrassing fact that I really wanted to know.

Vernon shrugged. "Seems like a nice enough guy. A landlord. Owns a small hotel a few blocks from here, up on 94th Street. The German Hotel, I think it's called."

"Great," Destiny said. "You can press charges for the stolen credit cards. Maybe even get the money she scammed back."

"Give it a rest, Destiny," I said. "Can't you?"

Destiny almost spit up her wine. "No. Don't tell me." She put her glass down with a thud. "You still have feelings for that grifter, after all she's done to you?"

"Don't be ridiculous."

"So you'll press charges?"

"Look," I said. "I can't *prove* she stole the credit cards."

"What about the money she scammed?"

"She can keep it." I drank some beer. "Long as she owes me that money, she'll stay away. It's the price of getting rid of her."

Raised voices.

I looked to my right, located the source of the noisy exchange: a bickering middle-aged couple sitting at a four-top, against a brick wall beneath the montage of hardcover book jackets. I used friendly force to shift an acquaintance from my line of sight and focused on the couple—a frumpy, albeit attractive, older woman and a fat jerk sporting a ridiculous-looking red road-kill toupee and cheap suit. From their facial expressions, I could tell that Road-kill was berating the woman. His hands and mouth were working overtime.

"That looks like trouble," Destiny said.

"Yeah," I said.

"He's gonna hit her," Destiny said.

"We're off duty." I turned back to the bar, nursed my beer.

"Right," Destiny said. "Like you're gonna sit there and let some creep slug a woman."

"Slut!" the guy with the red road-kill toupee said, his voice now loud enough to be heard above Sinatra's The Lady is a Tramp. "You're a goddamned whore."

"Please," the woman said, mortified. "Let's go."

"I'm not going anywhere," Road-kill said. He tore his wide polyester tie loose and clawed at his collar.

A waiter intervened. "I'll have to ask you to lower your voices." He placed the couple's check on their table and added crisply. "I'll collect that when you're ready."

"I'm sorry," the woman said. "We're leaving."

"Fuck we are." Road-kill flung a scorched look at those sitting closest to him. "We're not going anywhere." He picked up his vodka on the rocks.

The woman snatched the drink from Road-kill's hand.

And Road-kill slapped her, hard, across the face.

There was an audible gasp and the room fell silent.

"Told you so," Destiny whispered.

But I was already off my stool. I cleaved though the bar crowd and pulled up a chair beside Road-kill.

"Fuck you want?" he said to me.

I smiled, then used my index finger and thumb to grab Road-kill's ear and slam his face hard on the table—plates and glassware rattled—applying more than enough painful pressure to hold him there, immobilizing him.

"Like to hit women?" I whispered harshly.

"Ohmygod," the woman said.

"Easy, Beckett," Vernon said from across the bar. "We don't want any trouble in here."

I looked up. Everyone in Elaine's was watching me.

"There's no trouble." I flashed my warmest smile and applied more pressure to Road-kill's ear. "You're not gonna cause any trouble, right?"

"No," Road-kill yawped. "No problems."

"Don't hurt him," the woman said.

It always killed me how quickly battered women came to their tormentor's defense. "This your husband?" I said.

The woman nodded.

"You all right?" I said.

"I'm fine." Angry red finger marks striped the side of her face. The shock of being struck was wearing off, and tears were beginning to well.

"You want to press charges?"

"No. He didn't mean it." She addressed those around her. "He's never hit me before." The purple remains of a poorly disguised black eye said otherwise.

"Why don't you go on home," I said kindly. "I'll entertain your hubby till he calms down."

"No. I can't," the wife said.

"Go!" Road-kill growled, "you fucking whore."

The wife bit her lower lip. "You won't hurt him?"

I assured her I wouldn't—*not much.*

Road-kill's wife left money for the check on the table, gathered her belongings, and hurried out the door.

"You gonna behave?" I asked Road-kill.

"Yes."

With a snap I released the jerk. He sprang up in his seat, massaging his ear. "That fucking hurt."

"That's the whole idea." The sound level and restaurant routine were slowly returning to normal. So was my surly new friend.

"Move aside," Road-kill said.

I almost laughed. "Not a chance." I sat back. "You heard what I told your wife."

"Gonna be my ex," Road-kill said. "The fucking whore. I could kill her for what she's doing to me."

I didn't like his tone or the intent look in his eyes. "Divorce," I said, "would be a more sensible option."

"Michael." Destiny gestured that Road-kill's wife had gotten into a cab and was gone.

"All right." I pushed my chair back, allowing Road-kill some space. "Get outta my sight."

Road-kill grabbed his coat and walked unsteadily out the door, most probably heading south to the sea of bars along Second Avenue.

CHAPTER 4

A COLD MIX of snow and rain battered Harlem just before dawn, purging the oil-slick streets and littered sidewalks. Shrouding me in welcome shadows as I climbed the rusty hurricane fence and dropped into the alley behind the tenement. I scanned the area for signs of guard dogs: chains, leashes, fresh excrement, gnawed bones.

There were none.

I pulled a kelly green wool ski mask over my face, checked my Browning 9mm, and took a deep breath. Then I picked my way through piles of fetid kitchen trash that I assumed had been thrown from the apartments above.

I looked up and noted that nearly all the interior lights were out in the five-story sludge tenement. The occasional room light indicated someone up early for work, or perhaps a junkie who could not sleep.

I loosened the wrist snaps on my old black leather jacket. Reaching up, I used my body weight to pull down a wobbly fire escape ladder. That's when a thought occurred to me—since Tesser told me this operation was supposed to a "piece of cake"— why had he offered to supply me with semi-jacketed hollow point ammunition?

The ice-covered iron fire escape was treacherous. I watched my steps, ascended slowly, keenly aware that if a building occupant heard me, they could very well think me a burglar and call the police, or maybe pull a gun and open fire.

As I passed a second-floor window, I lost my footing, slipped and stumbled. I heard a dog bark inside the apartment. A light came on, a curtain parted. A window opened. I stepped back into shadow and stood perfectly still.

"Somebody there?" a gravelly man's voice said. Light from the apartment illuminated a narrow section of the fire escape. I flattened myself against the building's brick wall, hoping that the man would not open his window any farther and stick his head out.

"I'll sic the dog on you," the man warned.

I heard the window open wider. Heard the dog growl. I tensed and thought about what to do if the guy spotted me. Should I flash my NYPD ID and make up a story? Or run like hell back down the fire escape, up and over the fence? But the man did not stick his head out. After a moment the dog stopped growling, the window closed, and the curtain fell back into place.

I let a long-held breath out. Making sure to keep a tight grip on the fire escape handrails, I continued to climb.

From my frozen perch outside the fifth-floor target apartment, I looked past a flimsy metal security gate through threadbare pink curtains, and spotted an Hispanic man dozing on a plastic-covered couch. I guessed he was in his late thirties. He wore a New York Mets sweatshirt, jeans, and sneakers, and clutched a semi-automatic in his hand. Drug paraphernalia—a digital scale, miniature spoons, glass pipes used to smoke crack cocaine, and what looked like methamphetamine—were visible on the coffee table in front of him.

I heard a knock on the apartment's front door. It was a soft knock—in code—and the dozing man startled awake. He checked his wristwatch, then relaxed his gun hand. He shoved the automatic under his ample belly, into his waistband, moved to the door, and looked out the peephole.

"Keahy?"

The tin door came crashing in, its wood frame shattering. Four "rockers" brandishing wartime weapons, wearing ski masks similar to mine, rushed into the apartment.

As I kicked in the security gate and stepped into the over-heated apartment, a man I hadn't seen bolted from a chair across the living room, shouting something in protest. To my horror, one of the masked rockers drew back his Uzi and slashed the barrel across the man's face. He collapsed on the floor, spitting broken teeth.

"You crazy?" I screamed at the attacking rocker, but my words were drowned by a third man who ran in from the kitchen speaking rapid-fire Spanish. Another rocker doubled him over with a kick to the stomach, then hammered him to the floor with the butt of an AK-47.

What had I gotten myself into?

Sounds came from another room—men yelling, a woman shrieking, and children crying. Three more sleepy, dark-skinned men marched into the living room, hair and sleepwear askew, arms raised in soft surrender. They were ordered to lie on the floor.

One of the rockers held the captives at gunpoint while the others entered the bedroom and returned with a pajama-clad young woman and four little girls, all howling, terrified.

"Shut those fucking kids up," a voice said.

All eyes turned to the front door.

Mark Tesser's hulking frame filled the doorway. He swaggered into the apartment brandishing an enormous handgun with exaggerated gestures that left no doubt as to who was in charge.

The young woman quickly gathered the children around her, and hugged them, saying in broken English that everything would be all right.

I noticed a couple of the prone male occupants exchange glances and nods, but no one rushed to grab a weapon, thank god. That would have been suicide.

Tesser stepped over to the petrified young woman. He lifted her chin, gently stroked her face, and said though his ski mask, "You're a very pretty lady."

The children whimpered.

One of the men said something harsh in Spanish, an objection to Tesser's inappropriate behavior toward the woman.

Tesser bent down, grabbed him by the hair and yanked him to his feet. "Where're the drugs?"

"*No sé.*" The man was defiant.

Tesser cracked the man on the head with his handgun. "That's from your landlord," he said as the man hit the floor.

The young woman screamed hysterically.

"Shut her up," Tesser barked.

And she stopped screaming—just like that.

Tesser walked over to the coffee table, picked up the digital scale, and studied it. He used a finger to wipe a white powder residue from a measuring tray and tasted it. "Cocaine."

Tesser randomly chose another victim, dragged him off the floor, and stuck the barrel of the gun under the man's chin, raising him on tip-toe. "You *comprende*," Tesser said with a deadly gentleness. "Don't you?"

The idiot must've had a death wish, because he spit in Tesser's face. Tesser lost it. He slammed the guy against a wall. Stuck his gun into the guy's mouth. Cocked the hammer.

"Don't!" I said, convinced that Tesser was about to blow the asshole's brains out. "You listening? Don't!"

"Let it go," another rocker chimed in, backing me up.

Tesser paused to give us a look, his eyes wild. Then he hurled the spitter across the room. He bounced face first off a wall and timbered to the ground. The young woman rushed to the guy, cradled his head, shook him, spoke frantically in Spanish.

"Search the place," Tesser said.

Tesser's rockers began ransacking the apartment.

A rocker tore apart a closet, pulled out coats, and threw them around the room. "Guns," he said, holding up a stash of weapons and ammunition.

Another rocker searched the refrigerator, turned it over, and dumped its contents on the floor.

A third rocker emptied the cupboards, ripped open cereal and cookie boxes. Yet another used an assassin's knife to gut the couch.

"Nothing," the rocker with the knife said.

"They're holding out," another rocker said.

I didn't like the sound of that.

"Up," Tesser said. "Get 'em up on their feet."

The rockers dragged the men upright.

I took this opportunity to pull the young woman away from the barely conscious spitter. I hustled her and the children into a corner of the room, out of harm's way, and stood between them and Tesser's men.

"We can do this the hard way, or the easy way," Tesser said. "The one that gives up the drugs takes a walk."

The victims remained silent, eyes on the floor.

"All right, the hard way." Tesser threw the first punch. Hit the guy closest to him; his nose splattered.

A tall rocker cracked a guy on the head with a shotgun. Blood spurted from the laceration. Another rocker swung his AK-47 like a baseball bat, and broke a guy's jaw. Still another rocker kicked and stomped a fallen body.

I couldn't believe my eyes—the insane brutality. I could see myself being arrested, dragged before a grand jury, indicted as an accessory to murder.

"Mercy! Please! *No más!*" a bald victim cried, cowering in a corner, covering his shiny head in an attempt to cushion the unrelenting blows.

Tesser held up his hand. The assaults stopped.

The bald guy dropped to his knees, clawed aside a frayed throw rug. With frantic fingers he pried up several splintered floorboards, reached into the opening, extracted and held up a black satchel.

Tesser grabbed the satchel, looked inside, smiled. "Get them out of the apartment."

"Get dressed," the rockers told the victims. Held them at gunpoint while they quickly pulled on pants, slipped on socks and shoes.

I took the woman and children to the bedroom. Stood guard outside as the woman got dressed and then dressed the children.

"Move," a rocker said and gestured with his shotgun toward the door. The bruised and bloodied males, young woman and children were herded out without a hint of resistance.

"*No más, no más,*" the men kept saying as they walked down the hall and descended the stairs, begging for mercy every step of the way. When they finally reached the frigid sidewalk, Tesser took the man who'd spit in his face aside and jammed the barrel into the man's stomach.

"Consider yourself evicted," Tesser said, the black mask unable to hide his smile. "If you ever go back in that building again, your woman and children die." Tesser shoved the guy away roughly and gestured with the gun for him to go. He and his companions limped down the street through a maze of yawning slush puddles.

"Don't shoot. Don't shoot," the woman kept calling over her shoulder.

Tesser's rockers stepped to the curb where a nondescript gray van waited. A black guy and a Puerto Rican pulled off their black hoods, laughing and exchanging high-fives, thrilled that the operation had gone so well.

"I'd say we 'rocked' their world." Tesser slipped off his own hood. Dark, cold, expressionless eyes scanned the area for dangers: witnesses, unfriendly on-duty cops.

"Won't see those dirty spics back again," a blond with blue eyes chuckled.

"Hispanics to you," the Puerto Rican said, not joking.

"Touchy," the blond said, "aren't you?"

"Hey, fuck you."

The black guy broke the tension by stepping between the two snarling men and saying he wanted to go get breakfast. Tesser and the blond were all for it.

"Can't." I pulled off my kelly green hood, stunned by the brutality I'd just witnessed. I searched the eyes of the other cops and ex-cops, most of whom I'd met only an hour ago. "I've got things to do." I couldn't hide my contempt. "Appointments."

"Fuck's with you, Beckett?" Tesser said.

"You." I thumbed to his men. "And these psychos."

The blond spun. "You got a problem, Beckett?"

"You didn't have to beat those men."

"So, you *do* have a problem," the blond said.

"Hey, Beckett," Tesser said, "ain't you the guy looking to avenge your sister?"

"What?" I could feel my face flush, my temper start to slip. "I never told you that."

"You didn't have to," Tesser said.

"Way I heard it, Beckett," the blond guy said. "You had no problems busting heads when you were working the street."

"Fuck you." I regarded Tesser with disgust. He was holding the black satchel he'd taken from the apartment's inhabitants like a streetwise woman holds a purse on a crowded subway: under his arm, tight to his body.

"What's in the satchel?" I said.

"None of your business," Tesser said.

I got in Tesser's face. "I ain't gonna ask again."

"You don't wanna know," Tesser stammered, his composure wavering. He took a step back in an attempt to put some distance between us. I made a grab for the satchel, stopped when I felt a gun jammed into my back.

"Cool it," the guy with the gun said.

Now, I really didn't think that the rocker with the gun pressed to my back was actually going to shoot me. We all knew how messy that would be. Then again, Tesser's men were unpredictable whack-jobs.

I stepped away from Tesser.

The gun disappeared from my back.

"Look, let's end this before things get out of hand." Tesser reached into his pocket, counted out some cash. "Here's what I owe you."

"Shove it," I said. "Sideways."

"Ain't you the guy was crying poverty?"

I stuck a finger in Tesser's face. "Lose my phone number, asshole."

CHAPTER 5

THIRTY BLOCKS SOUTH, crumbling Harlem tenements gave way to immaculate multimillion-dollar Park Avenue cooperative—therefore exclusionary—apartment buildings. I moved cautiously across freshly shoveled and salted sidewalks down the picturesque, steeply sloping block of East 92nd Street and saw the vibrant glow of a promising sunrise over the East River.

A massive commercial airliner, taking off from LaGuardia Airport, seemed to be struggling as it powered its way into the orange-hued sky.

With a loud whistle a regally attired doorman hailed a cab for a sleek businesswoman who high-heeled across the sidewalk—her legs were very good.

An L.L. Bean-outfitted professional dog walker, pulled by several purebreds, trudged across the slushy avenue, heading toward Central Park.

A gleaming limousine rolled by, probably carrying someone to their seven-figure job in the Financial District.

Sirens.

I stepped out onto Park Avenue and watched the flashing

dome lights of two police cars that raced up the avenue. A sudden sadness overcame me. My heart was with those guys.

An honor.

That's what being a New York City police officer had been to me. As a rookie I'd had the good fortune to work with a squad of old-time cops who were not unlike my father: principled men who treated suspects, as well as a thankless, wary and often hostile public, with patience, compassion and dignity. And I strove to be exactly like those old timers.

Until my sister Shannon died.

I'd never forget that night.

"Get to Metropolitan Hospital," my father told me in a panicked cell phone call. "It's your sister."

Destiny and I were on routine patrol in our 19th Precinct sector car. "What happened?" I said.

"They say she overdosed," my father said.

"Shannon?" I felt my insides tighten. "Not Shannon." I pressed the cell phone closer to my ear. "Shannon doesn't use drugs. You hear me?"

"Just get over there," my father said, his voice thick. "Your mother and I will meet you in a half hour."

"What is it?" Destiny said.

"Metropolitan Hospital." I put my cell phone away, switched on the RMP lights and sirens. "Fast."

Minutes later, our RMP raced into Metropolitan Hospital's 97th Street emergency room entrance. I threw the passenger door open, stepped out before the car had come to a complete stop. I sprinted up some stairs and burst into the bustling emergency room reception area. Shoving several people aside, I collared a nurse.

"Where's Shannon Beckett?"

"What was she brought in for?"

"Overdose," I said, fighting to control a surging panic.

The nurse walked over to the reception desk, picked up and scanned a clipboard. "Shannon Beckett. Down there," she pointed. "Through the corridor. Area G."

I had to force myself to look to where the nurse was pointing. "Thanks," I said.

I walked slowly, purposefully across the gleaming white linoleum floor, my stomach in knots, my world filling with dread. I made it through a short corridor, turned right into Area G. I stopped at a drawn curtain and stood stone-like, mustering my courage.

"Michael." Destiny came up behind me. "I'm here."

I braced myself, pulled the curtain aside.

A body lay there, covered head to toe with a white bed sheet. I let out an involuntary moan. With a trembling hand I lifted the bed sheet, exposing a young woman's face.

Shannon's face.

"I'm sorry, Michael," Destiny whispered.

I felt like I'd been shot in the stomach. I had trouble breathing. I leaned heavily against a tiled wall and buried my face in my hands.

Destiny remained at my side but didn't say anything.

There was nothing to be said.

Since that night my life had been filled with an overwhelming sadness, bouts of anger, and sudden flares of hatred. Sure, I wanted those responsible for my sister's death—all drug dealers, for that matter—put out of business, which was what that morning's operation was supposed to be about. But what I'd done was inadvertently help Tesser's rockers commit a home-invasion style armed robbery. Yes, the drug dealers were evicted from the apartment and out of business for now, but I felt no satisfaction. Not assisting a sadistic head-case like Tesser.

Everything Tesser's rockers had done was overkill. The military-issue weapons, the totally unnecessary brutal assault on the occupants. The pilfering of the satchel that must have contained money or drugs or both. Was Tesser a user or a dealer?

By the time the sun was fully up, I was in my East 47th Street apartment. I walked into the master bedroom. As was her recent habit, my girlfriend Solana had already left for work. I looked around for a note; she used to leave me romantic cards and love notes. Magnet them to the refrigerator, leave them on the bedroom pillows, tape them to the bathroom mirrors—not any longer.

I checked my answering machine, checked my computer e-mail. But the only message had come in yesterday. It was from the client who owed me money. Julie Gunder, the Elaine's regular and former naval intelligence officer, had called to confirm our 4:00 P.M. meeting today at the Plaza Hotel.

I walked into my living and dining room area, slipped off my black leather jacket, hung it on the back of a chair. My eyes were drawn to a glass-enclosed armoire.

There were photos on display of my deceased parents, of my sister Shannon laughing it up during a family outing. There was a gold-framed Catholic high school graduation photograph of Shannon. She was eighteen years old when the picture was taken. Thanks to a Harlem drug dealer, she never saw nineteen.

I turned away from the armoire and felt pangs of regret.

I hadn't been the best of older brothers. I never remembered Shannon's birthday, or brought her Christmas gifts. I recalled the time I convinced her that the house we grew up in the Woodlawn section of the Bronx was haunted—she had nightmares for years. I was the one who told her there was no Santa Claus, ditto for the Tooth Fairy. Then there was the time a boy showed up at our house to take Shannon on her first date. I cornered the nervous youth in the kitchen, asked him about his intentions, then grabbed him, placed him in a painful headlock, and told him: "Whatever you do to my sister, I'm gonna do to you." Then I kissed him on the lips and the poor kid ran out of the house screaming, never to return. Shannon never forgave me for that.

Maybe if I hadn't been such a practical joker, if I'd found the time to get to know Shannon, spent more time with her, taken an interest in her life, I would have discovered that she was using drugs. And I would have saved her, guaranteed.

But at the time, she'd been living with my parents who were fighting terminal prostate and heart problems, respectively. They never even suspected that their daughter—a straight A student who'd won a full scholarship to Marymount College—was addicted to Vicodin and OxyContin.

I unstrapped my weapon and headed to the bedroom closet where I kept my other weapons: a Browning 9mm automatic and a Beretta .22 which were locked inside my weapons safe. I noticed Tesser's business card lying where I'd left it by the bedroom phone. I picked up the card, which was embossed with an "NYPD Retired" logo, tore it in half, and threw it in the trash.

CHAPTER 6

ABRILLIANT WINTER sun broke through receding snow clouds and woke Destiny Jones. She fought her way through layers of sleep, rolled over, and realized that her degenerate gambler husband, Fernando Garcia, was still in bed, snuffing up the furniture, as usual.

Destiny forced one eye open, glanced at the nightstand alarm clock and groaned. She buried her face in the pillow, dreading the thought of having to get up. The idea of leaving her idyllic Hastings on Hudson apartment with its pine-scented air and panoramic river views to run a dozen tedious domestic errands, then driving down to Manhattan and donning her police uniform, made her want to stay in bed forever.

Destiny flipped the pillow atop Fernando's drooling face—he didn't budge—and rocked herself from bed. She dragged her shivering carcass across the cold parquet floor, into the bathroom. The familiar headache struck. Destiny used both hands to rub her temples and thought once again that the migraines seemed to becoming more frequent and severe.

She opened the medicine cabinet, found a bottle of aspirin, and swallowed two along with a glass of water. Then she turned the shower on and let it run to hot.

Destiny wiggled out of her nightgown and looked at herself in the mirror—okay, so she was not fashion model skinny. But years of aerobics had preserved her womanly curves, which was why men, shallow creatures that they were, paid her attention—although the pressures of police work had slashed premature age lines in her face.

Destiny stepped into the steaming hot shower and soaped up. She was shaving her legs when she felt a stabbing pain in her lower back. She considered calling in sick, but knew she couldn't get away with it. Even though the back pain was caused by a prior line-of-duty injury—while she and Michael Beckett were wresting a knife from a fleeing felon, she'd fallen down a flight of concrete stairs—she was already on the department's chronic sick list. That was a negative if she ever hoped to be assigned to the detective division or achieve promotion.

Destiny dried off, stepped back into the bedroom, and looked at Fernando—the lazy prick. Feeling mean, she switched on the stereo, found a soul music station, turned the sound level up to loud. Fernando groaned, rolled over and pulled the covers over his head—the guy could sleep through an earthquake.

Destiny styled her hair, put on earrings. She pulled on a pair of worn jeans and a heavy wool sweater, stuck her off-duty weapon in her waistband and thought about how she and Fernando would survive when she retired, or if she ever decided to resign from the NYPD. As a bread winner, her husband was about as useful as an erection at a lesbian convention. Her teaching credentials would be of value landing a job, but they'd be worthless if she decided to start her own business; she and Michal Beckett often discussed quitting the NYPD and opening their own private investigation firm.

Destiny missed working with Beckett, an armed robbery specialist and veteran of a dozen shootouts—a proficient "gun slinger"—although they spoke almost every day, saw each other three or four times a month, much to the consternation of both Fernando and Beckett's neurotic girlfriend Solana.

Destiny headed to the kitchen and switched on the overhead fluorescent lights. Pulling a checkbook from her purse, she wrote two checks. One would go to her retired parents in Margate, Florida, to help with their monthly expenses, mostly the outrageous costs of prescription drugs. Thanks to her father's company pension plan failure, he and Destiny's mother were living below poverty level. The other was a household expense check to her husband—Fernando had agreed to do the food shopping—and left it on the white Formica counter.

Destiny recorded the two transactions in her checkbook ledger and noticed something odd—strands of a torn-out check were protruding from the middle of the book. Destiny flipped to the spot. Indeed, a single check had been removed. *Strange*. Well, maybe not so strange. Fernando had access to her check book.

"Fucking Fernando." Destiny shoved the checkbook back into her purse, stormed into the bedroom, and switched off the stereo.

"Fernando!" Destiny kicked the bed. "Hey, wake up." She yanked the covers off.

Fernando bolted upright. "Hey, you fuckin' beetch," he said, fury on his sleep-lined face. His thick Ricky Ricardo accent made even profanities sound somehow comical, although Destiny had stopped thinking her husband's antics amusing long ago.

"I know about the check you stole."

"I didn't steal no stinking check." Fernando found the sheets, yanked and covered up. "You crazy, beetch."

"I'm calling the bank, putting a stop payment on it. Don't bother trying to cash it."

Fernando shot to a sitting position, grabbed the bedside alarm clock, and threw it, full force.

Destiny ducked. The clock struck the wall, shattered, leaving a deep gorge in the plaster.

"Get the fuck away from me," Fernando screamed. "I kick your black ass."

Destiny almost laughed: same old Fernando. Confront him and he loses it. She backed out of the room and closed the door thinking: Why do I put up with this asshole? She grabbed her coat from a hall closet and headed to the building's underground parking garage.

Fernando Garcia and Destiny Jones had gotten married in a classic hot-pants haze. Even though he was uneducated and spoke broken English—Fernando was raised in poverty in the hills of Cuba—they had seemed well suited for each other. An NYU graduate, Destiny was an alpha female and had a strongly developed male side. Her husband was innately fashionable, sexy and, some would say, a tad effeminate.

Their first years together were filled with romantic candlelit dinners, long loving nights, rooftop champagne-drenched sunsets, and plans for the future—they both wanted children. But once it became apparent that Destiny couldn't conceive, the honeymoon was over.

Fernando began berating her. Accused her of being barren. Implied that she was somehow less of a woman. The fact that Destiny had passed a fertility test meant little to Fernando—*machismo* forbade him from assuming any responsibility.

The killer, though, was his gambling addiction, a major embarrassment for a police officer spouse. Although he'd sworn countless times to give up gambling, the addiction had caused Fernando half a dozen jobs. Last year he'd been arrested for running a dice game for a local hood.

And so, like many marriages, their relationship evolved from red-hot to simply convenient. Destiny began spending more time at work and hanging out with Beckett and the other cops. While her husband became self-absorbed, and immersed himself in absurd fantasy—his dream was to be a Formula One race car driver. He didn't even have a driver's license.

They no longer spoke about having children.

Destiny pulled her VW from the underground garage, took 9 to 9A to the Taconic State Parkway, settled into the speed lane, and decided she couldn't take being married to Fernando anymore.

She'd lived in denial for far too long, made lame excuses for his self-centeredness, larcenous ways, and hair-trigger temper. Although deep down she feared he was nothing more than a common thief, he'd never actually stolen from her. The missing check changed all that. Not to mention the distressing fact that they hadn't made love in seven months.

"I'm divorcing you, Fernando," Destiny said out loud. In that instant she felt her mood brighten and her headache nearly vanish.

CHAPTER 7

J ULIE GUNDER HANDED me a check. "Sorry it took so long."

I scanned the check, placed it in my suit jacket pocket.

We were seated at a table in the newly renovated Oak Room bar at the Plaza Hotel. Gunder sat across from me wrapped in expensive brown cashmere, sipping a dry vodka martini, enjoying her version of a snack: a thick, rare hamburger with the works, a side order of fries and onion rings. The establishment's indirect lighting accentuated Gunder's heavy, bloated features and perennial five o'clock shadow, reminding me that the former naval intelligence officer was the only woman I knew who actually shaved.

"Honestly, your invoice was misfiled," Gunder said. "I only just discovered you were never paid."

Bullshit.

I'd met Julie Gunder through Vernon the bartender, at Elaine's. Told her I was a cop interested in moonlighting, handed her my NYPD business card. She phoned me shortly thereafter, engaged me to conduct an investigation into, of all things, grocery store coupon fraud.

After completing the investigation, I sent Gunder a written

report, plus an invoice that went well over one hundred and twenty days past due.

"Now, about the new assignment." Gunder grabbed a fistful of onion rings and shoved them in her mouth. "You're of course familiar with my employer, Don Langlois?"

I didn't bother to respond to the rhetorical question. Everyone with a pulse was familiar with Langlois, one of the richest men in the world. His News Corporation owned more television stations, radio stations and newspapers—thus the grocery store coupon investigation—than Time Warner.

"What about him?"

Gunder made a production of checking the time, flashing her diamond-encrusted Cartier wristwatch.

"I want you to assess the security at his Manhattan residence." She crossed her fat, stumpy legs. "You'll work undercover, nights. That work with your schedule?"

I almost laughed. After Internal Affairs had received the anonymous tip about the heroin in my car, I'd been suspended, subsequently cleared of all criminal charges, reinstated, and then symbolically castrated—dumped, buried, along with other cops with disciplinary problems, into the basement of One Police Plaza. The Building Maintenance section was a place where I served no useful purpose other than to ensure the brass that I wouldn't be kicking down doors, cracking heads, or violating any more drug dealers' civil rights. On the upside, I had plenty of free time to moonlight.

"Not a problem," I said.

"You'll be assigned to the Langlois townhouse as one of his bodyguards. You report your findings to me, and only me. How's one thousand dollars a day sound?"

I feigned cool indifference. Twirled my beer glass. I thought about the stack of bills that were piled neatly on my kitchen counter. "I need to get paid within thirty days this time, Julie. No more of this one hundred and twenty days past due bullshit."

"Not a problem," Gunder said.

I heaved my best theatrical sigh and took a strategic moment to consider the job offer I knew I couldn't refuse. "A thousand a day works for me."

"Then we have a deal?" Gunder said.

"Depends," I said. "What are your concerns? I mean, what *exactly* would I be looking for?"

"I want you to evaluate the entire security setup."

That covered a very broad range. "Be more specific," I said.

"I need to know who frequents Langlois's townhouse," Gunder said. "And I mean everyone: personal assistants, domestic help, business associates, friends—anyone and everyone who comes and goes. I want a list of their names. Oh, and the alarm system—you familiar with alarm systems?"

I said I was.

"The alarm system is most important."

"That's it?"

"That's it.

"There's gotta be more for a thousand a day."

Gunder looked probingly at me, then swallowed whatever she was chewing and spoke behind her hand. "Someone's been trying to recruit a mercenary to break into Langlois's house."

I looked at her intently. "A kidnapping?"

Gunder gulped down her martini. "I don't think so." She signaled the waiter for a refill.

"What's worth stealing in the Langlois mansion?"

"Please! It's filled with millions in original art. And you must know Mrs. Langlois is a gossip columnist."

"I've seen her on TV." I pictured an attractive, gushy twit with a Hollywood insider's saucy grin.

"She stores sensitive information on her computer in her home office," Gunder said. "The names of secret sources. Probably even some names of organized crime, law enforcement, and confidential government informers."

"You mean rats," I said, starting to get the idea. "Don't you?"

"Some people would pay almost anything for the names of those sources."

I sat back, still somewhat puzzled. Honestly, this whole deal sounded like so much bullshit, but I played along. "Will Langlois know who I am, what I'm up to?"

"No." Gunder shook her head. "No one will know. Only me. And no one can know of our association."

"So how do I get hired, assuming there's a job opening?"

"There're always openings, thanks to Mrs. Langlois. Claudia's, uh, difficult."

"How difficult?"

Gunder grimaced. "Menopausal."

"Yikes."

"Langlois's director of security here in New York is a former NYPD Chief named Vogt."

"I know the name," I said, "I think."

"He does all the hiring. It's done word of mouth. You have to be recommended."

"You can't recommend me?"

"Not a chance. Vogt would resent me telling him who to hire. If he thinks I'm meddling, that could cast suspicion on you. Your undercover status could be compromised."

"I see the problem," I said.

"You know anyone close to Chief Vogt?"

"I dunno. I'll make some calls."

"Remember not to mention me," Gunder said. "To anyone."

"Got it." As I sipped my beer a new contingency occurred to me. "If I discover anything criminal, will I be burned?"

"I'm afraid I don't understand."

"Burned," I said. "You know, reveal my true assignment and testify in court."

Gunder looked off. "It's possible."

"I get twenty-five hundred a day to testify in court as an expert witness."

"Twenty-five hundred. A day?"

"Julie, there're cops with civil service mentalities who'll work for you for a hundred a day."

She waved away that idea. "I don't want them. I want you."

"Why?" I said.

"You did a great job with the coupon fraud investigation. To tell you the truth, you made *me* look good. And I know I can depend on you."

What I did was uncover the fact that thousands of Arab-owned mini-marts across the United States were involved in a massive criminal conspiracy. They would clip grocery store coupons from the Sunday and Wednesday newspapers, cut, stack, cash them in the usual way (without actually selling the products), and send the proceeds, tens of millions of dollars a year, to Al-Qaeda. I was able to prove to Gunder, beyond any doubt, what she already suspected: that Al-Qaeda had partially funded both World Trade Center attacks through coupon fraud. Gunder then handed over my reports and other information to the FBI, which made numerous arrests.

"The security men," I said. "They cops?"

"Some are." Gunder again checked the time, flashed the watch. "Some are ex-cops," she said impatiently. "Why?"

"I won't testify against them, no matter what."

Gunder sat back at this demand. "But what if they're involved in the conspiracy?"

"I won't testify against cops. Period."

"Do you know any of Langlois's security staff?"

"Not that I'm aware of."

She frowned. "But you're saying that, even though you'll be working for me, your loyalty is to men you've never met, strangers?"

"You got it." I leaned forward. "Plus I want a nonrefundable retainer for the new assignment, now."

"Michael." Gunder made an awkward attempt at femininity, batting her sparse eyelashes. "You don't trust me?"

I almost retched but remained stone-faced.

"All right." Gunder bent forward, reached into her purse; the valley between her two-ton breasts deepened. She took out a checkbook, wrote a check and handed it over.

I accepted the check with theatrical reluctance. I looked it over, considered the high pay and the fact that she'd agreed to my unrealistic demands—this was all too easy. My instincts told me that there was a lot Gunder was not telling me.

"We have a deal?" she said.

"Yes," I said. "We have a deal."

CHAPTER 8

GERMAN HOTEL PROPRIETOR Alex Schultz saw the Belfast Boys and their two pit bulls leaving the grounds of the Isaacs Houses housing project from half a city block away. The collection of about twenty young native-Irish and Irish-American thugs sauntered arrogantly across York Avenue, forcing all traffic to a brake-squealing standstill. The motley crew of discontents wore tight jeans and heavy black leather jackets adorned with a single green shamrock on their backs.

According to the newspapers, the Belfast Boys, like the ruthless Hell's Kitchen gang The Westies, were associates of the city's five organized crime families. Over the years several Belfast Boys were arrested for kidnapping, extortion, assorted conspiracies, and contract killings. However, since witnesses had a habit of disappearing, or flatly refusing to testify, few gang members were ever convicted. Their present leader, a rock-star handsome, thirty-five-year-old sociopath named Lochlainn O'Brian, was reputed to have served hard time in a British prison for his part in an IRA bank robbery.

The bodega owner across the street spotted the Belfast Boys as they made their way down the middle of East 94th Street and motioned frantically for his pretty young daughter to come inside. "Now!"

A cobbler closed and locked his shop's front door, turned the "open" sign to "closed" and pulled down a long shade.

A dry cleaner exited his store and stood sentry at the front door, the butt of a handgun visible under his jacket.

Schultz, paintbrush in hand, put the finishing touches on some window trim, one eye on the gang.

A hatchet man and lackey he knew as "Rat", stopped a passing preppy teenager and ripped a pricy-looking overcoat off the boy's back. The teen, quaking with fear, did not protest. Rat tossed the coat to Lochlainn O'Brian.

Lochlainn, an ever-present, unfiltered cigarette dangling from the corner of his mouth, inspected the teenager's coat inside and out with the eye of a street corner haberdasher. He nodded approvingly, then handed it back to the youth. "Nice coat, lad."

The teen nodded a tentative thanks and hurried away.

A car horn blared, the driver shouting that the gang should get the hell out of the goddamned road.

The gang cursed the impatient motorist, took its sweet time stepping aside, clearing the road. The car roared down 94th Street.

A sundried raisin of a woman, a fixture on the block known simply as "The Old Woman", shuffled along the street with the aid of a walker, a bottle of German beer protruding from a cup holder affixed to the walker's handlebar. She said something to Lochlainn who stopped, smiled warmly, gave her a cigarette, and then lit it for her.

Schultz's breathing quickened as the gang continued in his direction. He put his paintbrush down and backed away from the window—too late.

"Schultz!" Lochlainn called from the street, all smile and charm, his arms open wide. "My old mate." He waved amiably for Schultz to come outside and join him.

Schultz knew it was futile not to obey; there was no escaping the Belfast Boys. He walked to the back of the newly renovated hotel suite where his wife Enia was painting baseboard trim. Soulful jazz oozed from an iPod, which was set on a windowsill echoing in the empty space.

"I'm goin' downstairs for coffee. Want one?"

"No," Enia said absently, focused on the task at hand.

Schultz regarded his wife for a brief moment. She was wearing tight, low riding jeans, a baggy sweatshirt that could not hide her ample curves; shimmering blonde hair, deep blue eyes, lush, sinful lips that not only pleased him during intimacy but, he loathed to admit, controlled him.

Schultz stepped back into the front room, puffed up his five-foot-seven, sinewy frame, opened the door and headed for the stairs. The Belfast Boys were waiting for him on the front stoop.

Lochlainn, a vision of leather and denim, was leaning against the top step railing, greasy black hair pulled back in a ponytail, a pretentious diamond-stud earring in his right ear.

"Whaddaya want, Lochlainn?" Schultz said as he stepped outside. Even though he wore a paint-stained t-shirt and the temperature was hovering around freezing, sweat trickled down his face and neck.

"Always working," Lochlainn said with a lilting Irish brogue, referring to the paint splatter on Schultz's t-shirt and hands. "Your work ethic comes from the fatherland, eh?"

"Fuck you talkin' about? I was born here in Yorkville. I ain't never been to Germany." Schultz's eyes were on the two pit bulls. They were guard dog-alert, straining at their leashes, anxious to attack and rip apart anything that moved. "Well, whaddaya want?"

"It's good to have a hotel proprietor who is so—". Lochlainn stroked the stubble on his cleft chin. "So bloody concerned with the welfare of his guests."

"You're not a guest. You're a squatter."

After selling his share of a dot.com startup company and acquiring the leaky rooming house in Manhattan's Yorkville, Schultz, the grandson of German-Jewish immigrants, invested a full year and his dot.com profits in pursuit of a romantic notion: restoring the very building his grandparents had once lived in after passing through Ellis Island. He planned to turn the former grunge tenement located in what was once a slum into a boutique hotel.

Since this had been a multinational ghetto, Schultz wanted his inn to represent the immigrant experience. The resulting blend of preservation and design was a five-story, sixteen-room guesthouse, which merged modest period details with a few modern luxuries: steam room showers, hi-definition televisions, broadband internet service.

Although there had been significant cost overruns, the renovation had been more or less on schedule. Schultz and Enia had taken up residence two months ago and over twelve of the guest suites had already been rented when Lochlainn and his Belfast Boys appeared. They rented a suite, overstayed their time, frightened off other guests, and then "squatted." Soon, the constant comings and goings of street thugs and pit bulls encouraged most of the other potential guests to look elsewhere for lodging. As a result, Schultz was on the verge of bankruptcy.

Lochlainn sat on a gray concrete step and patted the spot beside him. "Have a seat, lad."

Reluctantly, Schultz sat.

"What a world we live in, eh?" Lochlainn said, his eyes on the streets, missing nothing. "So much bloody hatred, corruption, religious and racial unrest—Arabs killing Jews. Protestants killing Catholics. Bloody conflicts raging all over the globe. Why can't we all get along, eh?" Lochlainn took out a cigarette, placed it in his mouth. Rat rushed to light it.

"Whatever happened to personal responsibility, eh?" Lochlainn blew a long stream of smoke through his nose. "People blame fast food restaurants for getting them fat. Some guy gets a speeding ticket and he sues Porsche, blaming *them* for making *him* get the speeding tickets. A woman throws a glass of water in her boyfriend's face, then she slips on the water and sues the bloody restaurant! People should accept responsibility for their own actions; you concur?"

Schultz nodded cautiously.

"Good. Because, you see, lad, you are *personally* responsible for all the bloody police scrutiny that I am experiencing. And a man in my profession cannot prosper under police scrutiny, you understand?"

Schultz didn't know how to respond. He had indeed gone to the cops, several times in fact, to complain about the Belfast Boys. But the cops told him that, if he had no firsthand knowledge of the gang's criminal activities, squatters were a civil matter. That if Schultz wanted the gang evicted, he'd have to file a suit in civil court; a cruel joke.

"You're runnin' a criminal enterprise out of my hotel," Schultz said defiantly. "No one will rent with you here. You're puttin' me in the poorhouse. I got no choice but to go to the cops."

"We all have choices, lad. Yours is a very simple one." Lochlainn's eyes turned hard, the affable manner and smile disappeared. "You want to live or die?"

Schultz's stomach did a flip-flop. This was the first time that Lochlainn had threatened him directly.

Freckles, a shapely young Irish gang girl, stepped out of the hotel, sat alongside Lochlainn, kissed him on the lips.

Behind her a door opened, then closed.

"The bitch's coming," Freckles said, gesturing behind them.

"You!" Enia came screaming out of the hotel. She knocked Freckles aside and hurled herself at Lochlainn, slapping, kicking, clawing at his eyes. The pit bulls went berserk, straining at their leashes, attempting to get at her.

Rat took Enia by the hair, pulled her off Lochlainn, flung her to the ground. Enraged, Schultz charged Rat. Threw an overhead right. But another Belfast Boy caught Schultz in mid-swing and doubled him over with a short punch to the stomach, followed by a chop to the back of the neck.

Enia came hell-catting off the pavement. Freckles pulled a knife and slashed. Enia screamed, grabbed her arm and fell to the sidewalk. Blood seeped through the gash in her sweatshirt.

"Stop!" Schultz limp-crawled to his wife and covered her body with his. "No more. Please."

"That's enough," Lochlainn said lightly.

The Belfast Boys backed off.

Freckles wiped the bloody knife on her jeans and glared at Enia. "You're lucky this time. Cunt."

Lochlainn chuckled. "You'd better take your wife in hand, lad." He dabbed at a scratch Enia had carved into his face. "She'll be the bloody death of you."

The Belfast Boys snickered as they stepped around Schultz and Enia and entered the German Hotel.

CHAPTER 9

ENIA USED HER uninjured arm to push into a sitting position on the sidewalk. She winced in pain as she watched Lochlainn and his gang climb the hotel's interior stairs.

"Lie still." Schultz pulled out a handkerchief, used it to put pressure on Enia's wound, a six-inch long cut on her forearm. "I'll kill that son of a bitch someday."

"That gang stays much longer," Enia said, her accent Romanian, "You'll be ruined. *We'll* be ruined."

Schultz knew what she meant: She was upfront about the fact that she'd married him for financial security. Had even *demanded* that he purchase a five million dollar life insurance policy naming her as the sole beneficiary before she'd marry him.

"*When no money comes in the front door, love goes out the back door*," was the adage she used. There was no question, if he filed for bankruptcy, Enia would leave him.

"Maybe they won't stay," Schultz said. "Lochlainn said the cops're watchin'. They can't stay in one place too long."

"We can't afford to wait 'til they leave."

"What else can we do?"

"We?" Enia said angrily. "You're the man." She sat up, yanked her injured arm away from her husband. Snatched the bloody handkerchief, applied pressure to the wound herself. "I can't believe I married a coward."

"What did you say?"

"You're a coward."

Schultz felt as if he'd been slapped in the face. A mix of emotions struck: hurt, humiliation, anger. He wondered, and not for the first time, why he loved this woman who was so capable of emotional cruelty. And deep down he wondered if she was right, wondered if he was indeed a coward.

"That really what you think of me?"

"What else if you let them steal our livelihood?"

Schultz's heart sank.

A real estate neophyte, Pace University-trained visual artist, and former dot.com entrepreneur, Schultz was no match for any gang of thugs. True, he'd been wild in his youth. He and his friends had stolen cars, dabbled in drugs, had their share of fistfights. But maturity and fear of prison eventually overcame any desire Schultz had to continue a life of crime. Then again, where Lochlainn O'Brian was concerned, if he had the opportunity and some backup, he'd plunge a knife into the gang leader's heart and feel absolutely no remorse.

The bodega owner, cobbler, drycleaner, and other shopkeepers and neighbors straggled out of their hiding places and gathered around the Schultzes.

Schultz helped Enia off the ground, sat her on the hotel stoop. "Someone call an ambulance."

A neighbor took out a cell phone and dialed 911.

The bodega owner looked up to the suite the Belfast Boys had commandeered. "We have to do something about those punks."

"Yeah," a Korean neighbor said. "But what?"

"They came into my place last night," the bodega owner said, "took cases of beer, insulted my daughter, took liberties. Told me if I went to the cops they'd kill her."

"I've had it. I'm gonna move my business," the cobbler said. "Open somewhere else."

"Fight," the drycleaner said. "We have to fight."

"Like her?" the cobbler said, referring to Enia. "Take on twenty armed hoodlums? Talk some sense, will you?"

"We can go to the cops again," the Korean neighbor said. "See the precinct captain, keep complaining until they assign an officer here."

"They're not gonna station a cop here twenty-four hours a day," the cobbler said. "Even if they did, and the cops made an arrest, who's gonna testify in court, you?" He looked to the bodega owner. "Or you?"

"I'll testify," the drycleaner said. "No one's running me off. I'm gonna fight 'em, that's what I'm gonna do."

"You've been talking that shit for months," the cobbler said. "That's all it is—talk."

"I've got a gun," the dry cleaner said, patting his waist.

"So what?" the cobbler said. "They've got twenty guns, probably have explosives for all we know."

"You don't have a choice," a rasping, thickly accented German voice said. The Old Woman stepped into the circle of frightened men.

"Look, this is men talk, Old Woman," the cobbler said. "Drink your beer and be quiet."

"Watch your tone," the dry cleaner said.

"I'm just saying," the cobbler said.

The Old Woman took a long drag from the cigarette Lochlainn had given her, a pull from her beer. "We had problems with hooligans back in the eighties. They terrorized the neighborhood. Police couldn't or wouldn't help. The merchants got together, hired men, drove them out."

"That's taking the law into your own hands," the Korean said. "Vigilantism. I'll have no part in breaking the law."

"We don't know any gunmen," the cobbler said. "This isn't the Wild West."

"They weren't gunmen," the Old Woman said. "Not exactly."

"What were they?" Schultz said, really wanting to know.

"New York City cops."

"Police officers?" the Korean said.

The Old Woman nodded. "If I remember correctly." She took a drag on her cigarette. "The merchants called them 'Rockers.'"

"Rockers?" the drycleaner said.

"What's that mean," the cobbler said, "Rockers?"

"Alex," Enia motioned to Schultz to come closer.

Schultz bent forward. "Yeah?"

"I don't recall if I ever mentioned it to you," Enia whispered. "I once dated a New York City cop."

CHAPTER 10

"JONES?" SERGEANT HILL called out.

No response.

Hill, a thirty-year NYPD veteran, checked the roll call that he held in his hands, leaned on the podium, and glanced around the jam-packed muster room, picking through faces. "Jones! I just saw you—Destiny Jones?"

"Here!" Destiny said.

The 19th Precinct's four-to-twelve roll call was proceeding as usual. Between cell phones ringing, fart noises, and airborne rubber bands, Sergeant Hill was doing a pretty good job of maintaining order and calling the fifty-man roll.

"I'm taking you off your foot post, Destiny," Sergeant Hill said. "You'll be working with Moynihan in Sector Peter. His usual partner's out sick."

Destiny searched around the muster room, located Moynihan—a Lou Costello from Abbott and Costello fame look-alike—and waved. Although they'd worked in the same precinct for years, the only things Destiny knew about Moynihan was that he loved food—obviously—and he usually reeked of cigarettes.

Destiny entered the post change in her memo book. She actually didn't mind filling in for the occasional sector car vacancy, especially on cold winter nights. Besides, her normal foot post was teeming with not-a-clue tourists, hookers, street hustlers, three-card Monte dealers, and the occasional purse snatcher. Whereas Sector Peter, more a residential section, was quiet, home to upscale boutiques, restaurants like Elaine's, and the beautiful people.

Hill continued calling the roll.

The 19th Precinct's 1.754 square miles had one of the densest populations in the nation: 217,063 residents. The southern part of the precinct—Destiny's usual post—-had a large commercial area, the famous avenues of Madison, Lexington, and Third, and were well known for their high-end shopping. Many dignitaries, diplomats, A-list actors and corporate bigwigs resided or owned real estate within the precinct. There were currently thirty-two foreign missions, twelve consulates, and seventy ambassador and counsel general residences.

"If there's nothing else?" Sergeant Hill checked the room for raised hands. "No? Then that's it, people. Take your posts."

Destiny met up with Moynihan at the rear of the muster room and exchanged pleasantries. As they exited the station house, portable radios and keys to their assigned RMP in hand, Moynihan talked about all the great Italian restaurants along Second and Third Avenues. He promised dinner would be a gastronomical event.

"I know a place." Moynihan grinned and patted his well-upholstered stomach.

Moynihan wanted to drive and Destiny had no objection. She was fairly certain he didn't know that some people—some nit-wits—had problems with her driving over the years.

They headed to the East Side, did a thorough sweep of Sector Peter and made small talk, that is, Moynihan made small talk. Destiny watched the streets, barely listening—preoccupied with her gloomy marital situation—while he prattled on about some racetrack opening out in Del Mar, California.

It was common knowledge that half of all marriages end in divorce. But Destiny never thought divorce would happen to her. When she married Fernando, in a small ceremony at Marble Collegiate Church on Fifth Avenue, she was positive that their love would last a lifetime. They would be that one in a million couple who would work out any difficulties, give birth to a house full of beautiful children—she deeply regretted not having children.

Moynihan steered the RMP toward Second Avenue, made a left, drifted to the right, slowed in traffic. He stopped behind a double-parked car, honked the horn, gestured to the driver to move on.

"If you feel like a burger, we got Kinsale, JG Melon, and Luke's on Third Avenue," Moynihan said as he steered the RMP to a couple of special attention locations, trouble spots that he kept a close eye on. No drug dealers, lookouts, or runners were out in the cold. All in all, it was as Destiny expected: a clear, quiet winter evening.

"We got Rathbones on Second and Peking Duck," Moynihan pointed out. "And you can't beat Totonno's for pizza or Milano for hero sandwiches."

"Whatever you think," Destiny said absently.

"*Central to 19 Peter.*"

Destiny picked up the radio. "19 Peter."

"*10-1. Call your command.*"

"10-4." Destiny replaced the radio, took out her cell phone just as Moynihan stuck a cigarette in his mouth.

"You gonna smoke that in here?"

Moynihan sighed, pulled to the curb at East 92nd Street across from a Key Food supermarket. "You can make your call outside," he said with a smile, "if it bothers you."

Destiny made a face. "It's your sector car." She opened the door, stepped out, and dialed the station house. "Jones here. What's up?"

"Mail run," the switchboard operator said.

Destiny heard someone behind her clear their throat. She glanced over her shoulder and a woman wearing a dark blue work smock and light blue slacks stepped into view. She was short, thin, around forty years old with dyed black hair. Her even facial features hinted she'd been a hottie in her youth.

"Pick up the mail at borough HQ," the voice at the switchboard said. "Drop it off here."

"Got it," Destiny said and hung up. She shivered from a sudden gust of winter wind and turned to the woman behind her, fully prepared to hear yet another sob story about an inconsiderate neighbor, abusive husband, or complaint about an undeserved parking ticket.

"What can I do for you?" Destiny said. Then she noticed that the woman's eyes were Frisbee wide, pupils dilated. She was obviously on drugs or suffering from some sort of shock.

"Three black guys just held up the supermarket," the woman said rapid-fire.

"What?" Destiny listened up. "What supermarket?"

"Key Food." She pointed across the street with a trembling hand. "They had guns."

"When?"

"A few minutes ago."

"Anyone hurt?" Destiny said.

"No." Her eyes darted off to one side. "They went that way in a car." She pointed south on Second Avenue.

"What kind of car?" Destiny said.

"A dark car. Tan, I think."

"A Ford, Chevy, what?"

"I don't know."

Destiny's eyes swept the area. She speculated that there could be more than one car and more than three perps. According to Michael Beckett—*the* expert on armed robbery—armed backups were common with stickup teams.

Destiny opened the police car rear door. "Get in."

"What for?" the woman said apprehensively.

"If we catch up, we need you to identify them."

Reluctantly the woman stepped into the back of the RMP. Destiny slid onto the front passenger seat, filled Moynihan in on what was going on, and grabbed the radio.

"19 Peter to Central, k," Destiny said.

"*Go ahead, Peter.*"

"10-20, past robbery at the Key Food supermarket, Second Avenue and 92nd. Less than five minutes old. We're looking for three armed male blacks driving a dark, possibly tan car. No make or model. Last seen driving south on Second. We have a female witness in the car."

"*10-4,*" Central said and then repeated the broadcast to all units citywide.

Destiny opened her memo book, took out a pen, turned around and looked at the woman. Even though it was dead of winter, she was sweating profusely. She smelled faintly of perfume and cigarettes.

"What happened?" Destiny said.

"Two of them walked in, went into Anna's office. "

"Anna?" Destiny said, scribbling notes.

"Anna, the bookkeeper." The woman shivered at the memory. "They told Anna to give her the money. She did and they ran out of the store."

"Then what?"

"I saw them getting into the car. There had to be another guy in the car driving, but I couldn't see. The windows were really dark, tinted."

"Anything else you can remember?"

The woman thought a moment. "One of them had a shotgun."

At this news Moynihan and Destiny exchanged a glance. They were armed only with handguns: Glocks. Did they really want to take on three or more gunmen armed with at least one shotgun? Destiny didn't, and not just because they were outgunned.

Like most cops, Destiny had joined the police force for all the right reasons: to put the bad guys behind bars, to save lives, make a difference in the world. In the beginning, she and Michael Beckett had been aggressive cops. She'd lost count of the number of fugitives they'd apprehended, weapons and drugs they'd confiscated. They'd stopped, frisked, and run off every dangerous punk in their sector at every opportunity. Although they kicked ass only when absolutely necessary. They showed up for work early, stayed late.

But after Beckett was mistreated by the department brass, suspended, and persecuted, Destiny reevaluated her priorities.

She no longer went looking for trouble. She did her job to the best of her ability, took what came, but never went out of her way to break balls—just the opposite. In lieu of arrests, she preferred to chase hookers, bookmakers, squeegee men, unlicensed peddlers, and floating crap or card games off her post. She rarely issued parking tickets. And, based on the disheartening fate of some of her fellow police officers, she was most cautious when dealing with the general public. Because even a reasonable error, questionable decision, or misspoken observation uttered under the most extreme circumstances could place a cop's future in jeopardy.

Moynihan pointed the car south on Second Avenue and hit the gas. They drove a short distance to 86th Street then made a left, heading to First Avenue.

"They went down Second," the woman protested. "Why're you turning?"

"Simple," Moynihan said patiently. "Second Avenue is always gridlocked. The robbers would head east, hit the FDR Drive, or head up First into Harlem and dump the car. If they did their homework they'll know that the other northbound streets have construction delays. First Avenue is the only sensible route."

Destiny nodded at Moynihan's assessment. She pulled her

weapon, checked that it was loaded—she had never fired at a person before and had serious doubts that she was even capable. She could never rationalize the taking of a human life, of dealing with the psychological aftermath—there were always non-lethal alternatives.

Destiny vividly remembered the time she responded to a family dispute and was attacked by a schizophrenic parolee who was high on crystal meth. When she walked into that sweltering walkup apartment, she discovered a young woman clutching an infant, cowering behind a torn couch, and the parolee stalking them—he held a butcher knife in his hand.

"Police!" Destiny shouted, and ordered the psycho to drop the knife. The way the guy reacted, it was as if Destiny had startled him from a sordid dream. He blushed like he was embarrassed that he'd been caught. And then he charged, knife slashing the air. Destiny had every legal right to shoot that crazy son of a bitch, but the thought never occurred to her. Instead she sidestepped and cracked the guy on the head with her gun. Not that Destiny thought she'd be forced to use her gun that winter day. Common sense told her that the Key Food robbers were long gone.

"Traffic's heavy," Moynihan commented. He negotiated around a conga line of city buses, slowed at each intersection along First Avenue so they could check the cross streets for the tan car. He looked left, Destiny looked right.

"There they are!" The woman was pointing straight ahead.

Sure enough, one block north, a tan 1993 Plymouth with tinted windows turned off 94th Street onto First Avenue, raced to the 96th Street intersection, and stopped in heavy bus traffic.

"You sure that's them?" Destiny said.

"That's the car," the woman said. "I'm sure."

"The mopes must've tried to go up Third," Moynihan said. "Got stuck in construction traffic and had to double back."

"Think they saw us?" Destiny said.

"If they did, they're playing it cool."

"So can we." Destiny reached for the radio. "19 Peter to Central, K."

Central did not respond. "Central, 19 Peter is in pursuit of three armed male suspects. Request immediate backup."

No response. They had to be in a dead radio zone.

"Forget backup," Moynihan said. "Let's take these mutts while we can."

Destiny looked at Moynihan; they didn't know for sure how many, or what types of weapons the perpetrators had. Besides, two cops attempting to arrest them now might force a bloody confrontation. Waiting for backup, a show of overwhelming force might give the robbers pause and avoid bloodshed.

"19 Peter to Central, K." An urgency had crept into Destiny's voice. "In pursuit of three armed suspects. Request immediate backup. Ninety Sixth and First."

"We're wasting time," Moynihan said. "Traffic starts moving they'll take the FDR Drive and bolt. Or worse go up First Avenue, abandon the car and disappear into the projects. Either way we could lose them."

Much as she loathed to admit, Moynihan was right.

"Let's do it," Destiny said.

Moynihan tapped the gas, eased the RMP to the curb and killed the engine.

Destiny turned to the witness. "You stay put."

The woman nodded.

Portable radios in hand, the two cops stepped cautiously out of the RMP. Moynihan crossed to the left side of First Avenue, the driver's side. Destiny remained on the right. If all went well, they'd surprise the robbers, come at them from two directions, disarm them, have them out of the car and under arrest within seconds.

The bus traffic inched up First Avenue. Motors rumbled. Air brakes hissed. All at once an eighty-foot bus rolled forward and obstructed Destiny's view of the suspects' Plymouth.

"Shit." Destiny ran up the street, passed the bus. She leapt over the hood of an occupied car and stopped—the Plymouth's doors were wide open. The occupants had fled.

Destiny spun around, scanned the area.

A woman in colorful Haitian garb was pushing a baby stroller along the icy sidewalk. Three black kids were dribbling a basketball, tossing it to each other. Two bundled-up elderly women sat on a bench, deep in conversation. A tall black male wearing a skullcap and long brown leather coat was walking east on 96th Street, toward the FDR Drive. He wasn't running, exactly, but he was walking fast, head down.

"Police." Destiny pointed her Glock. "Freeze!"

The Haitian woman pushing the stroller froze. The three kids with the basketball stopped in their tracks and went wide-eyed. The two old women ceased their conversation and gaped at the female cop.

But the male kept walking.

Destiny raced onto the sidewalk, sidestepped the Haitian woman with the stroller, and came to a skidding stop about twenty-five feet from the suspect.

"Police." Destiny crouched into the combat position, cocked her weapon. "Stop, or I'll shoot."

The man turned slowly and smiled innocently at Destiny. He was light-skinned, round-faced, owl-eyed, with good teeth. He was holding a canvas money bag in his left hand. His right hand was down, behind his back. Whatever he was holding was hidden from Destiny's line of sight by the long leather coat.

"Lemme see your hands," Destiny said. "Do it now!"

The guy dropped the money bag.

Raised a shotgun.

Fired.

Destiny heard the blast. Saw the shotgun muzzle flash.

She steadied her Glock and squeezed out five shots. Two hit

the suspect in the face. He was blown back against a parked car and crumbled awkwardly to the sidewalk. He did not move again.

Destiny raced forward, Glock at the ready, checking herself for injury; miraculously, the owl-eyed gunman had missed. Approaching the gunman, she kicked the shotgun out of reach. Looked down at the bloody mess. The gunman was lying on his side. His face was half gone, but he was still breathing. The stench of spent gunpowder was thick in the air.

More gunfire.

Destiny spun and saw pedestrians scattering along First Avenue. Drivers were honking horns. Some abandoned their cars, trucks, and vans, running for cover.

The Haitian woman draped her body across her infant. The two old women dropped to the sidewalk. The three black kids with the basketball ran toward Destiny, dove to the frozen ground, and cowered behind her.

A bus lurched forward and Destiny saw two male blacks firing handguns at Moynihan. Moynihan returned fire. Ducked behind a bus. Fired. Ducked. Fired.

Destiny keyed her portable radio. "10-13! 10-13! 10-13! First Avenue and 96th. Shots fired. 10-13!"

"*10-4,*" Central said. "*What units responding?*"

"*19 Adam.*" "*19 Frank.*" "*19 Boy.*" "*19 Charlie.*" "*19 Henry.*"

And so on.

The sky filled with the sounds of approaching sirens.

The two gunmen fled north across 96th Street.

The taller of the gunmen absorbed a glancing blow from a skidding taxi. He rolled to his feet and hobbled north. The other gunman leapt over a car hood, slipped on ice, twisted his ankle, and limped on—-right into a beehive of uniformed beat cops. The two perpetrators never knew what hit them. They were tackled, disarmed, then hammered and stomped into bloody submission.

"*19 Peter,*" Central said. "*Any officer injury?*"

"Stand by." Destiny looked for Moynihan, saw him walk across 96th Street to help cuff the bloodied prisoners.

"Negative, Central," Destiny said. "No officer injuries." She heard gagging; the armed robber she'd shot was choking on his own blood. "But I need an ambulance, forthwith, Central."

"On the way," Central said.

"Let the mutha-fuckin nigga die," a voice said.

Destiny turned.

The three black kids with the basketball were staring defiantly at her.

CHAPTER 11

I WALKED INTO One Police Plaza, waved at the security guys at the front desk who were manning the metal detectors, checking IDs. I sidestepped and ducked a few unfamiliar superior officers as I walked through the employee gate—I didn't know them and there was no reason for them to know me—and headed to the basement stairwell and the building maintenance office.

The Building Maintenance Division was comprised of cops who were injured in the line of duty, or were burnouts, or were considered violence prone, like me. Some had had their guns taken away and were jokingly referred to as being members of the "rubber gun squad". Most were on limited or restricted duty and were counting the days, waiting to retire. Me? I'd been forced into full-duty limbo; told that, although I was allowed to keep my guns, my days as an active cop making felony collars was over; I'd never see the street again.

We'd see about that.

I used a key to open the door to the building maintenance office. Flicked the overhead lights on, took a seat at one of the six empty desks, opened the sign-in log, and scratched my name at the appropriate place. Using different pens and writing styles, I signed in three other cops who were scheduled to work the four-to-twelve tour with me, then signed out the three cops assigned to the eight-to-four tour, all co-workers who would not be coming to work that week. Since we were basically unsupervised "brooms" and served absolutely no useful function, we decided collectively that only one of us would show up each day and sign the others in and out. This week it was my turn.

I closed the sign-in log, turned out the lights, locked the office. On the way out I checked that the security guys at the front desk had all my contact numbers, just in case an emergency arose and someone needed a fucking light bulb changed.

I left One Police Plaza, headed to the IRT subway station.

A stampede of screaming, panicked people, rushing out of the subway station, greeted me as I legged down the stairs—first thing I thought was: *terrorist attack.* I sidestepped the horde, grabbed a panicked transit worker by the arm, asked him what the hell was going on.

"I heard a gunshot," the transit worker said. "People started running so I ran with them."

"Call 911," I told him, and he said he would.

I stayed to the side of the staircase, allowed the people to exit as I made my way into the bowels of the station. I jumped the turnstile, stopped to allow my eyes and ears to adjust to the sights and sounds. I heard a woman scream and raced across a bridge that took me over the express tracks to the uptown local platform.

The brain-rattling sounds of train traffic actually camouflaged my descent. I looked straight ahead and saw a tall Hispanic man pointing a gun at a woman who was lying prone on the ground. I pulled my gun.

"Freeze! Police!" I said, my shield in my left hand, my gun in my right. But my voice was drowned by the approach of another train. "Drop your weapon. Now!"

The man reacted, looked around, trying to locate the source of the voice. He saw me pointing my gun at him, lowered his weapon, and backed away from the woman, his eyes darting, searching for a way out. There was none.

"Drop it!" I repeated.

But the man did not drop it. Instead he leapt off of the platform, onto the tracks, and dashed into the subway tunnel.

Shit.

I raced to the woman. She was semi-conscious, bleeding from a gash on her head, but I couldn't see any gunshot wounds. I felt for her carotid artery; her pulse was strong.

"I'm a police officer. Can you tell me what happened?"

The woman only groaned.

"Freeze!" a voice said. I turned to see a uniformed transit cop pointing a Glock at me—Christ, he looked about eleven fucking years old. I held up my shield. "Take care of her," I said. "And get the power turned off." I leapt off the platform, and followed the gunman into the tunnel.

I caught a glimpse of the gunman, in silhouette, and then he vanished. I squinted into the darkness, the sounds of trains obscuring any telltale sounds of his movements. I moved cautiously down the middle of the track, careful to stay clear of the deadly third rail: six hundred and twenty volts of lethal electricity. The tunnel was cold, damp, and smelled of death—most probably the decomposing bodies of poisoned rats. Darkness enveloped me as I crept deeper into the gloom.

A huge rat scared the hell out of me as it scampered across the tracks, its tail impossibly long, eyes red as a demon's. I stepped to my right, took a position with my back to an enormous concrete support stanchion, my eyes fighting to pierce the murky darkness—why hadn't the electricity been turned off yet?

The train tracks at my feet creaked. Then creaked again. *Uh oh.* Headlights. Noise. I looked south—a train was barreling into the station—this was not going to be fun.

I plastered myself against the stanchion, braced myself. The turbulence from the speeding train nearly sucked me under and onto the tracks. The shooting sparks from the third rail almost set my pants on fire. And then the train was gone, stopped in the City Hall station.

I stepped back onto the tracks and stumbled over a dozen or so surplus railroad spikes; six-inch long, steel, chisel shaped nails. I picked one up—a formidable weapon.

I shoved a spike in my coat pocket, continued into the tunnel.

There were no shortages of places for the gunman to hide. Massive concrete support beams lined the tunnel and there were countless archways and doorways leading to who knows where. I heard what sounded like a thud then there was a disconcerting and absolute silence. The third rail electricity had finally been turned off—no more train traffic to worry about. I cocked an ear and heard water running. Saw more rats.

Voices. Spotlights. I looked behind me and saw that dozens of transit cops were flooding the tunnel. The gunman must have seen them, too, because he sprang from behind a stanchion, no more than twelve feet ahead of me, and started running.

"Freeze, asshole!"

He didn't.

I couldn't chase him without falling and breaking something, and I wasn't about to shoot the fucker in the back. And so I pulled out the railroad spike, threw it—*missed.* But the guy stumbled, lurched forward, arms wind-milling, fighting to maintain his balance. He fell flat on his face.

I came down on him like a ton of bricks, jackhammered my knee between his shoulder blades, my .38 pressed to the back of his head. I yanked the gun from his hand. And that's when the transit cops swarmed us.

"Son of a bitch," a transit sergeant said as we shoved the handcuffed gunman down the tracks, up a short set of concrete stairs, onto the platform, and into the light. "Know who this is?"

I looked closely at the guy's pockmarked face.

"The Soho rapist," the sergeant said.

"No shit." I had to keep from shouting *Yes!* and from fist pumping and kissing the Soho rapist—this was a high profile felony arrest that would make all the newspapers and TV news shows—my sure-fire ticket out of the Building fucking Maintenance Division. The fast track back to patrol, guaranteed. I spun the prisoner around, patted him down, and began going through his pockets; a cell phone, lip balm, a small hand sanitizer, but no ID.

"What command're you assigned to, officer—?" the sergeant said, memo book and pen in his hand.

That's when it struck me: There was no way in hell I could take this collar. I had only just signed myself and six other cops in and out. I had no reason to be in the subway, no excuse for being "off post." If I took the collar, I might sink every man I worked with; we could all be suspended, brought up on departmental charges, maybe even be prosecuted for Theft of Services.

"I'm, uh, off duty." My eyes found the cop who looked like an eleven year old. "I came to the aid of that officer. It's his collar."

The kid cop's mouth dropped open. He was shaking my hand, still thanking me profusely when I stepped onto the next uptown train.

I was surprised to find Solana at home. She was sitting in front of the fifty-two-inch HD TV watching a *Law & Order* episode that she'd co-written, attired in one of my starched white dress shirts; as usual her cell phone was in her hand. Her toned, bare legs were tucked under her, long black hair lay across her shoulders, her large, dark brown eyes were dreamy.

I glanced at the screen, looking to see if it was one of the *Law & Order* episodes that I'd acted on. It wasn't.

"Hey, babe," I said.

"Hey," she said. Her cell phone chirped. She flipped it open, read the text message, then answered, her fingers a manicured blur. Gone were the days when she would run into my arms, kiss me feverishly, tear at my clothes, and drag me into the bedroom.

I'd first laid eyes on Solana when I attended an open-call *Law & Order* audition. I responded to the nationally advertised newspaper ad on a lark, stood in line with a thousand other hopefuls; my only interest was meeting women. No one was more surprised than I when I actually landed the featured role.

Although I was attracted to the Latina beauty from the get-go, Solana paid me no attention during my first few days on the show; that was, until she became the victim of a diabolical murder, arson conspiracy, and, knowing I was with the NYPD, sought my help.

I walked into our bedroom, put my gun away, and thought that perhaps we'd become too involved too soon. I'd known Solana for only a short time when I came to her rescue, actually saved her life—a long story. A whirlwind romance followed and we decided to move in together. Rented the two-bedroom apartment, set up house, bought all new furniture. Furniture we might soon be fighting over.

Not that I blamed Solana.

Catastrophes in my life had caused me to neglect her.

The suicide of my friend and partner, Vinnie D'Amato, had had a lingering psychological effect, caused me to brood, become withdrawn; to this day I sometimes blamed myself for his death.

But the worst was when my sister Shannon died.

I'd embarked on a three-month-long crusade, determined to locate and punish whoever sold my sister the drugs that killed her. I kicked down doors. Made threats. Cracked heads. Then heroin was found in my car and I was suspended. Although I was eventually cleared of criminal charges, I was buried in the Building Maintenance Division, no longer a threat to Harlem drug gangs. Even though I never did find out who planted the drugs in my car (Destiny insisted it was a dirty cop) or the culprits who supplied my sister, I came close.

Then both my parents died.

And I stayed drunk for months.

Which brought us to our current state of affairs.

I found a lone can of beer in the back of the refrigerator, popped it open and felt disheartened about the fact our relationship was deteriorating. And there didn't seem to be anything I could do about it. Or was there?

I swallowed some beer, checked the bread box for some Entenmann's and decided that Solana and I had to talk. I needed to know how she felt, if she thought our relationship was worth saving—I did. Find out whether she wanted me to move out, or whether she wanted to do the moving, take a chance with the new guy in her life; whoever he was.

My cell phone rang.

"Hello?"

"Hey, Beckett. Mark Tesser here."

I couldn't believe my ears. "Hold on." I walked into the master bedroom so Solana could not overhear. "Thought I told you to lose my phone number."

"I called to apologize," Tesser said.

"OK. You've apologized."

"Look, you were right, my guys went overboard," Tesser said. "There was no reason for them to come on so heavy."

"No shit," I said.

"Look," Tesser sighed. "There's another reason I'm calling."

I waited for him to get to it.

"I've got another rocker raid, up on 124th Street, tonight at midnight. Gonna need an extra hand."

"That means what to me?"

"I need a guy with your temperament," Tesser said. "You know, to keep the lid on things."

Had to admit, Tesser had balls. "You gotta be desperate calling me."

"So, you'll do it?" Tesser said.

"Are you out of your fucking mind?" I said.

"I'll double your pay."

"Not interested."

"How 'bout I triple it?"

"You don't listen, do you?" I felt my face flush. "Don't call me again, dickwad, and I mean ever."

I didn't wait for Tesser's response. I hung up. Took a few deep, calming breaths. I realized for the first time that I had reason to be concerned about Tesser; he wasn't going away. And if he kept committing home-invasion-style armed robberies, it was only a matter of time before he would be caught. And he'd be the first one to make a deal with the district attorney. He'd give his rocker team up in a heartbeat. *Maybe even give me up.*

"News bulletin, Michael," Solana called out from the living room. "Police shooting in Manhattan."

I hurried back and saw the news unfold on TV.

"*…a blazing gun battle that sent pedestrians diving for safety,*" an onsite newscaster said. "*One alleged perpetrator was shot by police and taken by ambulance to Metropolitan Hospital.*"

The news cut to an ambulance speeding away from camera. Cut to a cop I knew, Moynihan, placing two battered prisoners into the back of a police car. Cut to uniformed cops administrating crowd control. Cut to cops stringing yellow crime-scene tape across the entrance to a supermarket.

"*Recapping the story,*" the newscaster continued. "*Police exchanged gunfire with three armed men who allegedly robbed a Manhattan supermarket.*"

"Hey, isn't that where your girlfriend Destiny works?"

"Don't start, Solana," I said, watching the screen intently.

"Well, isn't it?"

The newscaster moved on to another story.

"It's in the 19th Precinct, north side." I sipped my beer. "Destiny works the south side."

"There a rule she can't work the north side?" Solana said.

"No," I said. "But I know that cop on TV. Moynihan's had the same partner for years. Destiny works a one-man foot post."

"Don't you think you'd better check?" Solana said.

She was right. I reached for the phone, was about to call

Destiny's cell, but then decided to call the precinct desk officer first; he'd know all.

"Not that I care," Solana said.

I stopped mid-dial. "Now, what's that supposed to mean?"

Solana locked eyes with mine. "What word," she said, "didn't you understand?"

I had no answer to that.

CHAPTER 12

DESTINY DROVE TO Hastings on Hudson in a daze. She parked her VW in her building's underground garage, locked it, and headed to the stairs. That was when she realized that she'd been so spaced out since the shootout, she couldn't recall how she'd gotten home, what route she traveled.

Destiny climbed the brightly lit concrete stairwell to the lobby, checked her mail, took the elevator to the fourth floor, and entered her residence. It was 11:30 P.M. and the apartment was dark, empty, quiet except for the loud rap music that emanated from an upstairs apartment.

She hated rap music.

Destiny turned on the lights, tossed her mail on a hall table, hung her coat. She looked around, made a disgusted face. Fernando had left the apartment a mess as usual. "Fucking Fernando."

Destiny secured her off-duty weapon, clicked on a trigger lock, and placed the gun on a high coat closet shelf. She walked into the kitchen, switched the fluorescent lights on, and checked the answering machine for messages.

She was waiting anxiously for the results of a background check on the guy she'd shot, Gregory 'Sonny' McFarland. His criminal past, if he had one, would greatly affect the focus and politics of the Key Food robbery investigation.

And she wanted desperately to hear from Michael Beckett.

As a veteran of a half-dozen shootouts, he'd know firsthand what she was going through: the surrealism, mixed emotions, and the feeling of being alone.

The upstairs neighbor turned the rap music off.

"Thank you," Destiny said to the ceiling.

She opened the refrigerator and took out a tray of ice. In a cupboard she found a bottle of Mount Gay rum. She dropped a few ice cubes into a glass and covered them with the rich brown liquid. Took a long pull and noticed that her hands were trembling.

Destiny's phone rang. "Yes?"

"Gregory 'Sonny' McFarland's a predicate felon," Sergeant Hill said without preamble. "The skell's been convicted of half a dozen robberies, couple of felonious assaults, gun possession. Been out on parole only a month. How he got outta prison at all is a mystery to me."

"Thanks, Sarge." Destiny breathed a sigh of relief.

She figured that the NYPD and District Attorney's investigators, as well as the news media, would now, most likely, spotlight McFarland's criminal record and not look to find fault with her actions.

A knock—Beckett's knock—at Destiny's front door. She quick-stepped across the room, looked though the door's security peephole, and opened up.

CHAPTER 13

"HOW'S IT HANGING, Dead Eye?" I walked into Destiny's apartment, slipped off my coat, hung it on the back of a kitchen chair, and made myself at home. "I tried reaching you at the station house a couple of times. Your cellphone was turned off."

"Oh, shit." Destiny stepped over to the closet by the front door, opened it, pulled her cell phone from a coat pocket and turned it on. "I was inundated."

"Yeah, I know the drill." I sat on a stool at the kitchen counter and noticed the apartment was a freaking mess; clothes strewn around the living room, magazines, men's underwear, shirts, and shoes littered the floor. Definitely not Destiny's style.

"Talk to me, partner."

Destiny was staring at her cellphone screen. A bell tone rang eight times; she had eight messages. Three were from me.

"Dead eye?" She looked at me. "Did you just call me dead eye?"

"Your new moniker," I shrugged.

"How—?"

"The guy you shot—?"

"Gregory 'Sonny' McFarland," Destiny said. "He's got a rap sheet long as my legs."

I pulled tomorrow's early edition of the *Daily News* from my back pocket, tossed it on the counter, turned the pages, pointed to the article that included photos of her and Moynihan. "You blew McFarland's eyes out."

"Christ." Destiny glanced at the newspaper then massaged the bridge of her nose. "Dead Eye," she said. "I hate that nickname."

Time to change the subject. "You got anything wet in the house, beer, wine?"

"Mount Gay rum."

"Sold. On the rocks," I said. "Then you can tell me what happened."

Destiny got the ice, dumped it into a glass, covered it with rum. "I can't go over it again." She handed me my drink. "I already had my G.O. fifteen interviews," she said. "Told the same story two dozen times."

"So you were interrogated by the duty captain. The squad. A couple of creeps from Internal Affairs."

"An ADA," Destiny said. "A PBA lawyer. And Moynihan said there was some suit from the mayor's office listening to his interview."

"Well, how'd Moynihan do?"

For the first time Destiny smiled. "The guy's about as intimidating as Gumby." She sat on the stool alongside me. "Built like him too. But when the shooting started, he stood his ground, went toe to toe with the perps."

"From what I hear," I said, "you both did."

"I swear to God, I don't remember what I did."

"That what you told the brass?"

"Yeah." Destiny swallowed some rum. "Why?"

"'Cause they sometimes twist things." I took a minute before adding: "You give them an opening, they could make it look like you provoked the shooting."

"But that's not true."

"So? Politics has nothing to do with truth. If the brass has a reason to destroy you, they'll find a way. Remember what they did to me."

Destiny picked up the bottle of Mount Gay, topped off her drink. "Lemme ask you something, Michael. How'd you feel, you know, after you shot those men?"

How did I feel? I looked into my drink, my thoughts turning inward. I was still coming to terms with the moral implications of being a killer of men, second-guessing myself. And then there were the sleepless nights, although they were coming less frequently. "Immediately after the shootings, numb," I said honestly. "I felt numb."

Destiny was staring into her glass. "Am I gonna be able to sleep? I mean, I keep seeing McFarland's face, the look in his eyes."

"Don't do that to yourself, partner; I mean it. You did what you had to do. It was you or him."

"Yeah," Destiny said. "I know."

I placed my hand on hers and squeezed.

"Hey, almost forgot," I said, "You wouldn't happen to know a former NYPD chief named Vogt?"

"Everyone knows him," Destiny said.

"What I mean is, does he know you?"

"I worked in his office for a few months when I was a rookie," Destiny said. "Along with a couple hundred others."

"Would he remember you?"

Destiny shrugged. "There must've been twenty female cops. The horny old geezer was always trying to corner one of us in his office. We didn't know whether to call a lawyer or IAB."

"You leave on good terms?" I said.

"He'd think so."

"All right if I call him, use your name?

"What for?"

I trusted Destiny, but in a "need to know" world there was

no reason to tell her the details of the Julie Gunder undercover investigation. "I need a recommendation for a security gig. The old chief does the hiring."

"Use my name, then. Be my guest." Destiny's cellphone rang and she checked the caller ID. "I gotta take this call. It's my folks."

I got off my stool, opened the freezer, pulled out a tray of ice and added several more cubes to my drink.

"The news is exaggerated, Mother, as always," Destiny said, rolling her eyes. "We were really never in any danger."

I sat back down and gave Destiny the thumbs up sign. Playing down the very real dangers of police work was the right thing to do, be it with strangers, friends, and especially family members.

I listened to my former partner speaking patiently to her parents and had to smile. She was a good daughter. She called her folks most every day. She sent them money to help with their bills. Her father, a retired businessman whose company's pension system had failed, was in ill health. As was her mother. The fact that her parents were living in a rundown trailer park was a source of sadness in Destiny's life; not to mention her putz husband. Fernando was an unstable oddball who I'd just as soon punch out as look at. Destiny was too good for him.

I heard keys in the front door. Fernando walked in carrying a bag of groceries, some dry cleaning—speak of the devil.

Destiny waved to her husband.

"Fernando's home," Destiny said into the phone. "Yes, I'll tell him you said hello. All right then. I'll call you tomorrow. I love you. Bye, Mom. Bye, Dad."

I eyeballed Fernando as he walked into the apartment. He was wearing a long leather coat and his hair was styled back off his face; he looked every bit the glossy Latin lover.

"Hey, honey," Fernando said pleasantly.

I cleared my throat.

Fernando looked startled. "Beckett."

"You remembered the dry cleaning," Destiny said. "Good."

Fernando draped the plastic bags over a chair, placed the groceries on the kitchen counter. "How you been, Beckett?"

I stood and shook Fernando's hand. "Doing OK." I threw back my drink, then touched Destiny's shoulder. "I gotta run. I'm around if you need me." I grabbed my coat, said bye to Fernando, and let myself out. I walked down the hall, pressed the elevator down button.

"What the fuck was he doing here?" Fernando's voice boomed in the empty hallway.

CHAPTER 14

I WALKED INTO the Java The Hut coffee shop around 11
A.M., looked toward the newspaper rack, and saw Destiny
and Moynihan's photo on the cover of the *New York Post*.

The Hut was crowded as usual that morning. The tables were
occupied by laptop users. A few customers were reading books or
the *New York Times*. I noted that the median customer age was
about thirty. Although there were a few eagle-eyed Romeos stalking the place, no one seemed to be mingling.

I took my place at the end of the line, glanced idly out of the
coffee shop window and spotted the fat jerk with the red road-kill
toupee who'd struck his wife in Elaine's. He was skulking in a restaurant doorway, across First Avenue at 49th Street. Road-kill had
his coat collar turned up, hands in his pockets. The red toupee was
perched impossibly high on top of his head. From where I stood, it
appeared that Road-kill was focused on the entrance to the Beekman Tower Hotel, twenty paces or so east of his location.

"One half-white mocha, half-caramel, half-caf venti frappuc-
cino," a woman in the line ahead of me said. "Two grande mocha
coconut frappuccinos and one grande cappuccino."

What?

I checked my wristwatch, heaved a sigh. I didn't like the bitter taste of designer coffees, would certainly never wait on a line for one. But Solana, who was upstairs getting ready for work, loved the café latte.

The coffee line inched forward. I picked up an abandoned copy of the *Post* from an empty table, flipped some pages, scanned a few articles, and saw an interesting headline.

MASKED MEN ROB HARLEM DRUG DEALERS

A gang of heavily armed masked men invaded a Harlem apartment around midnight, brutally assaulted the occupants, and made off with an undisclosed amount of cash, drugs, and weapons, a confidential police department source said.

The article went on to state that the drug dealers were then marched out of the 124th Street apartment, onto the street, and told not to return to the building.

Tesser's Rockers strike again; I was certain of it.

"May I take your order?" a young, fidgety Java The Hut employee said. Her thickly gelled hair was swept back away from her oft-pierced face. Her smile was radiant, ridiculously broad, and white.

I said, "Lemme have a grande, non-fat, decaf latte."

She tapped the cash register keys.

I paid an outlandish amount for the cup of coffee, then wandered to the front of the store to wait, stood between two laptop users and looked across the street. Road-kill was still watching the Beekman Tower Hotel entrance.

My cell phone rang. "Beckett."

"Bill Santic here," a male voice said. "From Chief Vogt's office."

"Oh, right." I stepped into the coffee shop foyer where I had some privacy. "Thanks for getting back to me."

As instructed by Julie Gunder, I'd called Chief Vogt, left a message with his secretary that I was interested in working for Langlois, that I'd been recommended by Destiny Jones. The secretary said that a guy named Bill Santic would call me back ASAP.

"I understand you were Destiny Jones's former partner," Santic said.

"We worked a sector car together, 19th Precinct."

"Good cop, that Destiny. I like her. And because I like her I'm gonna be straight with you—fuck you wanna work for Langlois for?"

I kept my eyes on Road-kill. He was acting squirrely, popping in and out of the doorway, talking to himself.

"I need the job," I said. "Got bills."

"Look, do yourself a favor," Santic said. "Get a job digging graves. Hell, go door-to-door and sell Al-Qaeda memberships. I guarantee you'll be happier, you know?"

I stifled a laugh; Santic was a funny guy. "From what I hear, the hours are flexible, which is good for me."

"Don't think you're gonna make friends with Don Langlois. Some guys take the job thinking they're gonna get close to Langlois—guy's got billions, but he's one-way. Does shit for no one. Wouldn't spit to give a bird a drink of water, you know?"

"Like I said, I *really* need the work."

A silence on the other end of the phone.

"You still there?" I said.

"Where else you work?"

"The 41 Precinct."

"Oh. You're *that* Michael Beckett."

"Yeah. That a problem?"

"Not for me," Santic said, "but you gotta talk to the chief."

"Great," I said. "When? Where?"

"I'll check, see if there's an opening, let you know."

"I was told there're always openings," I said. "That there's a high turnover."

"Who told you that?"

I had to be careful. "I think Destiny mentioned it. Is it true, there's a high turnover? How come?"

"Langlois's wife, Claudia. She's the reason everyone quits."

"What's her story?" I said.

"I'll give you an example. They have a movie theater in the basement. I mean a first-class setup that would impress Spielberg. Twenty seats, 35mm projector, Dolby sound system. And just outside the theater they've got a professional concession stand; old-fashioned soda fountain, candy display, popcorn machines, the works. Claudia keeps it padlocked. Sometimes she sneaks down to the basement in the middle of the night, unlocks the concession stand, and counts every single candy bar to make sure the security men didn't steal anything. Can you imagine? They got billions and that paranoid bitch is counting candy." He paused. "And then there are her midnight fire drills."

"Fire drills?"

Santic snickered. "You get the job, you'll find out." He hung up. I put my cell phone away, walked back into the coffee shop.

"Non-fat, decaf, grande latte?" another ultra-bright coffee shop employee called out. I picked up my order, walked out onto 49th Street, glanced across the avenue.

A black Lincoln Town Car stopped in front of the Beekman Tower Hotel. A woman who looked an awful lot like Road-kill's wife, and a tall man with a thick mane of gray hair, got in. The Town Car pulled out, crossed three lanes of light traffic and made a quick left on east 51st Street.

"Taxi!" Road-kill raced into the street. As he raised his arms in a frenzied attempt to hail a cab, his coat fell open.

There was a gun tucked into his waistband.

CHAPTER 15

DESTINY DROVE TO work at the 19th Precinct that morning in a post-coital haze. She parked her VW in the precinct parking lot and ambled into the station house.

"Hey!" A veteran cop stopped her at the door. "Why didn't Moynihan kill those mutts when he had the chance?"

"Duh? Let me think," Destiny said. "Cause he didn't have to, you idiot." She shoved past the cop and made it to the stairwell.

"Hey, Dead Eye," a rookie cop collared her on the stairs. "You carve any notches on your gun?"

"You call me 'Dead Eye' again, shit for brains, and I'm gonna carve a notch on your skinny white ass."

A potbellied detective came up behind her. "Your boy Moynihan needs to spend more time at the shooting range."

"And you need to go on a diet, you fat fuck."

Destiny pushed past several other insensitive cops with stupid questions and comments. She hiked up to the locker room and changed into uniform—her mind not on the Key Food shooting, but on last night and Fernando.

Fernando had flown into a jealous rage over Beckett having been in the apartment. He'd kicked furniture, punched walls. But instead of quarrelling with her husband, getting in his face, going toe to toe as usual, Destiny had sat motionless at the kitchen counter; she was too emotionally drained to fight. She found she could not control the tears that rolled down her face.

"What is it?" Fernando had said, softening.

Destiny drew a deep breath, composed herself. "I was in a shootout." She pointed to the copy of the *Daily News*.

"You could've been killed," Fernando said after reading the *Daily News*. The article chronicled a fairly accurate version of the armed robbery, the search for the perpetrators, and the ensuing gun battle. He put his arms around Destiny, held her tight, rocked her back and forth.

"I'm so relieved you were not hurt," Fernando said. "I love you, Destiny. I'll always love you. You know that, don't you?"

"Yes, I know that," Destiny said softly.

"I'm sorry I lost my temper," Fernando said. "And I'm sorry about this morning. Sorry I threw the alarm clock."

They had sat at the kitchen table, held and rocked each other for what seemed like a very long time.

Later, in bed, a migraine kept Destiny awake.

She tossed and turned and couldn't stop thinking about the fact that if Gregory "Sonny" McFarland hadn't missed her with his first shot, she'd be the one who was lying half dead, or worse, in a hospital bed.

Destiny's restlessness woke Fernando.

"Are you all right?" he said sweetly.

Destiny said she was tense, that she couldn't sleep.

"Roll over onto your stomach," Fernando said.

Fernando had found a tube of warming body lotion in a bedside table drawer, squeezed some into his hand. Leisurely, methodically, he massaged Destiny's back, worked his way down to her buttocks, thighs, calves, feet. Then he turned her over, ran his fingers lightly over the front of her body circling her nipples, worked his way down her stomach to her pubic area; he gave her chills. Then he pulled her close, kissed her slowly, softly, then passionately, until she was writhing with anticipation. They'd made love for the first time in seven months—no, they'd screwed like minks until the wee hours of the morning.

Afterward, Destiny lay there with her sleeping husband's head resting on her shoulder, thinking that if Fernando was always this sweet, attentive, and understanding, they'd have few marital problems. And she wouldn't be planning on divorcing him.

She caressed Fernando's hair, stared at the ceiling, listened to foghorns booming from ships moving along the Hudson River.

Destiny dressed in her police uniform, strapped on her off-duty weapon—her on-duty Glock was with Ballistics—and headed down to roll call.

The muster room was packed with day-tour cops assigned to routine patrol, cops with criminal court and grand jury appointments. A contingent of Warrant Squad cops and Manhattan Task Force cops were also in attendance.

"Viselli?" Sergeant Hill said, calling the roll.

"Here."

"Harth?"

"Here, boss."

"Moynihan?"

"Yo."

"Jones?"

No response.

"Jones?" The sergeant looked around, saw Destiny, seated in the last row, last seat, staring out the window, daydreaming.

A cop nudged Destiny and she snapped out of her reverie.

"What?" Destiny said to the cop.

The entire muster room cracked up laughing.

"You with us, Destiny?" Sergeant Hill said.

"I'm here," Destiny said, embarrassed. "Sorry."

"You and Moynihan will be on light duty the next two weeks,"

Hill said, "until the shooting investigation is closed. Report to the desk officer for assignment."

Roll call broke up, and Destiny and Moynihan reported to the desk officer. The lieutenant offered them their choice of several "winking" clerical posts.

Moynihan chose to act as the 19th's assistant "broom," which meant he would hang out in the basement, help cook a station house meal, maybe organize a card game.

"Whoever's in favor of lasagna for lunch," Moynihan said, patting his stomach. "Speak up." Instead, a group of young cops surrounded him and began asking questions about the Key Food shooting. Destiny wanted no part of that.

"Well, what's it gonna be, Destiny?" the lieutenant said.

"Anything outside the station house, L.T.?" Destiny said. "Mail runs, transporting evidence, guarding a ripe DOA?"

"Hey, L.T.," the civilian working the switchboard said. "The cop guarding the prisoner over at Metropolitan Hospital's ICU needs relieving."

"I'll take it," Destiny said. The lieutenant assigned a radio car to drop Destiny at the hospital.

A cop stood up when he saw Destiny enter Metropolitan Hospital's ICU. "Hey, you shouldn't be here, Dead Eye."

"Don't call me that."

Destiny looked at the prisoner. He was in the last bed. Thick white bandages were wrapped around his head and face, covering his eyes—Destiny would never forget those owl eyes. Tubes were stuck in his mouth, nose, and arms. Electronic monitors were everywhere; Gregory "Sonny" McFarland was handcuffed to his bed. The cop was right. Destiny shouldn't be there guarding the man she'd shot.

"What's his prognosis?" she said.

"The scumbag's in an irreversible coma," the cop said. "He's dead already."

Dead already. The words reverberated like church bells as the consequences of firing her weapon struck her—she'd actually killed a man. She felt her insides knot and she vibrated with emotion. She made it over to the cop's desk and fell onto a chair.

"Hey, you all right, Dead Eye?" the cop said.

Destiny squinted at the cop.

"Can I bring you back anything?"

"Coffee," Destiny said. "Extra sugar."

"Sure thing." The cop grabbed his newspaper, memo book and hat and headed to the hospital cafeteria.

Destiny placed her elbows on a desk, glanced around the dimly lit, hushed ICU ward and the three or four other patients, and didn't think for a good fifteen minutes. Then she leaned back in the chair and stared at the man whose existence she had severed.

She told herself that McFarland deserved to die. He was a violent predicate felon. And he had tried to kill her. He had given her no choice. But those truths didn't make a damned bit of difference. Destiny felt like she'd done something immoral.

Another thought was bothering her. McFarland had fired a shotgun at her and from less than twenty-five feet away. How could he have missed? Was McFarland a lousy shot? Or had McFarland missed on purpose? Maybe he would rather have died than go back to prison. Maybe he fired at Destiny knowing the cop would shoot back—suicide by cop. It happens.

The migraine struck without warning. Destiny dropped her head in her hands, let out a soft moan.

"You all right, officer?" a male voice said.

Destiny looked up and saw a tall, handsome, square-jawed doctor smiling down at her.

"Just a headache," she said.

"Headaches can be a good thing."

"You're joking." Destiny noted the twinkle in the doctor's large brown eyes. His skin was a flawless deep black, his smile broad, his teeth were even, perfectly white.

"They alert us to things like too much stress, allergies, vitamin deficiencies," the doctor said. "Sometimes conditions far worse. If the headaches are frequent, you should see someone."

"Right now I'll settle for a couple of aspirin." Destiny flipped back her hair and sat a little straighter in her chair. "You wouldn't have some aspirin, Doctor—?"

"I'm Marcus." He extended his hand, let go with an enticing smile. "Doctor Marcus Ian."

"Destiny Jones," she said and shook.

"I'll ask the nurse to bring you some aspirin," Dr. Ian said. "Although Tylenol might be better."

"You!" a woman said.

An older, gray-haired woman was glaring at Destiny, hatred in her owl-shaped eyes, a newspaper clutched in her fist.

"Murderer!" the woman screamed. "You're the mutha fuckin' nigga shot my son. Murderer! Murderer!"

Dr. Ian intervened. "That will do, Mrs. McFarland!" He and a nurse took Mrs. McFarland by the arms and ushered her out of the ICU.

"What the hell was that all about?" Sergeant Hill had entered the ICU and was standing behind Destiny.

"That's the prisoner's mother."

"Oh." Hill sat on the edge of the desk. "Look, whenever you're ready, come see me and we'll write up your application for department recognition. You and Moynihan'll get an Honorable Mention Medal for the Key Food robbery shooting. Maybe even the Combat Cross."

"I don't want any medals," Destiny said, still reeling from McFarland's mother's outburst.

"It's not up to you," the sergeant said flatly. "Department recognition makes the captain look good, which makes the inspector look good, which makes the borough commander look good, which makes the commissioner look good. You're getting medals whether you like it or not—by the way, what're *you* doing here?"

"Relieving McFarland's guard."

"You shouldn't be guarding a guy you shot."

"Tell me about it."

CHAPTER 16

RETIRED CHIEF DOM Vogt was a round, pleasant-looking, grandfatherly type, and I liked him on sight. We met in the Madison Avenue offices of News Corporation, one of the many subsidiaries of Langlois's holding company, Langlois International. Vogt, dressed in an expensive looking gray suit, sat behind a wooden desk in a tiny, dimly lit cubicle office, scanning my resume. He wore a thick wedding ring, and a solid gold NYPD inspector's ring on his right hand.

I sat directly across from him in a navy blue suit, starched white shirt, and black knit tie. I glanced around the office, noted the chief's impressive array of police department memorabilia. Vogt's shields: police officer, sergeant, lieutenant, captain, deputy inspector, inspector, assistant chief inspector, and chief inspector, were mounted on a single plaque, documenting his rise through the NYPD. Photos of the chief with politicians and celebrities were scattered around the room. A Bachelor and a master's degree in criminology from John Jay College hung on a wall behind his desk. On a windowsill stood a photo of the chief with his family; wife, children, and grandchildren.

"How *is* Destiny?" Chief Vogt said.

"She's pretty shook up by the shooting, Chief."

"That's to be expected."

I added, "She's a tough one, though."

"Pretty, too." He looked up, signaling a change of subject. "You ever work for anyone like the Langloises before, pally?" the chief said. "I mean, with their kind of money?"

"No." Which was technically true. I'd socialized on occasion with very wealthy people, but never actually worked for any of them.

"The rich are different," the chief said. "Don't have the same insecurities the average person does. Few years ago the biggest thing in the Langlois's lives was finding the 'right' guru. Then it was the 'best' psychic. Then the 'most popular' plastic surgeon. Now it's who in their social circle has the best Pilates instructor. It's a competition. Seems everything to them is a competition."

"I understand."

"Do you?" The chief laid down my resume and picked up and opened a folder with "Beckett" written across it in neat block letters—was that my official NYPD personnel folder?

"Look, pally, says here you're one hell of a cop."

"I did all right," I said.

"Worked the Bronx. Medal of Honor. Averaged seventy felony arrests a year, ninety-percent conviction rate; six confirmed kills."

I shifted uneasily in my chair. I'd never spoken to anyone about winning the Medal of Honor, or the men I'd wounded or killed.

"I see you've had your share of disciplinary problems." Vogt flipped a page, raised an eyebrow, shook his head. "Now they've buried you. Building Maintenance; no place for someone as active as you." He closed the folder. "You know, they would've fired you if you weren't a Medal of Honor winner."

I felt my eyes turn hard. "Is that right?"

"Relax." The chief held up his hands. "I got no problem with you, pally. Matter of fact, you're my kind of cop." He picked up a piece of paper, handed it over. "Here, sign it."

"What is it?"

"A standard non-disclosure agreement. It states you will not speak or write anything negative about Don Langlois and his family. If you violate the agreement, he'll sue your ass into the afterlife. I guarantee it."

I glanced over the agreement, signed it, and handed it back to the chief. Vogt checked the signature and then gave me a cop's practiced once-over.

"I won't bullshit you, pally," the chief said. "You have the corporate look the Anglos want. Just between us, they won't have blacks or Hispanics in the house." The chief sat back. "You've probably heard about Mrs. Langlois. She's not easy on the help. How do you feel about that?"

"Long as I get paid."

The chief smiled. "Good answer." He stood up and held out his hand. "You're hired, pally."

We shook.

"Oh, there's another former 41 Precinct guy working here, senior man, runs things at the Langlois residence. Hans Kohlman?"

"The kraut?" I said, perking up. "Sure. Retired last year. He still the NRA pistol shot champion?"

"Not since his son's accident," Vogt said.

"Oh," I said. "Right." I vaguely remembered that after Kohlman retired from the job, a car accident had rendered his adolescent son a paraplegic. As a result, Kohlman, the undisputed best pistol shot in the NYPD, was forced to abandon competition and return to full-time work. It was the only way to keep up with his son's appalling medical bills.

Vogt waved a summons to a man seated at an obscure desk at the far end of a field of desks. "You'll report to Bill Santic. Know him?"

"We spoke on the phone," I said.

"He's a retired detective out of Manhattan North. Good man.

Handles the payroll and scheduling for the security teams." The chief patted me on the back. "Do me a favor, pally. Don't make me regret hiring you."

"I won't," I said, though I wondered why he said that.

Bill Santic, an affable, gap-toothed ex-jock gone to pot, wore a suit that needed pressing and a shirt that needed laundering. After some department small talk, I accompanied Santic to his desk. I sat across from the ex-detective and filled out the necessary forms: W-2, emergency notification in case of injury.

"You aware you'll be making eleven-dollars an hour?" Santic said.

I started. Julie Gunder had not mentioned that the regular pay was so lousy.

"Reason I mentioned it," Santic said. "I was told you were a high roller; weren't you an actor on *Law & Order?*"

"Yeah," I said. "I was in half a dozen episodes. Made enough money to pay my cell phone bill. Now I'm a flat broke high roller. A legend in my own mind."

Santic chuckled. "Long as you know; I mean, supervisors can make upwards of forty an hour, but that's after a few years."

"I understand," I said.

"When can you start?" Santic said.

"Right away."

Santic placed my paperwork in a desk drawer. "I'll take you over to the residence now if you have the time. We'll start you tomorrow night."

"Works for me."

We left the News Corporation building, bundled up, and walked through driving snow up Madison Avenue to the Langlois residence on East 65th Street.

"Langlois's got over fifty full-time armed security men," Santic said, "and, believe me, he needs them. He has enemies. You'll be assigned to his elite personal team. His 'Praetorian Guard,' which numbers about twelve men." Santic managed to light a cigarette from the glowing butt of another in the high wind.

"There are two men in the residence at all times," Santic said. "That's twenty-four hours a day, seven days a week. You'll be one of them. Two more men are assigned to Langlois personally, a driver and a bodyguard, both armed. Mrs. Langlois has an armed driver at her disposal. There's an extra driver for incidentals, case there's an errand to be run, or one of Mr. Langlois's, uh, lady friends needs something."

"I hear ya."

"Look," Santic said as we negotiated a filthy snowdrift and stepped onto a sidewalk, "the Langloises are not what you'd call salt of the earth people. Off the record, they're fucking ass-wipes. But they've got the money, six billion dollars—."

"And we put up with them."

The Langlois residence was a stately, six-floor, thirty-thousand-square-foot stone edifice located at East 65th Street, between Park and Madison Avenues. As we approached, I noted that there were no windows at street level, only a large, regal front door, a smaller service entrance, and aged TV security cameras.

Santic rang the service entrance bell and we were buzzed in. We made an immediate left and stopped in the security office/command center: a tiny, ratty, walk-through room.

On a homemade plywood desk sat several ancient Sony surveillance monitors, radio battery charge racks, and piles upon piles of dog-eared magazines. The room had the feel of a ten-year-old's backyard tree house.

Santic introduced me to five beefy, dark-suited cops and ex-cops. Most were older than me. We exchanged handshakes all around. Suspicious eyes scrutinized me—the new hire. One guy repeated my name twice. Spelled it. I knew the moment I was out of earshot, every man present would be on the phone to check me out, determine if I could be trusted.

Santic led me through the security office and into the main house. Servants were scurrying about. Security men roamed.

Our footfalls echoed as we stepped across the formal entranceway: a vast, cold-tiled foyer with large paintings on the walls.

"Case you're wondering," Santic said. "Those two paintings're Picassos. That's a Van Gogh. That's a Monet—all originals, of course."

"Of course," I said. The joint was decorated to awe, staffed to intimidate, and was large enough to house the entire 19th Precinct.

Santic led the way to a man seated at a desk situated at the foot of an enormous, sweeping staircase that I could picture Norma Desmond swishing down. A private elevator was located directly across from the desk.

"Mario," Santic said. "Say hi to your new partner, Michael Beckett. He works down at HQ. Building Maintenance."

Mario, a studious, stiff sort, looked up from a book. The weak handshake and thin smile were an effort.

"Mario retired out of traffic," Santic said.

"How nice," I said.

I could feel Mario studying me.

"Report here to the security office tomorrow night at eleven P.M., Beckett," Santic said. "It'll give you an extra hour for Mario to show you around the house, teach you how to work the phones."

"Phones?" I said.

Santic pointed at a confusing-looking desktop switchboard with a dozen phone numbers listed on its face. "Every call for the Langloises comes through those phones. You'll know where they are at every moment, here or Palm Beach or the Hamptons, and you'll route the calls to them. It's a difficult system to learn, and Mrs. Langlois breaks water every time a new man loses a call or cuts her off."

"What's security doing fielding phone calls?"

"Everyone in the company seems to resent the security staff,"

Santic said. "Says we got a cushy job, sit around and do nothing, so they're constantly finding jobs for us to do."

"Didn't you work in the 19th?" Mario asked bluntly.

"Yeah."

"I know you," Mario said.

Here we go.

"You were in the papers. They found drugs in your car." Mario turned to Santic. "IAB found drugs in his car. They suspended him, brought him up on charges."

Santic cocked an eyebrow.

"Lemme ask you something, Mario." I could feel a blast of adrenaline hit my blood stream. "Being an asshole," I said a little too loudly. "It come naturally, or you work on it?"

"We have a problem?" a commanding male voice said.

I turned. A bear of a man, Hans Kohlman had stepped off the Langlois residence elevator and was towering behind us.

"Beckett?"

"Kohlman." I lit up with a smile of real pleasure. "You old jarhead."

"For the love of—". Kohlman planted his oversized fists on his hips. "We *gotta* be hard up to hire the likes of you."

"Stop with the praise." I chuckled. "You'll embarrass me."

We both laughed, shook hands, and embraced. This phony job might be some fun after all.

CHAPTER 17

"GIVE IT TO me straight, Beckett," Hans Kohlman said above Elaine's bar chatter. It was just after 9:00 P.M. Kohlman was working on his first scotch and water. I had ordered dinner; steak and mashed potatoes, and was finishing my second Coors Light.

"What's a high roller like you doing working at Langlois'?"

"Will you stop with the high roller shit? I'm broke. Period. Who isn't these days."

The actor Alec Baldwin and director Martin Scorsese were sitting at a table to our right with what appeared to be an entourage of staffers. At the other end of the bar Vernon was doing his best to quiet a group of sports geeks—grown men who were screaming and yelling at a college football game on the restaurant's only TV. Dressed like adolescents in various football jerseys, the man-children were so agitated with the score, you'd think a home team loss would have worldwide consequences.

"C'mon, Michael." Kohlman turned on his barstool and faced me. "This is *me* you're talking to."

I smiled at my old mentor. I hated having to lie to him, a man who not only helped train me, but whom I'd spent three weeks with, lying in ambush for a gang of armed thugs. My friend's craggy face reminded me of that 41 Precinct stakeout—one of the reasons Hans Kohlman was a legend in the annals of the New York City Police Department.

Late one New Year's Eve, me, Vinnie D'Amato, and Hans Kohlman were sequestered in the backroom of a Bronx liquor store, playing cards, five-shot-pump shotguns at the ready.

"I'm out." Kohlman threw down his cards, excused himself, headed to the men's room, and took his shotgun with him.

The two crackheads took us by surprise when they rushed in brandishing semi-automatic weapons. One of them shouted out their intentions to rob the place. He forced customers to hand over their cash while the other mutt pistol-whipped the proprietor for no reason.

Before D'Amato and I could spring from our hiding place, Kohlman charged in from the other side of the store. Yelled out: "Happy New Year, motherfuckers!" and opened fire. Both robbers died instantly. D'Amato and I never fired a shot.

When newspaper, TV reporters, and CSI investigators arrived on the scene and interviewed the liquor store proprietor and other witnesses, they quite innocently told what happened.

"Happy New Year, !@#$%^&*!" blared from the front page of every newspaper in town. A grand jury was paneled to investigate. D'Amato and I testified, swore on a Bible that Kohlman had done things by the book; that he'd identified himself. Gave the perpetrators a chance to surrender. That we did not hear anyone call out: "Happy New Year, motherfuckers!" That the liquor store proprietor's memory was in question because he'd been pistol-whipped. And that the customers/witnesses had to be either drunk or stoned on crack cocaine.

I had the distinct feeling that the grand jurors did not believe a single word we said, and I feared that our friend would be prosecuted, stripped of his badge, gun, and pension. How wrong I was.

As D'Amato and I passed Kohlman on his way into the grand

jury room, we watched just long enough to see the grand jurors jump to their feet and give the crusty old cop a standing ovation.

"Look, I ran up my credit cards," I said. "I've got creditors coming outta my ass. I'm desperate."

"Desperate enough to work for assholes like the Langloises, and for peanuts?" Kohlman said. "You won't last two weeks."

"*You're* working for them."

"And I hate working for them," Kohlman said. "But I've been there long enough to earn top wages. I wouldn't put up with them otherwise."

"It's not that I haven't tried moonlighting," I said. "I'm available for PI work. I'll play bodyguard. Hell, I even tried rocking."

Kohlman rose an eyebrow at that. "No shit?"

I sipped my beer. "Sounded good at first. We were supposed to evict a gang of clueless drug dealers, piece of cake. Five hundred dollars for an hour's work."

Kohlman was impressed. "Sign me up."

I shook my head at his enthusiasm. "Guy in charge assembled a team of sadists. You might know him, Mark Tesser?"

"Yeah." Kohlman looked off, trying to remember. "I think I know Tesser." He swallowed some scotch. "A shifty character, but a good cop, as I recall. He's rocking?"

"More like committing home invasion robberies," I said, scowling. "Not that I think rocking's a bad idea in general. But you need the right team. Not to mention clients with money."

Screams. The sports geeks went berserk. They hollered, mumbled, chanted, shouted hexes, rocked, hugged themselves, turned their caps upside down, inside out like fetishists.

"Hey!" Vernon said. "One more outburst and you're outta here, the bunch of you." The sports geeks dropped it a notch.

Kohlman's wristwatch alarm went off. "I'd better get going." He tossed back what was left of his drink. "See you at Langlois's." He started to get up, then stopped. "Say, Beckett." He placed a hand on my shoulder then whispered in my ear. "If you ever do decide to try rocking…"

"You'll be the first reprobate I call." I watched my pal walk out the door.

"Your dinner, sir." Vernon set a tray of food down in front of me: a broiled sirloin steak with garlic mashed potatoes and string beans. "You need anything else, sir?," Vernon said. "Butter, salt, fresh pepper, steak sauce?"

"Say what?" Vernon had never referred to me as "sir" before. "Come again?"

"You need anything else, sir?"

I eyeballed Vernon. "How `bout a knife and fork."

"Right away, sir."

"All right." I pushed my plate away. "That's it."

"Excuse me?" Vernon said.

"Lookee here, negro. I come in here to be picked on and abused. You start being nice, treating me like some nobody paying customer, I'm leaving and not coming back."

Vernon cracked a smile. "All right. Calm your pits." He set down the requested utensils and the usual accoutrements. He glanced around to make sure the boss Elaine was not watching. He set his elbows on the bar, leaned toward me, and lowered his voice.

"Remember I told you about Enia and her husband stopping by?"

"Yeah," I said warily. "I remember."

"Well, she came back yesterday. Alone. Told me that she and her husband're having problems with a street gang."

I knifed a dollop of butter, jabbed into the potatoes. "Yeah, so tell them to go talk to the gang unit at the 19th Precinct."

"I told her she should talk to you first."

"You what?"

"Hey, relax," Vernon said. "Just talk to her. Give her some advice. I mean, you can just talk to her, can't you?"

"Forget it." I shook a bottle of steak sauce, twisted the cap off, slathered some on my steak. "I want nothing to do with her. Case closed."

"Oops," Vernon said.

"Oops?" I said. "Oops what?"

"She's here."

"What?" My heart skipped. "Where?"

"That's her and her husband. In the back." Vernon gestured. "The four-top against the wall."

"Aw fuck, Vernon."

CHAPTER 18

I LOOKED TO a rear table and my stomach did something painful and unnatural. Enia's husband was facing me: an average looking forty-something year-old guy in a dark business suit. All I could see was Enia's back; it was an elegant back.

"Well?" Vernon said.

"If I do talk to her," I said, giving in quicker than I should have, "you gotta keep your big fucking mouth shut about it. Don't tell Solana *or* Destiny."

"Hey, I swear." He held up his hand; a pledge. "Not a word to anyone. That's why they call me 'the sphinx'."

"No," I said. "They don't."

Vernon used his pledge hand to wave to Enia's husband.

I put down my fork, took a deep breath, tried to prepare myself. The last time I'd seen Enia, she'd caused an embarrassing scene in a restaurant, thrown food in my face.

"Alex Schultz," Vernon said, his eyes over my right shoulder. "Say hello to Michael Beckett."

I turned to face Schultz.

"Hello." Schultz stuck his hand out. "Good to meet you."

I shook Schultz's hand, a strong workman's hand. He was balding, needle-nosed, slight of stature. The off-the-rack suit and tie he wore looked inexpensive. He wore a gold wedding ring. A Movado wristwatch.

"You already know my wife, Enia."

At first I averted my eyes. I hadn't seen Enia in a couple of years and I wanted her to be fat, unkempt, miserable. I wanted the satisfaction of knowing that her life had fallen apart after she'd ripped me off.

Enia stepped out from behind her husband and into view.

I felt my breath catch.

"Hello, Michael."

The sports geeks leered.

"Hello, Enia."

Enia was still savagely attractive with long blonde hair, large blue eyes, a wide mouth, and flawless skin. She wore a white, off the shoulder cashmere sweater that accentuated insistent breasts, and a tight, short navy blue skirt that revealed just enough of the toned, sensuous thighs that I once loved to kiss.

I stood out of habit because I was raised to stand in the presence of a lady. Not out of any kind of respect. "It's been a while."

"Has it?" Enia said. She tossed her hair, revealing large diamond earrings. A gold watch and other expensive looking jewelry dangled from her wrists.

"Over three years," I said and noticed she was wearing her trademark six-inch stiletto heels. "Bruno's Restaurant."

"Ah, yes, Bruno's," Enia said.

"We sat upstairs, corner table by the piano player," I said. "Shared the carpaccio di pesce appetizer, a rare porterhouse steak, a bottle of red wine."

"No dessert?" Schultz said half-jokingly.

I looked at him. "Warm truffle gateau." I turned to Enia. "As I recall, you threw it in my face."

She was entirely unfazed. "Seemed like a good idea at the time."

Schultz chuckled and put his arm around Enia. "She's done the same freakin' thing to me."

"Chianti," Enia said lightly, "makes me crazy."

Schultz laughed.

Vernon laughed.

I didn't.

"Join us when you're done eating?" Schultz said. "Please?"

I glanced at my wristwatch. "I'm late as is."

"Please," Enia said and touched my arm.

I looked at the flawless manicured hand making contact with my skin and felt the force of Enia's sexuality. I looked deep into her baby-blues and she looked back—she had a lot of nerve approaching me like this.

"All right," I heard myself say. And watched as she and her husband walked back to their table.

"Now." Vernon set down a fresh beer. "That wasn't so bad, was it?"

The look I gave Vernon sent him scurrying to the opposite end of the bar. I sat back down on my bar stool, picked up my knife and fork, cut a slice of steak, pushed it angrily around in the garlic mashed potatoes and string beans. I never thought I'd see Enia again, never wanted to.

I drank some more beer, played with my food, and couldn't stop myself; I stole a glance at Enia's table. She had her legs crossed, skirt hiked up. *Christ!* Was that for my benefit? Of course it was. Enia did everything for a reason.

I caught myself staring lustily, my eyes moving ever-so-slowly from Enia's hooker heels to her dainty ankles to her full calves. I snapped myself out of it, averted my gaze, pretended interest in my food, and recalled the day we met; it was the first time she conned me.

I was alone at Elaine's that summer evening when Enia breezed in, scented in lilac, dressed in tasteful business attire that did little to hide her knockout figure. She took a seat at the near empty bar, ordered a glass of champagne. I looked up from my Blackberry.

Enia glanced in my direction.

I smiled.

She nodded pleasantly. "It is my birthday."

Warning bells. Women were forever coming into Elaine's claiming it was their birthday; an obvious and annoying attempt at hustling drinks. But, then again, none of those women looked anything like Enia.

"Are you celebrating alone?"

"Yes," Enia said and let loose with a smile that simply bewitched me.

"I can't allow that."

Picking up on my cue, Vernon popped open a bottle of Crystal, poured Enia a glass. "This is with Michael." He gestured to me.

My man.

I moved down two bar stools. "I'm Michael Beckett."

"I am Enia Vladimirescu."

"Enia." I tasted her name. "May I join you?"

"You may," she said. "But you may not pay for my champagne." She reached into her purse, placed a credit card on the bar. "It is my birthday. I buy the champagne."

Vernon poured me a glass of bubbly. I settled in beside Enia. We slid into get-acquainted small talk; Enia was obviously educated, well mannered, charming. Her accent was provocatively foreign.

"What is your profession?" she said.

"I'm a police officer. And you?"

"In Romania I was a lawyer," Enia said. "Here I work for Mary Kay Cosmetics. I win pink Cadillac every year."

"Have you had dinner?"

She said she hadn't.

We sat at a table, ordered dinner, finished two more bottles of champagne—Enia insisted on picking up the entire tab. She wouldn't even allow me to leave a tip; a gesture that thoroughly impressed me. (And fooled me. Enia would never again pick up a check, or pay for anything with her own money ever again.)

Later that evening I coaxed her back to my apartment. And for the first time in my life I experienced life-altering, soul-penetrating sex; I did not know it at the time but Enia was to become my obsession.

During the next few months Enia proceeded to dazzle me with her sense of style, humor, and shrewd intellect. I saw her seven days a week, neglected my job, family, friends, even myself. Became jealous of everyone and everything that kept us apart; I couldn't get enough of her. The fact that she performed fellatio on me at every possible opportunity—in men's rooms, restaurant coat rooms, the back seat of taxi cabs—caused me to ignore the fact that she never did go to work. And, in contrast to her "big spender" routine our first night in Elaine's, she was always borrowing money from me. It also meant I paid no attention to my credit card statements.

"Must be mistake," Enia said when I finally came out of the sex-induced fog and realized there were bogus credit card charges on my bill. "Maybe identity theft." I called the banks and disputed each and every unauthorized charge. After a brief investigation it became evident that someone very close to me was using my cards.

It was time to confront my obsession.

I met Enia for dinner at Bruno's Restaurant. We ordered a four-star dinner along with a couple of bottles of red wine. Over dessert—that warm truffle gateau—I confronted her about her job; *did she really work for Mary Kay?* The frequent loans I'd made to her; *when would I be paid back the over $10,000?* And the unauthorized credit card charges; *who was responsible for them?*

Enia claimed she quit Mary Kay because of corporate politics; *people were jealous of her.* She said she'd pay me the money she borrowed as soon as she was able; *didn't I trust her?* And she vehemently denied ever using my credit cards, wove an intriguing tale of conspiracy and treachery, attempted to cast suspicion on everyone from Mary Kay herself, Destiny, even my sister Shannon; that did it.

"You're a liar," I told her.

And she threw the warm truffle gateau in my face, stormed out of the restaurant, never to be seen or heard from again—until tonight.

"Fucking Vernon," I grumbled.

No longer hungry, I laid down my knife and fork, pushed away my plate, took a deep breath, and made my way to the rear of the restaurant to Enia's table.

The Schultzes were seated between Leonardo DiCaprio's table and Julie Gunder's reserved table—Gunder had yet to arrive.

I pulled out a chair at the four-top and sat across from the couple. "So," I said. "Tell me about your gang problem."

Schultz said that after selling his share of a dot.com company, he'd purchased and moved into the very tenement where his immigrant grandparents had once resided and converted it into a boutique hotel.

"The German Hotel is on 94th Street between First Avenue and York Avenue," Schultz said. "Half a block away from the Isaacs Houses projects."

The idea actually intrigued me. "German Town," I said as a waiter brought me a fresh beer. "My father told me 86th Street was once packed with so many German restaurants and dance halls, it was known as Sauerkraut Boulevard."

"Everyone said I was nuts to buy the dump," Schultz said. "But they'll change their tune when they see what I've done. I reinstalled the original nineteenth-century oak and pine window and ceilin' moldings."

Enia said, "He found an ancient wooden door in the basement, restored it, and hung it in the entrance. Then he located period sinks, faucets, tubs."

Schultz chimed in. "I removed the fire escapes—my grandparents once slept on those fire escapes—and refurbished them."

"They're now called 'decorative balconies,'" Enia said.

"A financially risky project," I said.

"Not really," Schultz said. "I mean, the real estate market in Yorkville is holding steady. The area is still gentrifying. Upscale clothing boutiques and gourmet coffee shops're popping up. People're drawn by the neighborhood contrasts: you can buy gourmet foods or patronize the old mom and pop German delis. It's only a matter of time before the investment pays off."

Schultz said that it had taken a full year to renovate the buildings. He had begun to rent rooms to business travelers and tourists. But in the past few months, a gang from the Isaacs Housing projects had moved in, terrorized and run off the guests.

"What gang?" I said.

"The Belfast Boys."

The Belfast Boys? I knew them from when I was investigating my sister Shannon's death: an IRA-connected bunch of psychopaths on par with the infamous American born-and-bred Westies. But the gang's leader had been gunned down, their second-in-command was in some British prison, and so my investigation had hit a dead end.

"I'm on the hook for nearly two million," Schultz said. "We lose the hotel, we'll be destitute."

Despite my dislike of Enia, I found myself sympathizing with the guy. "I'll make a few calls," I said. "Put you in touch with the right cop, someone in the gang unit."

Schultz shook his head. "Show him, Enia."

Enia pulled up the sleeve of her white cashmere sweater and lifted a large bandage displaying an angry red scab with stitches on her forearm.

"They said they'll cut her throat if we go to the cops again," Schultz said, dropping his head. "I believe them."

"All right, I get the picture," I said. "But if you don't want me to use my connections, what do you want from me?"

Enia let her sweater sleeve fall back into place. She leaned forward and whispered, "We want you to help us rid ourselves of this gang."

I listened to Enia speak, watched those lips move, immersed myself in the sound of her voice, found I was awash with lustful memories: Enia nude, straddling me, her eyes closed, into her orgasm, repeating my name, "Michael." "Michael." "Michael," over and over.

I had a vivid flash of the first time we'd had sex: in my apartment. Enia was bent over my bed, her skirt pulled up to her waist, her silk-thong panties around her ankles. My windows were wide open—the possibility of being seen had only added to the excitement.

Schultz said. "I've heard about groups of cops called rockers."

Rockers. The word startled me back to reality. I took a moment, sipped my beer.

"I'd pay to clean my buildin' out," Schultz said.

"Thought you were broke," I said.

"We can raise *some* money," Enia said.

"Really," I said, an edge to my voice. Enia and I locked eyes and an electric flare passed between us. I didn't know whether I felt more like slapping her or tearing her clothes off and fucking her.

"There're other shopkeepers in Yorkville who have a vested interest in seeing the gang leave," Schultz said. "They'll contribute."

I still wasn't committing myself.

"Look, if you're sure you don't want to deal with the Gang Unit, all I can do is recruit a couple of off-duty cops, or ex-cops to hang around the buildings as part-time security guards. They'd make dealing drugs difficult, eventually starve or scare the Belfast Boys off."

"That'll take too long," Schultz said. "I'll be ruined. I want those bastards out. Now."

"Can't help you," I said.

"You know any rockers?"

I sat back in the chair.

If I didn't despise Enia, I might have actually considered recruiting Hans Kohlman, putting together a first-rate rocker team of my own, and rocking the Belfast Boys from the German Hotel; I could always use the money. As it was, the only rocker I knew was Mark Tesser. And for a fleeting moment I actually considered recommending him and his band of sadists. But I wanted nothing further to do with that whack-job. The memory of busted heads and spattered blood sent a shiver up my spine.

I shook my head. "Rockers are a myth."

Schultz and Enia exchanged a look.

"You're sure?" Schultz said.

"Trust me." I looked Schultz in the eye. "There's no such thing as rockers."

CHAPTER 19

"HERE'S THAT PUSSY from Building Maintenance," a big Irishman said with a wry grin when I came in through the Langloises' servants entrance at 11:00 P.M.

The other four men I'd met stopped and looked mildly at me. I said hello, forced a smile; not into it. My mind was still on my encounter with Enia.

I could tell she didn't believe me when I said I couldn't help with their gang problem. And so it was only a matter of time before she tried to contact me again, infiltrate my life—*What Enia wants, Enia gets.*

I slipped out of my overcoat, shook the snow off, hung it on an available hook in the foyer and stepped into the security office.

The Irishman stuck out a giant hand. "Kohlman said you can handle a shotgun and your beer." He shook my hand with a well-intentioned, bone-crushing squeeze. "We'll have to see about the beer."

The service entrance door swung open and a blast of cold air followed my new partner, Mario the Asshole, into the townhouse. He slipped off a ratty ski parka, hung it on a hook.

A telephone rang.

The five men straightened. A mustached guy seated at the surveillance monitors picked up the phone on the second ring.

"Security," he said, listened for a second, hung up. "That was Kohlman. Get ready."

All at once last gulps of water, soda and coffee were swallowed, coats and gloves hurriedly pulled on. The mustached guy remained at the monitors. The other men rushed from the office and out the service entrance door.

"What's going on?" I said.

"The Langloises are on their way out," Mario the Asshole said.

I checked the time: 11:02. "Where to?"

"Who the fuck knows."

Using the security video monitors, I saw that the men who'd rushed outside had taken posts on the street in front of the townhouse and by the Langlois limo.

"Say, Beckett," Mario said. "How 'bout you take the front door post?"

"Me? I'm here for orientation."

"You're getting paid," Mario said, "aren't you?"

The mustached guy smiled. "Think of it as a form of indoctrination, Beckett. Baptism by fire."

"Yeah, yeah."

"Listen up," Mario said in that charming way of his.

"I'm all ears."

"When you see the Langloises approach, open up the door, let 'em out, then close it fast. Don't speak to them unless spoken to. Got that?"

"Yeah." I took up the position at the front door. After a moment I heard the elevator rattle, then voices, watched as a stone-faced Hans Kohlman, Don Langlois, his wife Claudia, and a nurse carrying an infant exited the elevator.

The Langloises were casually dressed. He was a short man, bald, had a long, fat lit cigar stuck in a friendly-looking face.

Claudia was not unattractive. Doe eyes, full lips, slim. She looked better in person than she did on TV.

The Langloises walked to a hallway closet, grabbed their coats—hers a full-length fur, his a fleece-lined Marlboro— and straggled toward me.

I opened the front door.

"What're you doing?" Claudia shrieked.

"Excuse me?" I said.

"You're letting heat out, you idiot." Claudia spoke as if to a retard. "What the hell is wrong with you? Are you stupid? Addle-brained? You have any idea what it costs to heat a home this size?"

"Sorry," I said, thoroughly humiliated. I closed the door, waited as the Langloises bundled up, and assembled at the door.

"Now," Claudia said, dripping sarcasm. "I said, n-o-w. Open the goddamned door now!"

I did as told, stepped aside as the Langloises, escorted by Kohlman, exited their house.

"So, whaddya think of Mrs. Charm?" the mustached guy said when I walked back into the security office. "Me?" he said. "I hate her fucking guts."

"She always so pleasant?" I said.

"You got off easy," Mario said. "She fired the last new guy for letting heat out sixty seconds after he started work."

"So," I said. "You set me up."

Mario smiled smugly. "C'mon."

Mario led me out of the security office, back to the rear of the house, and down a set of concrete stairs to the basement. We passed the plush home theater and concession stand Bill Santic had mentioned. Pushed open a door and entered an overheated, makeshift locker room that smelled of last year's air with a hint of coal gas.

Mario showed me where to stow my gear, a rusty locker. There was an old coffee machine, refrigerators: padlocked. Mario pointed out the toilet. I looked inside and grimaced. I'd seen cleaner toilets in ghetto gas stations. I would soon learn it was the only toilet that security was permitted to use.

"I guess it's a good time to show you the house with them out," Mario sighed. A burden.

Mario led me back up the rear stairs, through the security office and into the foyer. He introduced me to the four-to-midnight man sitting at the desk at the bottom of the sweeping staircase. We would relieve the man at the desk and the mustached man who was sitting at the monitors in the security room in less than an hour, at midnight.

I followed Mario into the Langloises' elevator, rode it to the sixth floor, then walked one flight up to the roof. The roof door was alarmed and the roof itself monitored by motion detectors. As we descended via the stairs and stopped at each floor, I discreetly checked windows and door locks, needing to see if alarm contact points were intact, and scanned for functioning motion detectors.

In addition to a well-equipped gym, a library and an elaborate playroom, the fifth, fourth and third floors contained guest rooms, twelve in all, most of which, according to Mario, were rarely used.

"Why's that?" I said.

"Far as I know," Mario said. "The Langloises have no friends."

The second floor was the Langloises' main residence.

"All windows on the second floor are bulletproof," Mario said. "There are panic buttons everywhere wired to us downstairs. The floor is soundproof. You could set a bomb off down on the first floor and they wouldn't hear it."

Mario guided me through the Langloises' enormous master bedroom. The carpet was beige, wool and thick. A plush king-size canopy bed was the focal point of the surprisingly sparse room. The large, draped floor-to-ceiling windows, which were also soundproof as well as bulletproof, faced the street. The few furnishings, which I assumed were over-the-top expensive, were muted in color.

"That bathroom also functions as a safe room," Mario explained, gesturing to a closed door on the south side of the bedroom.

Thirty steps took me to the bathroom. I opened the door, switched on the lights and had to shield my eyes.

"Yikes," I said. The gold fixtures and seemingly acres of gleaming white tile and mirrors were blinding.

"The word 'garish' come to mind?" Mario said.

I stepped inside. There were reflections of our reflections of our reflections. "Tell me about this place."

"In case of emergency," Mario said, "the Langloises would run in here and seal it off." He demonstrated by closing the door and tripping a lock; six steel rods engaged the door frame.

"The doors and frame are reinforced steel," Mario said, "as are the walls, ceiling and floor." He opened a linen closet's doors revealing neat, precise stacks of white towels. He pressed a button and pulled. The shelves swung out and open, revealing a hidden chamber. We stepped inside what was a good-sized room. There were six bunk beds. Some basic furniture. A stand-alone generator.

"They have cellular communications," Mario said. "There's enough food and water in here for seven days." He pointed to a flat cherry wood cabinet mounted on the wall. "The weapons are in there."

I took it all in without comment, although I couldn't imagine being this paranoid. "What's that in the corner?" I pointed at a large black box with a digital keypad on its face.

"Some sort of high-tech safe. I'm told it's burglar proof, if there is such a thing."

We stepped out of the hidden room. Mario gently pushed the shelves back in place, closed the linen closet, and walked through a door on his left.

"This is the infant's room."

The Langlois infant's room was overdone in pink. The crib was situated in the center of the room and had a video camera positioned on the ceiling directly above it.

"The baby is watched and tended to day and night by twenty-four hour nurses," Mario said. "Claudia is not what you'd call a 'hands-on mother'. She's never changed a diaper in her life. The kid gets cranky or sick, Claudia dumps her on the nanny."

At the rear of the second floor was a full kitchen that would impress a certified master chef. It was independent of the large professional restaurant kitchen Mario told me was on the main floor.

"The Langloises spend most of their time in this kitchen," Mario said. "Watching TV, gorging themselves on junk food." He looked at a digital wall clock. "Time to relieve the four-to-twelve guys."

We relieved the man at the stairway desk and then the man at the security monitors. Mario pointed at the stack of six video monitors and told me that each one displayed a separate video feed from cameras placed strategically around the outside perimeter of the house. Then Mario demonstrated how to set the wall-mounted alarm system. I noted that the system was old, ancient by today's standards.

"What do those red lights mean?" I pointed at the two lights, knowing perfectly well that the system was not set properly.

"Those are motion-detector sensor indicators. Falling snow or leaves set off the roof alarm, so we keep that one turned off. Mrs. Langlois demands we check the rear of the house every fifteen minutes, so rather than turn off the sensors in her office and dining room four times an hour, we keep them off too."

Mario led me back to the stairway desk and pointed at the foyer elevator directly in front of us. "Now, this is important," Mario said. "Anywhere between three to three-fifteen every morning, the baby's night nurse feeds the infant, then unlocks the elevator and sends it down, empty. The Langloises won't hear it, but you will. Makes a racket that time of morning. The newspapers are delivered to the service entrance at five-thirty, and one of us has to stick them in the elevator and send it back up. Understand?"

"Got it."

Mario took his seat behind the desk. "Okay, here's the deal. The Langloises bolt themselves in on the second floor around midnight and almost never come downstairs. It's like lockdown in a prison."

"The paranoid elite," I said.

"Yeah. Unless Mrs. Langlois is in one of her moods." He raised a finger. "Hits a panic button. That happens, you run up the back stairs to the second floor, I go up the front."

"Why would she hit a panic button?"

"To break our balls. Make sure we're alert. See how fast it takes us to get upstairs and locate her."

"She do that often?"

"When she and her husband are fighting; often enough." Mario leaned back, crossed his legs. "About tonight: We both stay at our posts tonight until the Langloises get home. Once they're settled in, I'll stay awake all night here at the desk, man the phones, check the back of the house, put the papers in the elevator at five-thirty. You can go downstairs to the movie theater, stretch out, and get some sleep. Tomorrow night, it's your turn to stay up and I'll get some sleep."

I said, "What about the security monitors?"

Mario raised an eyebrow. "What about them?"

"Who's watching them if you're at the switchboard and I'm downstairs?"

Mario gave me a wary look. "You wanna stay up all night and watch monitors, be my guest. Me? For eleven bucks an hour, the Langloises are lucky I even sleep here."

"Sounds good to me," I said.

"But one of us *has* to stay by the phones at all times. Even though it almost never rings past eleven. We miss a phone call, we're both fired."

Mario pointed to a room across the vast foyer by the front door. "See that door? That's the foyer toilet. Don't use it, ever."

"Why?" I noted the toilet was only twenty paces from where we stood, and far more convenient than trudging through the foyer, security office, back hallway, down the stairs, past the home theater, and through the locker room to the basement lavatory.

"Mrs. Langlois doesn't want security using it. Period. You get caught using it, you're fired." He thumbed to a room next to us at the rear of the house. "That's Mrs. Langlois's office."

I walked to the door and looked in. The office was an airy, art-strewn study, more of a living room with a large comfortable couch. Great for relaxing.

Mario read my mind. "Whatever you do, do not loiter in Mrs. Langlois's office for any reason. If you sit on her couch she'll know it—don't ask me how—and you're fired. Ditto for the room next to it, the dining room.

"The main kitchen is also off limits, as is the candy concession stand by the theater in the basement. Mrs. Langlois catches you behind the concession stand, or in the kitchen, she'll assume you're stealing food and-—."

"I know," I said, "I'm fired."

"Right. And she'll have you arrested for larceny."

I did a double take.

For the first time Mario smiled. "I kid you not."

CHAPTER 20

"JONES," SERGEANT HILL said.

"Here," Destiny said.

Hill checked the roll call. "You'll take the Metropolitan Hospital emergency room fixer. Sector Adam will drop you off."

Destiny wrote her assignment in her memo book.

Fifteen minutes later Destiny entered the emergency room; she was three floors below the ICU and the man she'd shot, Gregory "Sonny" McFarland.

Destiny introduced herself to the hospital staff, a mostly female crew that seemed friendly enough. She said hello to several hospital police officers, a ragtag crew of unarmed, low-paid, and therefore unreliable guards with limited police powers. One of the hospital cops directed her to a makeshift NYPD security office—a small room with a tin desk and rickety chair—where the city cops normally assigned to the post sat.

Destiny made herself comfortable in the small office. She drank coffee, read the papers. Spent the remainder of the morning flipping through medical reference books she'd found piled on the tin desk. Destiny thumbed past graphic color photos of cadavers, various body parts, internal organs, and paused at a section marked "neurology". She scanned the chapters, came across and read about the various origins of headaches. She picked a tin of aspirin from her uniform shirt pocket, tossed half a dozen in her mouth, swallowed them with some bottled water.

"Six aspirin are a lot."

Destiny looked up. Smiled. "Dr. Ian."

"Please, call me Marcus." He walked over and glanced at the medical reference book Destiny was reading. "Researching the cause of headaches, I see. What have you learned so far?"

"Well, my symptoms indicate a host of possibilities."

"What are your symptoms?" Dr. Ian pulled up a chair, sat across from Destiny, and leaned forward, elbows on knees.

"Well—." Destiny sat back. "The headaches keep me awake at night. Wake me in the morning. I've experienced some nausea."

"What would you advise someone with your symptoms do?"

"See a specialist," Destiny said.

"That will be seven hundred dollars," Dr. Ian said with a wink, "for the, er, consultation."

Destiny laughed; cute and a sense of humor.

"How do you feel right now? Are you hungry?"

"Why? Food a headache cure?"

"It is. Especially Mexican food."

"Are you asking me to lunch, Marcus?"

"Yes," Dr. Ian said. "I am."

"I'll meet you outside," Destiny said. "Ten minutes."

Destiny retreated to the emergency room's ladies room, fiddled with her hair, opened the travel size makeup kit she always carried. She reapplied her lipstick and couldn't help but compare Marcus to Fernando.

Marcus was taller, clean cut, athletic looking. First impression: He appeared to be the straightforward type, whereas Fernando was a sinewy, slick, cagey flirt.

Destiny studied herself in the mirror, saw wrinkles around her eyes that makeup could not hide. She worried that she was looking old, tired. She added a touch of mascara, a tad of eyeliner, a swish of concealer.

"You married, Marcus?" Destiny said as they strolled down Second Avenue to the Mexican restaurant. The day was clear, cold, bright.

"No." He looked toward some kids playing in Ruppert Park. "Never met the right one. You?"

"Yes," Destiny said. "Not happily."

They passed the infamous Key Food supermarket. There were still two NYPD vans parked out front.

"You like being a police officer?" Dr. Ian said.

"I've a love-hate relationship with the department."

"What do you love?"

"Oh, things like rescuing an abused child. A battered woman. Catching a felon in the act. Aiding the sick or injured."

"What's to hate?"

"Department politics. The potholed criminal justice system. Having to notify a relative that a loved one is dead."

The Mexican restaurant was decorative, festive. A manager seated them at window seats that overlooked a small, well-tended backyard garden. Destiny glanced around the room, commented favorably on the authentic-looking décor and the mouth-watering aromas coming from the kitchen.

"You a regular here?" she said.

"I was raised close by, up in Harlem," Dr. Ian said. "Still live there."

A busboy brought them two glasses of water and a basket overflowing with tortilla chips and two types of salsa.

"I'm curious, Marcus," Destiny said. "Did you always want to be a doctor? I mean, when did you first know?"

Dr. Ian said he'd known since he was a boy. "My mother suffered from a debilitating form of diabetes. As a kid I felt helpless, tormented by the fact that I couldn't do a thing to relieve her suffering. After she passed on, I vowed to become an MD. Figuring if I couldn't help my mother, at least I'd be capable of helping others."

Destiny reached in her purse for the tin of aspirin, popped several in her mouth and washed them down with the water.

"Why don't you tell me more about your headaches?"

"I can't afford your fee," Destiny said and they both laughed. She noticed that the sexy laugh lines around his brown eyes and the cleft of his chin were more pronounced in the restaurant's moody light.

"Throbbing?" Dr. Ian said. "Affect one side of the head?"

"Yes. Sometimes I get sick to my stomach. Light hurts my eyes. I can't see."

"Probably related to a hormone imbalance or stress," Dr. Ian said. "You been under any stress lately?"

Destiny almost laughed. "Let's see; did you read about the Key Food robbery, the police shooting?"

"Sure." Dr. Ian gestured across and up the street. "Key Food on 92nd. We just passed it."

"I shot one of the robbers."

"Really. Well, how has that experience affected you?"

Destiny thought it over. "I haven't slept much since."

"Drinks?" A smiling waiter appeared at their table.

"A frozen margarita," Destiny said. "No salt."

"Just water for me," Dr. Ian said.

The waiter departed.

"You know, Destiny," Dr. Ian said. "Alcohol's not good for headaches."

"*One* can't hurt," Destiny said. "Right?"

The waiter brought Destiny's drink along with two menus.

"Your mother ever complain of migraines?"

"Not that I recall," Destiny said.

"How long have you had the headaches?"

"They started about a month ago." Destiny paused to sip her frozen drink. "Mild at first. But they're getting worse."

The waiter reappeared and they ordered lunch. Salsa music of some sort played softly in the background.

"You should consult a neurologist." Dr. Ian dipped a tortilla chip into a green salsa. "I know a good one."

"He'd have to be part of the city's insurance plan." Destiny tried the red salsa.

"May not be wise to use insurance."

"Why's that?"

"You use insurance—". He hurried to sip some water—the green salsa was delightfully hot. "Your employer will be aware of any negative results."

"You trying to scare me?"

"I'm sorry," Dr. Ian said. "Didn't mean to. It's just—my uncle worked for the city. A transit worker. He went to a doctor, used insurance. His supervisors became aware that he had leukemia. They forced him out on a paltry, nominal disability pension. With treatment the cancer went into remission and he lived cancer free for the next twenty years. Hell, he's still alive and kicking."

"He got the shaft," Destiny said, sourly.

"I didn't mean to sound alarmist."

"No, I appreciate the advice."

"I'm sure you have nothing to worry about," Dr. Ian said. "And if the results are negative as expected, you can always file an insurance claim later."

Destiny used a chip to scoop up more salsa. "Where's the neurologist located?"

"Here in the city. He's a medical school classmate of mine. A leader in his field. I can make an appointment for you, get you to the front of the line."

"I'll think about it."

"Let me know." Dr. Ian pulled a business card from his jacket pocket. "Call me anytime."

Destiny accepted the card, placed it in her purse.

"Excuse me, please," a smiling waiter said and served lunch: two heaping taco salads, burritos, chalupas.

"Bon appétit," Dr. Ian said.

Destiny saw the 19th Precinct RMP parked at the entrance to the emergency room when she and Dr. Ian turned right onto 97th Street. She looked at her wristwatch; she'd been gone for nearly two hours. She checked the RMP number. *Shit.*

"What's wrong?" Dr. Ian said.

"That's a supervisor's car," Destiny said. "I'm only allowed an hour lunch."

Sergeant Hill was sitting in the emergency room waiting area, reading a newspaper. He saw Destiny walk in, checked his wristwatch, folded the newspaper and tossed it aside.

"A two-hour meal period, Officer Jones?" He gave Dr. Ian a glance. "How's it hanging, doc?"

"Don't blame Officer Jones, Sergeant," Dr. Ian said. "I'm afraid I imposed upon her, complaining about some parking tickets."

"No problem, Doc." Hill turned back to Destiny. "You got a minute?" The sergeant led her into the security office.

"Listen," Hill said. "The perp upstairs in ICU, Gregory 'Sonny' McFarland, took a dirt nap about an hour ago."

"Oh," Destiny said, expecting it but still sickened.

"That's one skell we don't have to worry about anymore."

Destiny didn't know how to respond. She leaned against the desk, emotion clouding her eyes.

"Hey," Sergeant Hill said, "you all right?"

"Yeah," Destiny said. "Sure."

"Well, cheer up," Hill said. "I guarantee you and Moynihan are gonna get medals for this."

Destiny did an eye-roll and twirled her finger in the air. "Whoop-de-fucking-do."

CHAPTER 21

THE THOROUGHLY ANNOYING high-pitched whine of my building intercom system startled me awake. I rolled out of bed, grabbed a robe that was hanging on the back of my bedroom door and headed to the kitchen, where the building's intercom was recessed into a wall by the front door.

"Yes?" I said, my eyes still pretty much closed.

"Mr. Beckett, there's an Alex Schultz here to see you," the doorman said.

Enia's husband.

I checked the time. Recalled that I'd gotten about four hours sleep at the Langloises, another three at home.

"He alone?" I said.

"Yes," the doorman said.

I rubbed sleep from my eyes, scratched myself. "Ask him what he wants."

I could hear the doorman ask Schultz, then Schultz say he needed to see me immediately, that he was there at the urging of his wife.

No shit.

I should have known the ever manipulative Enia would send an envoy. She knew her added presence at my apartment could lead to an awkward, revealing confrontation, which was not in her best interest.

I said, "Tell him it's a bad time."

I heard the doorman speaking.

"Mr. Beckett, the guy says he has to see you, says he won't leave. What should I do?"

I thought it over. Meeting with Schultz would only encourage Enia. But on the other hand, I didn't want the poor dupe causing a scene in my lobby, giving the doorman a hard time and disturbing my neighbors. And I *was* curious about Schultz. A perverse part of me wanted to know the man Enia had married; was their lovemaking as volcanic as ours had been?

"Send him up." I hustled into the bedroom, slipped on a set of sweats, gargled with mouthwash.

Moments later there was a knock at my front door. I opened up and stepped back, allowing Schultz to enter.

"Thanks for seein' me." Schultz was dressed in jeans and a turtleneck sweater. He carried a heavy looking down coat on his arm.

I led my unexpected guest into the living room and pointed him toward the couch. "Have a seat. You want something? I've got soda, bottled water. I can make coffee."

"No, thanks." Schultz sat on the leather couch, glanced around, and looked out the window. "The 59th Street Bridge, great view."

"Yeah." I sat on a leather easy chair facing Schultz, put my bare feet up on the coffee table. "So, what can I do for you?"

Schultz took a moment choosing his words. "The Belfast Boys won't leave my hotel," he said. "Therefore I can't rent rooms. There's no income. It's only a matter of time before the bank forecloses and we lose the place."

"We already had this discussion," I said. "Get to the point."

Schultz took a moment. "You've killed people."

That took me by surprise. "In the line of duty."

Schultz reached into his coat pocket, took out a thick business envelope and laid it on the coffee table.

"What's that?" I said.

"Ten-thousand dollars," Schultz said.

I bent forward, thumbed through the bills. $10,000 was most of what Enia owed me.

"Get the Belfast Boys out of my building," Schultz said. "I don't care how you do it. Put `em in the hospital, kill `em if you have to, but get `em out."

I tossed the $10,000 back to Schultz. Got to my feet, grabbed Schultz by his turtleneck, yanked him out of the chair, threw him against my living room wall, and roughly patted him down. "You wearing a wire, asshole?"

"A wire? No. I swear!"

I spun Schultz around, got in his face. "I'm a cop, you dumb fuck. You just offered to pay me to commit assault, murder—that's called solicitation, conspiracy; all fucking felonies."

"I'm sorry," Schultz said. "I didn't think—."

"No. You didn't." I released him. "You're lucky I don't put you in handcuffs right now, lock your dumb ass up."

"Really, I'm sorry."

"Just get the fuck out of my apartment."

Schultz straightened his sweater, moved timidly to the middle of the room, picked up his coat. "I can't believe this is happening: I'm finished." Schultz's voice cracked. "I can't take on Lochlainn O'Brian alone. No one will fucking help me."

I perked up at the mention of that name. "Who?"

"Lochlainn O'Brian. Leader of the Belfast Boys."

Right. Lochlainn O'Brian had been the gang's second in command, the one supposedly sitting in a British prison when I investigated my sister Shannon's death.

Schultz slipped on his coat. "Sorry I bothered you."

"Wait," I said. "What's this Lochlainn look like?"

Schultz stopped. "Why? What difference does it make?"

"Humor me."

"Like a freakin' rock-n-roll musician," Schultz said. "Older than the others. Greasy black hair, wears it slicked back."

"A diamond stud earring in his right ear?"

"Yeah," Schultz said. "That's the son of a bitch."

"Wait a minute." My mind raced. I'd seen Lochlainn O'Brian's mug shots. I couldn't be positive that he personally sold drugs to my sister, but he was at the head of one of the gangs that did. "Tell you what," I said. "I'll make a few phone calls, ask around, see if there's anyone who can help you."

"Help me?" Schultz was cautious. "How?"

"I don't know, yet." I walked Schultz to front door, ushered him out. "I'll be in touch."

"Wait." Schultz took out a business card, handed it to me. "That's my cell number. Call day or night."

"Yeah. Sure." I locked the door behind him.

I walked into the kitchen, started a pot of coffee.

I knew better than to trust anything Enia was involved in. I had to be certain that there really was a Lochlainn O'Brian, that he was the same Lochlainn O'Brian whose gang sold drugs to Shannon. For all I knew, Enia and her hubby were just another set of greedy New York City landlords, hell-bent on evicting law-abiding tenants from rent-controlled apartments so they could take over a building, renovate and raise rents. I had to be sure that Enia was not playing me for a fool once again.

I poured a cup of black coffee, took a cautious sip, decided that, after I'd done my sign-in and sign-out routine down at the Building Maintenance Division, I'd pay a visit to the German Hotel, conduct a mini surveillance, see whatever there was to see. Problem was, primetime drug dealing takes place after midnight. And I'd be working for Julie Gunder, the midnight shift at the Langlois's residence.

Mario the Asshole would just have to cover for me.

CHAPTER 22

"WHAT DO YOU mean, you're leaving?" Mario the Asshole said, incredulous. He slammed closed the book he was reading, shoved back from the foyer desk, jumped to his feet. "There's only the two of us. You can't leave."

"Why not?" I'd just left One Police Plaza and still had my coat on. "The Langloises are asleep. You told me they never come down after midnight, that the phones rarely ring."

"They find out, we'll both be fired."

"No, you won't," I said. "I get caught, I'll tell Chief Vogt I had a personal emergency. That I didn't tell you I was leaving."

"I don't believe this." Mario's voice echoed in the vast, church-quiet foyer. "It's your turn to stay up," he said. "My turn to sleep. I've got plans, things to do in the morning. I need my sleep."

"I'll make it up to you," I said, trying to calm him down. "I'll stay up the next two nights."

"No way." Mario shook his head. "I'm not changing my plans to suit you."

"Fine." I shrugged. "You need to sleep. Sleep."

"I can't. Not with you gone." Mario picked up his book and banged it on the desk several times like a spoiled child. "This is bullshit."

"You misunderstand me, Mario," I said, getting in his face. "I'm not asking your permission. I'm leaving. You got a problem, deal with it."

"Lower your voices." Hans Kohlman came from out of nowhere. He had his coat and gloves on, apparently on his way home. "You wanna wake the whole house up?"

"This one," Mario thumbed toward me, "is deserting his post."

Kohlman looked at me in surprise. "I said you wouldn't last two weeks, but this isn't even two days."

"C'mere." I took Kohlman to the side and lowered my voice. "Look, I didn't want to involve you, but remember you saying you might be interested in rocking? Well, I got a hot lead on a job."

"Really?" Kohlman raised both eyebrows, keenly interested. "How's the money?"

"They're offering ten thousand up front, plus whatever cash we find in the apartment—that's if they're for real. Which is what I'm about to find out."

Kohlman looked over at Mario sulking at his desk.

"This can't wait?" Kohlman said.

"Trust me," I said, "it can't wait."

"All right." Heaving a sigh, Kohlman pulled off his coat, tossed it on a chair, and addressed Mario. "I'll cover for Beckett till he gets back."

"What?" Mario said, outraged. "You're going along with this? I don't believe it."

"Thanks," I said to Kohlman and headed to the exit.

"Hey, Beckett," Kohlman said.

I stopped short.

"Don't keep me here all night."

I gave the thumbs-up sign.

"I don't believe this shit," Mario bellowed.

"Mind your own fucking business, Mario," Kohlman growled. He picked up Mario's book, shoved it into his midsection.

"Here, read. Try to relax for once."

I walked out of the Langlois townhouse, onto the street and hailed a cab. "Ninety Sixth street and First Avenue," I told the cab driver. "Take Madison up. Drop me on the south side of Ninety Sixth, near corner."

I took out my cell phone, checked for text messages, thought about Solana and felt a sense of loss. She used to text me "I love you" and "thinking of you" notes at least ten times a day. Not anymore.

I gazed out onto Madison Avenue and the high-end boutiques. Thought about what I'd do if Lochlainn O'Brian was *the* Lochlainn O'Brian. Putting Lochlainn out of business would be the first. Killing him a desirable, happy consequence. But Lochlainn would be protected by his Belfast Boys. I'd need more than just Hans Kohlman as backup.

I would need a team of rockers.

The cab dropped me off at East 96th Street. I pulled my coat collar up, stuffed my hands into my pockets and headed south along First Avenue. I took my time reconnoitering the area, alert for signs of drug dealing: cruising drug buyers, street dealers, fleet-footed lookouts or other gang activity.

I observed a group of homeless men in an empty lot, gathered around a trash can fire, warming their hands. Occasional pedestrians, hankered down in their coats, hurried by without acknowledging me.

Turning a corner, I saw that there were many newly renovated retail stores, now closed for the night, selling everything from designer clothing to cut crystal and art. Several trendy bars had lines of attractive, well-dressed people hanging outside, smoking or waiting to gain entrance. The bars appeared to be doing a respectable business.

94th Street between York and First Avenues had several businesses: a bodega, drycleaner, shoemaker, a German deli, a hair salon and a bar. To the east loomed the Isaacs Houses housing projects, home to gangs and many a convicted felon. I looked up at the streetlights; they appeared to have been shot out.

Up the block a couple of white, freckle-faced young clockers—cocaine or crack dealers—were leaning against the windows of a closed dry cleaning store. They appeared to move only to pop their hands in and out of passing cars that never completely stopped as they crawled down the street. Spotting me, the clockers halted their activities and hard-eyed me as I walked by.

Irish faces, I noted. It reminded me of the time I asked my father why the Irish all look so much alike. "The Irish are a poor race," my father had told me without cracking a smile. "They can't afford a lot of faces."

A quarter of the way down the block, I sidestepped a couple of hookers who were shuffling their high-heeled feet on the pavement in a futile effort to keep their half-naked bodies warm.

"Want some loving, baby?" a black hooker said. She was tall as a basketball player, dressed in a garish red ensemble.

I shook my head, kept moving.

A security bell chimed as I walked into a ramshackle bodega. Three geriatric, fist-faced men, playing dominos, gave me the once over as I stepped inside.

"How ya doing?" I said.

The old men kept their focus on their game.

"Right," I said.

The store was a dump. The ceiling and wall paint was peeling. The rickety shelves were nearly empty, stocked with a few dusty cans of vegetables and some dry goods. The filthy linoleum was chipped and had large pieces missing, exposing the splintered wood floor underneath. If I had to take a guess, I'd say that the place was yet another front for illegal clipping and cashing in valuable store coupons—"terrorists" weren't the only ones bilking the system.

I walked to the section where the cold beer was kept. I reached into a cooler and took out two cans of Guinness. In a grimy, curved security mirror above my head, I saw that the three old characters playing dominos were watching me.

The cash register was manned by a Hispanic man and a young attractive woman; his daughter? They were seated at a counter behind some sort of thick, scratched glass.

I stuck some bills into an opening. The young woman closed the opening on my side, opened it from her side and took my money out.

The security bell chimed.

And I saw fear on the young woman's face.

I turned around.

One of the young clockers sauntered into the deli like he owned the place. He graced everyone with a comical tough-guy smirk, then grabbed a case of beer from a floor display.

"Put this on our account," he said, his accent Irish.

The bodega owner said nothing.

The clocker walked out with the beer; a large green shamrock was stenciled on the back of his black leather jacket.

I left the deli with my Guinness and continued east. I saw an artful black sign with "German Hotel" in gold letters hanging above the entrance to a building across the street. I glanced around, checked for any undue attention, then I backpedaled into a tenement.

I jimmied the lock on the vestibule door, stepped inside, and gently closed it behind me.

The pleasing odor of cooking food greeted me. I climbed the old but spotless stairs and passed a snoring homeless man who was sleeping upright, cocooned in plastic dry cleaning bags. I heard loud televisions. A dog barked. A man yelled. A baby cried.

I found the fifth floor roof door latched but not alarmed. I flipped the latch, stepped out onto the roof and, hand on my gun, did a series of three-sixties. Like the building itself, the roof was clear, clean.

I scanned the other rooftops.

No one was visible.

I took a position at the front of the roof, behind a low brick wall that blocked the wind. I looked up at the clear night sky. Stars were shining, but fast-moving, churning clouds were off to the west. A yellowish crescent moon hung low in the east. Something in the air alerted me to the possibility of snow. I pulled my coat around me. It was eerie being on a strange rooftop at night.

As I settled in, I thought about how old the building beneath me was. It was probably built around 1850. How many German, Irish, and Hispanic immigrant families had passed through its portals: lived, worked, married, raised families, and died within its confines?

I peered over the building ledge, down to the street, and saw the hookers rolling a helpless drunk in the darkness.

A raucous fistfight between two college types spilled out of the bar. They danced around in the glow of the bar's exterior lights like ungainly boxers, then charged each other like bulls, butting heads, knocking themselves back and to the ground. Fight over.

I guessed that the cops assigned to this sector were stuck at a crime scene, guarding a DOA, or buried in paper work. I recalled the days when Destiny and I patrolled our own sector and felt a sudden, sharp longing. I missed working the street. Missed the action. Missed working with Destiny.

A snowflake landed on my nose, then another, and another. The sky was now totally overcast. I opened a can of Guinness, took a sip, watched, waited.

By 1:45 A.M. the snowfall had become heavy, wet.

It didn't stop the drug traffic, though.

I observed a steady stream of drug buyers, some of them white suburban teens driving late-model cars, stopping in front of the dry cleaners, across the street from Schultz's German Hotel. A clocker would approach the car, an exchange would take place, the car would drive off—like my sister Shannon's car had probably done.

Violence erupted without warning.

I heard the screams first. Then two young white females vaulted down the German Hotel stairs. A couple of thickly muscled pit bulls came charging out in hot pursuit, dug their fangs into the women's legs, and easily took the panic-stricken duo down into the slushy snow.

A man with greasy, slicked back hair, a diamond stud earring in his right ear—*the* Lochlainn O'Brian—strolled casually down after them.

"Jew bitches," Lochlainn said. He called to the dogs and the pit bulls halted the attack, retreated, and sat panting at Lochlainn's side. The crying women struggled to their feet, limped to a car, got in, and drove away.

I'd seen enough. I checked my wristwatch. It was time to head back to the Langlois residence and relieve Kohlman.

CHAPTER 23

FROM MY SHELTERED position outside the Metropolitan Hospital emergency room, I could not see the harsh morning sun that reflected off the freshly fallen snow and into the eyes of squinting hospital employees walking east on 97th Street.

I heard brakes screech, horns honk, and glanced toward Second Avenue. Destiny's VW cut off a red Firebird, made a hairpin turn off of Second, raced into the hospital parking lot and skidded to a stop in a *No Parking Doctors Only* zone.

The Firebird screeched to a stop at the parking lot entrance and a beer-gutted white guy stepped out of his car. "You drive like an lunatic, lady," the guy screamed at the top of his lungs, shaking his fist. "A fucking lunatic!"

Destiny stepped out of her car and flipped the guy off. Seeing the police uniform, the Firebird driver jumped back in his car and sped away.

"Hey, partner," I said as Destiny came toward me, looking thoroughly stressed and bone tired.

"You waiting for someone?" She seemed surprised.

"You."

"Must be my lucky day."

I followed her into the emergency room. She exchanged pleasantries with the hospital cops and the emergency room staff on her way to a tiny security office. Hanging her coat on the back of the chair, she tossed her memo book on the desk.

I looked around feeling uneasy. "The last time I was in this place was for Shannon."

Destiny frowned. "I remember."

I glanced down the hall toward Area G and my thoughts returned to the surreal horror of that night. The phone call from my father. Rushing to the emergency room. Seeing Shannon's body. The disbelief. My complete emotional collapse.

All at once pangs of guilt enveloped me. I realized that I'd never even visited Shannon's grave, or my parents', for that matter.

"Hey," Destiny said. "Whasssssssup?"

I shook the morose thoughts from my mind. "We gotta talk."

"So, talk."

"Over breakfast," I said.

Destiny made a face. "I'm not real hungry."

"When's the last time you ate?"

Destiny shrugged.

"C'mon. Let's hit the cafeteria. I'm buying."

Everything about the hospital's large cafeteria was rundown and institutional. Destiny and I stood on a short line. She chose a fruit cup and coffee. I ordered the triple bypass special: fried eggs, bacon, buttered rye toast and coffee. We carried our tin trays to an unoccupied table at the far end of the room.

"So, how you holding up?" I said as we sat.

"Everything's fine."

"I'm here for you, you know that." I took a bite of my toast; it was cold.

"I *said*, I'm fine. Stop bugging me."

I was taken aback. "I'm not bugging you."

"You are." Destiny took in a breath, let it out. She looked down at her coffee, added cream and sugar. "Sorry."

I salted my eggs; they were cold, hard. The bacon was nearly raw. "It was on the news. The guy you shot, McFarland dying. I just wanted to see how you were handling it."

"They wanna give me and Moynihan a medal," Destiny said ironically. Tears came to her eyes. "Can you believe it? You kill someone, you blow their fucking eyes out, and you get a medal."

"Don't do this to yourself," I said.

Destiny used a paper napkin to dab at her eyes. "So," she sniffled, "you ever speak to Chief Vogt? How is the horny old coot?"

"I got the job," I said brightly.

"Do tell."

"Guarding Don Langlois's residence. Kohlman's my supervisor."

"Hans?" Her eyes lit up at that name. "How is the kraut?"

"He's fine," I said, working my way toward why I'd come to see her in the first place. I leaned forward, rested my elbows on the table. "Say, remember when I was investigating Shannon's death? There was a gang member, an IRA associate in jail in England we never got to interview?"

"Yeah, I remember." Destiny looked off in thought. "Lochlainn something. Right?"

"Good memory. Lochlainn O'Brian. He's back in the USA."

Destiny looked probingly at me. "Yeah?"

"Lochlainn's gang, The Belfast Boys, took over a small hotel over on East 94th Street. I met with the owners the other night at Elaine's. They asked me for help."

"94th Street?" She looked askance hearing the address. "What hotel?"

"The German Hotel."

"Enia's place? Fuck, Michael." Destiny slammed down her spoon. "You should have your head examined, you get involved with that bitch again."

I put up my hands to stop the lecture. "I'm not getting 'involved' with Enia, believe me."

"What're you doing then?"

"Putting Lochlainn O'Brian out of business."

She stopped to factor in this information. "How?"

"I'm forming a team of rockers. I want you in."

"Forget it," Destiny said.

"Should be at least two-thousand a piece for a couple of hours' work," I said. "Probably more."

She shook her head. "Look, being a cop's not my whole life, but it's all I have right now. I'm not taking chances; especially for that low-life cunt, Enia."

"I already told you, I'm not doing it for her."

"Maybe not." Destiny sat back and folded her arms across her chest. "But she's part of it."

I worked on my dry eggs, underdone bacon, and cold toast. "I'm heading out to Hans Kohlman's place in New Jersey in a couple of days," I said after a few bites. "Meeting up with some guys from the 41."

That piqued her interest. "Which ones?"

"McKee. Serria."

"Your rocker team, I take it?"

"Maybe. Wanna come along?"

Destiny stared into her coffee, not ready to commit.

"C'mon," I said. "The guys miss you."

"And I miss them." Destiny shrugged at last. "What the hell. A chance to see the kraut, the mick, and the spic? How can I refuse?"

We ate in silence after that. I made a few attempts at small talk, asked about her parents, her husband Fernando, but Destiny offered only cryptic responses. I could tell there was something on her mind, probably the death of McFarland. Regardless, I knew better than to pressure her. She'd open up to me when she was good and ready.

"I'm bushed." I yawned and stretched. "Gotta head down to HQ later. Working at Langlois's place again tonight." We picked up our trays and dumped the remains in a garbage can.

"Say, Michael," Destiny said.

I turned to look at her.

"You know any good lawyers?"

"There are none."

"I need a divorce lawyer."

I stopped and faced her fully. "You mean…?"

"Yes, butt breath. I'm divorcing Fernando."

For the record I said, "Is this cause for condolences, or congratulations?"

"Congratulations."

"All right." I lit up with a big smile and we exchanged high-fives. "We gotta celebrate."

"We do?" Destiny said.

I threw an arm around her shoulder and guided her out the door. "Drinks. Tonight. On me."

CHAPTER 24

DESTINY WAS HALF in the bag when she steered her VW into her Hastings on Hudson underground garage around eight that evening. She pulled the Bug into her parking spot, thankful she'd made it home without being caught in a DUI trap by New York state troopers.

True to his word, Beckett had gone down to HQ, did his sign-in and out routine, then he'd come back to the hospital at the end of Destiny's tour. Rode with her back to the station house, waited while she changed. Then they headed to "21", drank copious amounts of champagne, and then went on to Kinsale's Irish Pub for a night cap, though she needed a nightcap like she needed to be struck by lightning. She'd left Beckett at Kinsale downing cups of coffee, trying to sober up. He had to go to work at Don Langlois's place later that night.

Destiny switched off the VW engine.

Her temples pounded.

She locked her car, climbed the stairs, and entered her building lobby. She claimed her mail—Fernando must not be home—stepped into the elevator, and heard loud music the moment she arrived at her floor.

"*I got my black shirt on. I got my black gloves on. I got my ski mask on. This shit's been too long. I got my twelve gauge sawed off. I got my headlights turned off. I'm 'bout to bust some shots off. I'm 'bout to dust some cops off. I'm a COP KILLER, better you than me. COP KILLER, fuck police brutality!"*

"Christ." Destiny massaged the bridge of her nose. "Not tonight." She dropped her mail on the burlap "Welcome!" mat on the floor in front of her apartment door. Heading up the stairs, she caught the strong scent of marijuana.

An elderly female neighbor in a baggy house coat, her face scrunched with anger and disgust, her hands covering her ears, was in the hall on the next landing.

"I can't take it, Destiny," the old lady said.

"I'll see what I can do."

"My adrenaline's pumpin'. I got my stereo bumpin'. I'm 'bout to kill me somethin'. A pig stopped me for nuthin'!"

Destiny rang the apartment doorbell, pounded on the door. Not surprisingly, the occupants could not hear above the ear-rup-turing noise. She pounded harder. Nothing. She tried the door. It was locked.

Last time she and Beckett were in this situation, she had climbed to the top floor, went onto the roof, down a fire escape, and knocked on the occupant's window. She scared the hell out of the inhabitants, but at least she got their attention.

Destiny told her neighbor what she planned to do and suggested she wait in her apartment.

"It's dark up there," the woman said. "Hold on." She stepped into her apartment, returned with a pretty good flashlight, and handed it to Destiny. "You might need this."

"Thanks." Destiny climbed two flights and stepped out onto the building roof. A cold river wind hit her in the face. Strangely, the music seemed even louder from up there.

"COP KILLER, better you than me. COP KILLER, fuck

police brutality! COP KILLER, I know your momma's grieving,
(FUCK HER!)

COP KILLER, but tonight we get even, yeah! DIE, DIE, DIE
PIG, DIE! FUCK THE POLICE!"

Destiny's eyes adjusted to the darkness.

The roof itself was flat and blanketed by an inch or so of snow.
A water tower loomed at the other end of the roof. A couple of
ten-foot-high ventilation pipes surrounded by brick reached to the
sky.

The first year she and Fernando were married, they'd bring
wine and cheese up to that roof and enjoyed the unobstructed
views and romance of the Hudson River: the intriguing boat
traffic, shimmering stars, and glorious full moons—now that all
seemed like a lifetime ago.

"COP KILLER, better you than me. I'm a COP KILLER, fuck
police brutality! COP KILLER, I know your family's grieving,

(FUCK 'EM!) COP KILLER, but tonight we get even, ha ha ha
ha, yeah! FUCK THE POLICE!"

Twenty paces placed Destiny a quarter of the way across the
roof. She switched on the old woman's flashlight, swept the beam
across the expanse, looking for the fire escape ladder, and noticed a
series of fresh footprints in the snow.

Noise.

Destiny saw sudden movement in the darkness ahead.

"Anyone there?" She swung the flashlight beam toward the far
end of the roof. Saw the guns pointing at her before she got a look
at who was holding them.

Destiny lurched to the side, skidding over snow and ice. She
switched off the flashlight and found only minimal cover behind a
ventilation pipe. She drew her weapon. "Police! Drop it!"

The shadows froze.

"Drop the guns, now!" Destiny said.

No response.

"Put the guns down," she screamed. "Now!"

Still no reaction.

Destiny's heart pounded. She looked desperately around: the exit was too far back. If she stepped out from behind that ventilation pipe, made a run for it, she'd be an easy target.

Destiny cursed herself. She would not have been this lackadaisical had she been in the city, where guns and predators were commonplace. But she could never have imagined stumbling upon people with guns on a residential rooftop in low-crime, manicured Hastings on Hudson.

"*FUCK THE POLICE, yeah! FUCK THE POLICE, for Darryl Gates. FUCK THE POLICE, for Rodney King. FUCK THE POLICE, for my dead homies.*"

Abruptly, the music stopped.

The sudden silence was unsettling.

Destiny squinted, fighting her headache, struggling to locate her adversaries in the darkness.

Noise to her left.

Destiny swung her weapon around. "Come out with your hands up. Now!"

No response.

But what was that noise?

Destiny cocked an ear.

Whimpering.

"Who's there?" Destiny switched on the flashlight and pointed it toward the sound.

A black kid about twelve years old was hiding behind a low, jutting wall. "Don't shoot, please," he cried.

"We're playing," Destiny heard someone to her right say.

She swung the flashlight beam around.

Two more preteens used their hands to block the flashlight beam from their eyes. They were absolutely terrified.

"Don't shoot," the younger of the two boys pleaded.

"Toss your guns over here," Destiny said.

Three plastic guns hit the snow at her feet.

Destiny drew in a deep breath, let it out.

"We were playing Cop Killer," the older kid said.

"It's all right," Destiny said as she stepped into the open and holstered her weapon. "I'm not gonna shoot."

The sudden muscle spasm felt like a punch. Destiny went rigid. A white-hot pain stabbed her brain.

CHAPTER 25

"**Y**OU HAD A seizure," an ambulance attendant said.

Destiny looked at the medic. Found she was having trouble focusing. Slowly she realized that she was lying on a stretcher in the back of an ambulance. An oxygen mask was affixed to her face. The attendant was taking her blood pressure.

"Thought I was shot."

"So'd everyone else." The attendant gestured, and Destiny glanced out the ambulance's open doors. A lone Hastings on Hudson police car's flashing lights pulsed off trees, cars, and the faces of concerned neighbors. Destiny searched the crowd for Fernando. He was nowhere in sight.

"You've been drinking," the attendant said.

"Some—where's my weapon?"

"The officer has it."

Destiny sat up, pulled the oxygen mask off her face. "I'm refusing medical aid."

"That's not smart," the ESU worker said. He pulled the blood pressure apparatus from her arm. "You need to be checked out by a doctor."

Destiny pushed to her feet but had to hold on to an overhead chrome rail in order to steady herself. "I'm fine." She stepped unsteadily to the rear of the ambulance.

The attendant helped her navigate the ambulance's steep steps to the street. Several neighbors were milling about, watching her.

"What do you think you're doing?" A military-fit Hastings on Hudson cop stepped in front of Destiny. "You should go to the hospital."

"Where's my weapon?"

The cop handed Destiny her gun.

"I'm fine, officer," Destiny said. "Really."

"Not according to those boys," the cop said, pointing at the three youths she'd encountered on the rooftop.

"The tall one said you had a seizure," the cop said.

"What, he a Doogie Howser?" Destiny said.

"His mother's an epileptic."

The tall boy smiled and waved at Destiny. She waved back.

"Well," the cop said. "I can't force you to go to the hospital."

"No," Destiny said. "You can't."

"You need to see a doctor," the cop reiterated.

"Thanks for your concern." Destiny turned and walked unsteadily toward her apartment building. She stopped to assure her fretful neighbors that she was feeling fine.

"Well, where's your husband?" an elderly lady said, accusation in her voice.

"I have no idea," Destiny said.

Destiny entered her building, stepped into the elevator, and got off at her floor. She picked up the mail she'd left piled on her welcome mat, unlocked, and opened her door.

She switched on the lights, looked around. The living room was even messier than before. More dirty dishes were piled high in the sink, overflowing onto the counter—fucking Fernando.

Destiny tossed the mail on the kitchen counter and thought about what had transpired on the rooftop. Had the stark reality of her nearly shooting three innocent boys, combined with the alcohol she'd consumed, caused her to blackout? Or had she had a seizure like the Hastings cop said—and if so, what had caused it?

Destiny opened her purse and found Dr. Marcus Ian's card. She picked up the phone and called his answering service. Left a message, thanking him again for lunch and saying that she wanted to take him up on his kind offer. "Would you please make an appointment with your neurologist friend ASAP? Thank you, Marcus."

Next, Destiny checked for messages on her answering machine. Michael Beckett had phoned twenty minutes ago: The rocker meeting was set. She thought about returning Beckett's call, then thought better of it. She wasn't about to tell her former partner, or anyone else for that matter, about her blackout.

Destiny heard the bedroom toilet flush.

"Hey, babe." Fernando walked yawning into the living room, clad in only Jockeys, rubbing sleep from his eyes, clawing at his crotch. "What's with all the fucking sirens outside? Woke me up." He flopped down on the couch and turned on the TV. He flipped to a sports channel, saw the scores, then flipped to a San Diego game, then a Green Bay Packers game—to Destiny, a sure sign that he was gambling again. The question was, where was he getting the money?

Destiny walked into her bedroom, reached into a dresser drawer, pulled out her jewelry box and opened it. It took her about five seconds to discover that a Seiko wristwatch plus a pair of diamond earrings were missing. Jewelry Fernando had given her.

Destiny closed her jewelry box, put it away, and fought to control her temper. Her head hurt. Her mouth was dry—a 14-carat hangover was overtaking her. She knew if she confronted Fernando he'd come up with a bullshit story. Probably claim that he was getting the jewelry cleaned, or fixed, or that they must've been— gasp!—burglarized. And if she pushed him, questioned his yarn, he'd go ballistic, maybe even get violent.

No, she wasn't up to a full-scale war that night. What she needed to do was stick to her plan: get a lawyer, divorce Fernando, walk out the door and never look back.

CHAPTER 26

MY KIDNEYS WERE floating when I entered the Langlois residence at 11:55 P.M.—a dozen cups of black coffee will do that to you. I waved to the mustached guy at the monitors, made a beeline for the basement lavatory, and thought about the fact that, after helping Destiny celebrate her pending divorce, I should not have come to work. I should've gone home to bed, slept it off.

I finished using the ratty lavatory, legged it back upstairs to the security office and relieved the mustached guy.

"Shithead One and Shithead Two went out to a party," the guy said, referring to Ron and Claudia Langlois. "I wouldn't leave the monitors till they're back, if I were you." He pulled on a wool watch cap and thick down coat, anxious to get out of there. "Mario's already at his post."

"Have a good night," I said.

"You too." The mustached guy walked out the service entrance door.

I stuck my head out of the security office. "Yo," I said and waved to Mario. He was seated at the bottom of the sweeping staircase, manning the phones. Mario looked up from a book, scowled and shook his head—multitasking.

I took a seat in front of the security monitors, put my feet up on the desk, sat back, closed my eyes hoping to catch forty winks.

The Langlois house phone rang.

Groan.

I could hear Mario answer on the second ring. A moment later he appeared before me in the security office.

"That was Kohlman." Mario spoke rapidly, his eyes darting about. "They're on their way home."

"Yeah?" I took my feet off the desk, sat up. "So, they're coming home."

Mario was practically shaking. "They're fighting."

"Married couples fight," I said. "So?"

"Mr. Langlois shacks up a couple of nights a week with one of his lady friends. Claudia isn't going for his line of bullshit tonight."

"Great," I said. "This should be fun."

"You don't get it, Beckett."

"Mario," I said. "Calm down."

Mario pointed at the bank of monitors. "Keep watch. When you see them pull up, get to the front door, fast. Open up. Let 'em in. Get back to the monitors."

The Langloises' limo rolled to a stop a few minutes later. I headed to the front door and opened up. Don Langlois and Hans Kohlman breezed past me. Claudia came rushing in behind them.

"Don't you turn your back on me," Claudia shrieked. She was followed by the nurse who was carrying the wailing infant.

"Shut that kid up," Langlois said.

I closed the front door, stepped back to the security office, but stayed by the entrance where I could hear; this was too good to miss. I peeked around the doorframe, saw that Kohlman was standing over by Mario's desk, looking at some paperwork, like he was trying hard to ignore the embarrassing scene that was unfolding.

"If I could stop babies from crying," Claudia said, "*I'd* be the billionaire." The infant's screams were ear-piercing.

"I can't stand it." Langlois threw up his hands. "I'm going out for some peace and quiet."

"You're not going anywhere." Claudia planted herself in Langlois's path. "You think I don't know where you go? The whole fucking world knows where you go."

"Take a valium." Langlois said and pushed past Claudia. He opened the door and walked out, Kohlman trailing behind him.

"Fuck you!" In her fury, Claudia threw her purse. It seemed to detonate when it hit the door. Its contents—a dozen different types of makeup—scattered and rolled around the marble foyer floor.

"That fucking, cock-sucking son of a bitch-bastard prick's not getting away with this," Claudia screamed.

I retreated to the monitors, attempted to look busy. Claudia's shrieks faded as she crossed the foyer and rode the elevator up to the second floor. A moment later Mario was picking up the contents of Claudia's purse.

"Need help?" I said.

"Just stay at your post," Mario said. "And stay alert. No one's sleeping tonight."

It was 2:32 A.M. when the first alarm sounded.

I checked the alarm system display panel: second floor, Langlois kitchen. I ran to the corridor, looked for my partner, but Mario was already racing up the sweeping stairwell. I ran back through the security office, down a long corridor, up the rear staircase, down a second-floor carpeted hallway to the kitchen where Mario was waiting. The room was empty.

Mario spoke in a whisper. "She's hiding."

"From who?" I said.

"Us. It's a game she plays."

We began searching rooms: the Langloises' master bedroom, safe room, baby's room—the infant was missing.

I raced into the hall and opened a closet.

"Time!" Claudia had a professional stopwatch in her hand. "Pathetic."

"Are you all right?" I said.

Mario came up alongside me, his gun in his hand.

"Where's *your* gun?" Claudia demanded of me. The baby's nurse was standing in the closet shadows, holding the sleeping infant, a hapless look on her face.

"My gun?" I patted my waistband.

"Your gun should be out, you stupid prick," Claudia screamed, "ready to shoot."

I squinted at Claudia, thought of a dozen responses, none conciliatory. "I understand, Mrs. Langlois."

Claudia pitched the stopwatch down the carpeted hall. "You." She stuck a finger in my face. "Go pick that up and bring it here."

"What is this," I tried a smile, "a game of fetch?"

"Do it," Claudia said, "or you're fired."

My first reaction was to tell Claudia to go fuck herself. But I walked down the hall, picked up the stopwatch, walked back and handed it to her.

"Now," Claudia said. "Both of you, get back downstairs."

Claudia tripped the panic alarm, timed our response, and verbally abused Mario and me six more times that night.

CHAPTER 27

"THANKS FOR THE drunkfest," Destiny said. "The champagne was delicious, from what I remember."

"Don't mention it."

"You know," Destiny said. "I never saw you shove two straws that far up your nose before. The bartenders at "21" were most impressed."

I spit up some coffee. "I did that?" I wiped the coffee off my sweater with a napkin. "Really? No kidding?"

Destiny smiled broadly. "Tell me something: Why the hell're we jackassing all the way out to *Noo Joisey*? I mean, the state's one big oil refinery."

We were sitting in Destiny's VW driving north on the Harlem River Drive heading toward the George Washington Bridge. As we drew closer, Destiny chose the bridge's outbound lower level. I tightened my seatbelt, dug my fingers into the upholstery, held on for dear life.

"What?" Destiny said. "Kohlman can't meet us in town?"

"We need privacy. Kohlman's is the best place." I glanced north at the white-capped Hudson River and the majestic New Jersey Palisades. Large ships steamed upriver toward the Tappan Zee Bridge and the United States Military Academy at West Point.

"You look tired, Michael. I mean it."

I fought off a yawn just thinking about it. "The battling Langloises had a little marital spat—she knows he screws around. So he storms off to his mistress's place, and fucking Claudia kept tripping the panic alarm, kept us up all night." I sipped some coffee and tried to keep my mind off Destiny's driving; she was speeding and tailgating like a madwoman. "It's the great equalizer," I said. "Bad marriages. Can happen to anyone."

"Tell me about it." Destiny took one hand off the steering wheel and sipped her own cup of coffee. "Fucking Fernando."

"Speaking of which." I reached into my shirt pocket, took out an attorney's business card and placed it in the VW ashtray.

"He handles a lot of cop and firefighter divorces," I said. "He's a real straight shooter, and he's fair."

"If you say so." Destiny downshifted, eased around a slow car, hit the gas and jammed it back into fourth.

I was happy that Destiny was acting like her trademark ornery self. She'd arrived at my apartment that morning on time, annoyingly alert, congenial, carrying three cups of designer rotgut coffee: two cups of the house blend and a café latte for Solana.

Destiny said, "Which way, Simba breath?"

"Take the Palisades Parkway to Exit 74," I said. "Take Route 303 South, Exit 5 South toward Tappan. Turn right onto NY-303. Turn right onto Kings Highway. Turn right onto Greenbush Road. Right onto Old Tappan Road East. Left onto Washington Avenue. Right onto Westwood Avenue. Left onto Clauss Lane. Now, repeat it back to me."

Destiny flashed a playful grin. "How'd you like five fingers shoved up your fucking nose?"

Thirty minutes later, we pulled onto a tree-lined street with deep backyards and ample new houses. Hans Kohlman's residence was at the end of the street: a shack compared to the new

McMansions on the block. Several cars crowded the short, snow-covered driveway.

Destiny pulled up and parked behind a nondescript van. We exited the car and threaded our way cautiously up the icy walkway. Plywood ramps—built for Kohlman's paraplegic son—overlaid the front stoop. Destiny rang the bell. Big Ben sounded in the background.

Opening the door, Kohlman brushed me aside, lifted Destiny off her feet and gave her a slobbering kiss, enveloping her in a bear hug. Destiny squirmed, giggled, and hugged him back.

"C'mon in, kids." Kohlman released Destiny, stepped aside allowing us to enter. "Got a call from Chief Vogt first thing this morning," he said to me. "Seems Claudia called him screaming, told him you were a lazy insolent prick."

"I could've told you that," Destiny said with a smile.

"What went on there last night?" Kohlman said.

I told him. "Am I fired?"

"No." Kohlman shook his head. "Not yet."

Kohlman put his arm around Destiny and ushered us both through an exposed-beam and wood-paneled living room, past an old stone fireplace. The Silver Star, which Kohlman won while serving in Vietnam, and a dozen sharpshooting trophies were set on the mantel.

Ernie Serria and his former partner Thomas McKee sprang to their feet when we entered a porch at the rear of the house. Hugs, kisses, and handshakes all around.

One part Julio Iglesias, two parts Bronx Puerto Rican, Serria was the diminutive, bitterly divorced father of a troubled sixteen-year-old son—a hopeless drug addict who had been in and out of rehabilitation programs. Serria had killed two armed robbers in as many shootings. Since retiring from the force he had launched a fledgling standup comedy career.

Thomas   McKee   was   a   chain-smoking,   wheezing, couch-potato-fat candidate for a quadruple bypass. A winner of the NYPD Combat Cross currently tied to a desk in the Chief of Patrol's office, McKee had survived being gunned down in the line of duty. Although he never spoke about the incident, I'd observed that the trauma had changed my friend; he'd stopped caring about himself and gained over 100 pounds.

Kohlman handed out German beers. Handed Destiny a glass of water. I watched her pop four, or was it five aspirin in her mouth and washed them down. *What was that about?*

I opened my beer, sat back and took a moment to regard my cronies. As decorated cops we'd been altruistic adrenaline junkies. And we all admitted to missing those days: the primal rush associated with the perennial possibility of a gunfight, the satisfaction of catching violent felons in the act.

Kohlman's plow-horse-thick wife entered the room and served overstuffed knockwurst and potato salad sandwiches while Kohlman tried explaining some sort of investment. "Stem cell therapy will be a billion-dollar industry," he said. "The investment of the future. In this country we have restrictions on stem cell research, but all forms of research are legal outside the United States. As a result, these startup companies are good speculative investments."

"Let me see if I understand you correctly," Destiny said. "You saying that stem cells could repair injured nervous systems, maybe even replace entire organs?"

"Right," Kohlman said. "The research is promising."

"Sounds good," Destiny said, "but whaddya want us to do?"

"Support the Stem Cell Research Foundation."

Dead silence greeted that idea.

"I don't have a pot to piss in," McKee finally remarked.

"Same here," Serria said.

"Then support elected officials who support the research."

The reason for Kohlman's interest and enthusiasm was obvious.

From what I'd read, stem cell therapy could someday revitalize his son's damaged spinal cord.

"Hans?" I gestured to Kohlman with a cocked finger to ask his wife to leave the room. "Whenever you're ready."

Kohlman said something guttural in German. His wife set down several more cold bottles of beer and headed to the kitchen, closing the door behind her.

"Want me to leave the room?" Destiny said.

"No." I shook my head.

"Why would you leave?" Serria said.

"'Cause I'm not involved."

"Involved in what?" McKee wheezed.

"I've got a job." I lowered my voice.

Everyone pulled their chairs closer.

"Pays twenty-five hundred apiece for a few hours' work. Plus whatever cash we confiscate. We split equal shares." I paused and added, "Could be dangerous."

Serria graced us with a maniac grin. "Count me in."

McKee looked crossly at him. "Dumb spic. You don't even know what the job is yet."

Serria grabbed his crotch. "Bite this, you potato-eating faggot."

The banter elicited laughs, just like old times.

McKee shrugged. "Serria's in—." He took a moment to cough his brains out. "Guess I'm in, too."

Serria said, "What is the job anyway?"

I looked around at all of them. "We're gonna be rockers."

It took a moment for that to sink in.

"Who we rocking?" Serria said, hesitantly.

"The Belfast Boys."

"The Irish gang?" McKee said.

"Their leader's from Belfast," I said. "Northern Ireland."

"IRA?" McKee said.

"There's probably a connection. But these guys're real

scumbags," I said. "Certainly not the patriots our grandparents idolized, believe me."

"Where?" Kohlman said.

"They're squatting in a boutique hotel in Yorkville."

"Sweet," Serria said.

"When?" Kohlman said.

"ASAP," I said. "Depends on your schedules."

"You check things out?" McKee said. "The client for real?"

"I did," I said. "They are."

As I detailed the eviction to the men, I felt an elation I hadn't experienced in a long time. Sure, I was going into a potentially deadly situation—the Belfast Boys would be formidable adversaries and well-armed. But these men, unlike Mark Tesser's ragtag team of former beat cops, were disciplined professionals. The best of the best. And soon I'd be face to face with Lochlainn O'Brian, the leader of a drug organization that sold the drugs that killed my sister.

"What about weapons?" McKee said.

I looked at Kohlman. "Hans?"

We grabbed our coats and Kohlman led us out of the house, across a small yard, and into an old barn that served as a workshop and garage. He pushed aside a handyman's wall unit, opened a hidden door, and we descended into a concrete bomb shelter that Kohlman had built with his own hands.

Lining the two-foot-thick cement walls were shelf after shelf, rack after rack, of weapons sophisticated enough to make a terrorist proud. There were AK-47s, shotguns, Uzis, laser-sighted sniper rifles and handguns, bulletproof vests and night-vision goggles.

Serria picked up a weapon, checked the action, smiled his approval. "Since when did you become a gun collector?"

"I'm not a collector." Kohlman pointed at a framed official-looking document that was nailed to the wall. "I'm a licensed dealer. I tried cutting all of you in a few years ago. Remember?"

"I remember," McKee said. "The government was planning to make it more difficult for someone to get a dealer's license. You wanted us to buy in before the new regulations went into effect."

Kohlman had told us that a gun dealer's license was like a New York City taxi medallion, that it would only go up in value and could later be sold for a huge profit.

"Right," I said. "But the government outlawed selling the old licenses."

"The government screwed me," Kohlman said, sighing.

"Seems everyone's always screwing you," Serria said. "You dumb kraut."

"All right," I said. "Any more questions?"

"Yeah," McKee said. "Not for nothing, but you sure the hotel owner's good for the money?"

"I'm sure, but if something happens, and they don't pay, I'll make good," I said. "This is more than just a rocking gig for me."

"What's that mean?" Serria said, suspicious.

"You saying it's personal?" McKee said.

Destiny put in, "The gang sold drugs to his sister Shannon."

Serria and McKee exchanged glances.

"Fuck the money," Kohlman said. "You don't get paid, I don't get paid. You owe me nothing."

"Me too," Serria said.

"I'm in," McKee said.

Honestly, I was speechless. I never imagined that level of support. I turned my back, picked up a weapon, pretended to check the action, all the while I fought to control my emotions.

Destiny came up behind me, rubbed my back.

"You all right?" she said.

I nodded, cleared my throat, turned back to the men. "I appreciate it, but no one's working for free." I placed the weapon back on its rack, pulled out my cell phone. "Time to call the client."

"There's no reception down here," Kohlman said. "You gotta go upstairs, to the foot of the driveway."

"Be right back."

I climbed out of the bomb shelter. As I walked over the hard snow, I breathed in the pleasant scent of wood-burning fireplaces. I glanced down the driveway and saw Kohlman's wife standing in front of her house, at the curb, waiting. Just then a yellow school bus pulled to a stop. The bus's rear doors parted, a lift extended, and a boy around thirteen years old in a motorized wheelchair was lowered to the street.

I checked my phone for reception, dialed Schultz's number.

"Hello?" Schultz said.

"Michael Beckett here. Look, I think I've located some people who might be willing to help with your problem."

"They rockers?" Schultz said, excited.

"I guess you can call them rockers," I said

"Well, how they gonna get Lochlainn out?"

I smiled pleasantly and waved to Kohlman's wife and son as they made their way up the driveway and into the house.

"They'll hit the hotel in the early morning hours," I said. "Take Lochlainn and his gang by surprise. Rough them up a little. Drag them out into the street. Threaten them with bodily harm if they come back."

Schultz didn't seem happy about that plan. "You don't know Lochlainn," he said. "You let him go, he *will* come back, come looking for *us*."

"No," I said. "He won't. But if it'll make you happy, I'll arrange for the local precinct to increase patrols around your hotel, give you special attention."

"Fuck that," Schultz said. "I want Lochlainn dead. I'll pay whatever it takes, and I wanna be there to see it."

This guy's hard-ass act wasn't doing it for me. "Look asshole.

First off, these aren't hit men. There's not going to be *any* unnecessary violence. As far as you going along, forget it."

I hit end, cancelled the call. Then I smiled—out there in the Noo Joisey country we'd just became rockers.

CHAPTER 28

DESTINY SAT IN the waiting room of the neurologist's office on Fifth Avenue, thumbing through fashion magazines, scanning articles like "What Makes You Irresistible to Him," "Confessions of a Reformed Bad Girl," "Sex Tips That Will Make Him Beg for More!" "Secrets to a Fabulous Orgasm".

Oh, pleeze!

A woman across the cold, impersonal room fought to control a demonic, totally out-of-control three-year-old. Several old-timers, accompanied by caregivers or family members, drooled as they slept through the nerve-wracking disturbance.

The three-year-old let out a blackboard-scratching scream that woke one of the old-timers, just as a spike of pain struck Destiny like a blackjack. She tossed the magazine aside, rubbed her temples, and tried to relax.

She checked her wristwatch. Dr. Goldsamp had examined her half an hour ago. She hoped they wouldn't keep her waiting for her results much longer. Her nerves couldn't take it.

Goldsamp had performed a neurological examination: checked the nerves of the brain that controlled her eyes and face. He'd checked for equal strength and sensation on both sides of her body, coordination and balance, memory, and judgment. He looked into her eyes for signs of increased pressure in the skull, such as swelling of the optic discs.

Destiny planned to take Marcus's advice, delay making an insurance claim, and pay for the initial tests with a nearly maxed-out credit card. And if the credit card company declined the charge, she'd work out a payment schedule with the doctor and worry about paying him later.

"Destiny Jones?" A woman in a white lab smock stood in a doorway. "Ms. Jones?"

"Yes?"

"This way."

Destiny was led down a short corridor and into a small consultation room. Goldsamp, a serious looking, bald white man, was sitting at a desk perusing some paperwork.

"Have a seat," the doctor said distractedly.

Destiny did her best to get comfortable. At times like this she really missed her parents. They were the only people in her world, besides Michael Beckett, who she could depend on, no matter what. As for Fernando? She hadn't told him that she was seeing a doctor, didn't plan to. He'd only find some way to exploit the situation.

The doctor flipped a few pages and took a moment before he spoke. "Some of the most common symptoms of a brain tumor are headaches that wake you up in the morning. Seizures in a person who does not have a history of seizures. Cognitive or personality changes. Eye weakness. Nausea or vomiting, speech disturbances, or memory loss."

"Whoa! Hold it, Doc, slow down," Destiny said, her eyes wide. "I've got stress headaches, maybe a hormone problem—right?"

"Based on your symptoms and the results of my examination," Goldsamp said, "I believe that there may be a tumor on your brain."

"Oh, sweet, Jesus. No."

"Next step," Goldsamp said, slipped off his reading glasses and sat back. "We must first establish whether or not you have a tumor, and the type. Only then can we discuss treatments."

The word "tumor" ping-ponged. "Come again?"

"Although surgery is the main form of treatment for some tumors, others are treatable with radiation therapy, chemotherapy, or some combination of all three." The doctor smiled reassuringly. "What I'd like to do next is schedule a CAT scan."

"Why? What will that accomplish?"

"CTs are necessary to provide basic diagnostic information. If the CT is positive, we'll schedule an MRI, which is very precise and sensitive. If we still have concerns, I'll take a biopsy."

"Of my brain?" Destiny said, horrified.

"It's the only way to be absolutely sure of what kind of growth is present, if there, in fact, is a growth at all."

"This can't be happening," Destiny said despondently.

"Not to worry. Nowadays biopsies are quite safe."

"Yeah," Destiny said. "Right."

"We use stereotactic guidance—a fine needle is placed into the tumor with the help of an MRI scanner."

"Oh. My. God." She almost jumped out of her chair. "You wanna stick a needle in my brain?"

"I'm just listing possibilities."

Destiny began to tremble. Tears welled.

The doctor leaned across the desk, touched her arm reassuringly, handed her a box of tissues. "You need some time alone?"

"No," Destiny said. "I'm all right."

Goldsamp gave her a moment. "Let's schedule the CT."

Destiny sniffled. "How soon?"

"Now," the doctor said, "if you have the time."

"I'll make the time."

Don't panic, Destiny told herself. Goldsamp said that she *may* have a brain tumor. And if she did, it might be treatable by non-surgical means. Didn't he?

The doctor hung the phone up. "The clinic is a few blocks away, over on Park Avenue." He took out a prescription pad and began writing. "They're expecting you."

Destiny bundled up, trudged the few blocks over to Park Avenue Radiology, thinking hard about how she could pay for the CAT scan. Fernando had stolen and hocked her only remotely valuable jewelry. She owned no real estate that she could mortgage. Her credit was in the toilet thanks to, guess who, fucking Fernando. Her parents were nearly destitute. She had no wealthy friends.

Destiny walked into the ground-floor offices of Park Avenue Radiology. She registered with a receptionist, took a seat in the waiting room and her cell phone vibrated.

Michael Beckett was calling.

"Where're you?" he said.

"I'm at the doctor's."

"The police surgeon?"

"Neurologist."

"About the headaches?"

"Yes."

"So, what'd the doctor say?" Beckett said.

"They're running tests."

"For stress headaches?"

"You know doctors," Destiny said, trying to sound appropriately cynical. "They say they wanna be thorough but all they wanna do is run up their bill."

"Thank God for insurance."

"Yeah." A light went off in her head. "Michael?"

"I'm here."

"I changed my mind."

"A woman changing her mind," Beckett said. "How un-freaking-usual, curious, strange, extraordinary."

"Will you shut the fuck up?"

He did.

"I wanna join your rockers—you still there?"

"Thought you didn't wanna risk getting caught," he said.

"I don't. But things've changed. I need the money."

"For the divorce?"

"Yes." Destiny could almost hear Beckett's thoughts as he considered her change of heart, factoring in the new dynamics.

"You understand," he said, "you'd be helping Enia."

"Yeah, I guess."

"You said you wanted nothing to do with Enia. Said you'd never help the low-life bitch, the cunt."

"I said, I need the money."

"That bad?" Beckett said.

"Yeah, Michael." Destiny's voice cracked. "I need the money that bad."

CHAPTER 29

I N THE FRIGID, pre-dawn hours the following day, a plain
brown van roared north on First Avenue, made a right at 94th
Street and came to a stop in front of Alex and Enia Schultz's
German Hotel.

"How's it look?" I said from the back seat.

"All the lights are out," McKee said, scanning the windows of
the five-story structure. "Except the Schultz apartment."

"Good," I said. "All right, once more."

"I take the fire escape." Kohlman, seated on my left, racked a
round into his shotgun. "Radio the status. Alert you if the coast
is clear."

"McKee, Destiny and me follow Beckett in," Serria said from
the driver's seat. "Standard attack formation."

With the logistics set, I moved onto the next step. "Night-
vision goggles?"

Destiny, sitting on my right, said, "Check."

"Vests?"

"Check."

"Sedative for the dogs?" I said.

"Liquid tranquilizer," McKee said. "Works much faster."

"Good. The van's license plates?" I said.

"Washington State," Serria said. "Borrowed from long-term parking, Kennedy Airport."

"Borrowed?" Kohlman snickered.

"I'll return them," Serria said, indignant.

"Remember," I said, "things go wrong, we get separated, we meet back here."

Everyone acknowledged that they understood.

"Time to check the area," I said.

Serria and McKee rolled down their windows and carefully inspected the streets for drug lookouts, whores, gang members and other forms of low life. Half a block away the looming Isaacs Houses projects were dark, silent. Across the street a sign hanging from a closed bar squealed as it swung in the stiff breeze. Loose newspaper pages swirled by. A light changed, and what little traffic there was began to move.

A news truck shifted gears, slowed, dropped a stack of papers in front of the bodega and sped off. A garbage truck and a gypsy cab raced by in quick succession.

"Lookout in the doorway." McKee wheezed, coughed, gestured across the street at a darkened storefront that housed a shoemaker.

"Ain't no lookout, you dumb donkey," Serria said. "That's a drunk. What's this world coming to when an Irishman can't spot a kindred spirit?"

"We gotta be sure," I said.

"I'll go," Destiny offered.

"Be careful," I said.

Destiny exited the van, zipped up her jacket, crossed the street, and approached the guy in the doorway, hand on the gun in her pocket.

"Hey, mister."

The guy was seated, propped up against a door frame, mouth open, head resting against the storefront door, eyes closed.

We all watched as Destiny squatted down beside the guy and

tapped his shoulder. No response. She touched his neck, felt for a pulse. Destiny looked in our direction, shook her head.

Destiny looked both ways before heading back to the van and climbing in alongside me. "DOA," she said, quietly.

"Probably frozen to death," I said, remembering those midwinter mornings when NYPD trucks would scour the ghettos, searching for poor unfortunates, those with nowhere to go: homeless men, women and children who didn't survive the frigid overnight temperatures.

"Two hookers down the block," Serria said, eyes on his side rearview mirror. "Could be lookouts. Hold it. A car just pulled up."

The hookers approached the car and spoke to the occupants. The women stepped back and pulled their skirts up to show their wares.

"Ah," Serria said. "Negotiations."

The car's rear door opened, the hookers stepped inside and the car pulled away.

"Clear," Serria said, smiling slightly.

"Hans," I said, checking my wristwatch. "Go."

Hans Kohlman, night-vision goggles hanging around his neck, radio in hand, pulled his black hood on and slipped out the back door on his way to the rear of the building and a second-floor fire escape—decorative balcony—landing.

The rest of us waited in edgy silence.

I shifted in my seat. My neck was stiff, my lower back sore. Thanks to me and my big mouth, I hadn't slept at all last night.

Instead of allowing Solana to think I was working at the Langlois's residence that night, I'd told her the truth, that I was moonlighting at yet another job, doing a security gig with Destiny. I mean, why would she care?

"Destiny?" Solana fumed. "You're getting up at three A.M. to meet Destiny?"

Taken aback, I explained that I was meeting a "team" of cops of which Destiny was a member.

"Destiny thinks I'm stupid," Solana seethed. "She buys me a café latte, chats me up and she thinks she's my pal?" Solana added with an emphatic thump of her fist. "She's after you, Michael. You're a man. Too damned dumb to know it. But she's after you."

Once in bed, Solana turned her back to me.

I had lain there unable to sleep, actually pleased by Solana's gross overreaction—which I took to mean that she still cared about *us*, that our relationship still had a chance.

I hoped so.

Soon I was attempting to tire myself, not by counting sheep, or bottles of beer, or bikini-clad vixens, but by running through the German Hotel rocker raid.

I pictured myself breaking into the target suite, pulling Lochlainn O'Brian from his bed, down the stairwell, into the street. Forcing Lochlainn to his knees. Pressing the barrel of my Browning 9mm to his head while Lochlainn blubbered and begged for his worthless life. Saying, "This is for Shannon," and pulling the trigger. Blowing Lochlainn's fucking brains out.

Although the homicidal scenario was wishful thinking, all that was necessary for it to occur was for Lochlainn to do something stupid: Go for a gun and I would have the excuse I needed.

Alongside me in the van, Destiny muttered something that sounded like a curse, then used her index finger and thumb to massage the bridge of her nose.

"How's the headache?" I said.

"Ever present." Destiny pulled a prescription bottle from her pocket, tipped some pills out, washed them down with a bottle of water.

"What's that?" I said.

"Vicodin," Destiny said.

The portable radio crackled. "*Stand by*," Kohlman said.

"Get ready." I drew in several deep, calming breaths.

In the reflected glow of streetlights, Serria, McKee and Destiny pulled on black ski masks and checked the action of their weapons.

"*Do it,*" Kohlman said.

"10-4." I pulled on my kelly green ski mask, checked that my Browning 9mm had one in the pipe. Positioned my backup .38. Checked my shotgun. "One. Two. Three. Go."

Careful not to slip on the ice, my rockers charged out the van's doors and into the building, staying low, in single file. We leapfrogged our way into the vestibule, rang the Schultz's "manager" bell.

Schultz appeared in silhouette, backlit by the glow from his apartment. He opened the heavy, antique wooden door, stepped aside allowing us to enter.

"You're sure Lochlainn's up there?" I whispered.

"I'm positive," Schultz said.

Enia stepped into the hall, dressed in tight low-riding jeans and a pinup girl sweater.

"Be careful," Enia said.

I looked at her. "Don't worry."

Destiny shoved me forward. "Move, idiot."

We continued up the stairs, the gleaming, refurbished wooden steps creaking nosily every step of the way.

"*Halt,*" Kohlman said over the radio.

I paused the rockers on the second-floor landing. "Talk to me," I whispered into the radio.

"*Pit bulls,*" Kohlman said. "*Front door.*"

"10-4."

We moved down the hall to the Belfast Boys' suite. I could hear the pit bulls snorting and growling on the other side of the door. McKee pulled a plastic bottle from a fanny pack, unrolled a long rubber tube, slipped it under the door, and squeezed a flavored sedative out.

"*Drinking,*" Kohlman said.

A few minutes later, we heard movement inside the suite and flattened ourselves against the wall.

The locks clicked, the doorknob turned.

Everyone pointed their weapons.

The door swung open. "Greetings," Kohlman whispered.

I let out a deep breath.

We pulled on the night-vision goggles, stepped over the snoring dogs, entered the suite.

In the first bedroom, we quietly weapon-nudged five Belfast Boys awake, frog-marched them into the main salon, and ordered them to lie face down on the floor. I checked a second bedroom. Lochlainn O'Brian was sleeping with his tattooed arms around a freckled girl.

Training my shotgun at Lochlainn, I moved silently across the bedroom floor, and then kicked the bed.

Freckles opened her eyes. Screamed.

Lochlainn bolted upright, gun in hand.

"Don't." I started the trigger squeeze. Stopped. I would've hit the girl. "Drop it, dick head."

Lochlainn dropped the gun.

"Up," I said.

Lochlainn and his girl rolled from bed.

I shoved them into the main salon.

"My dogs. You hurt my dogs, eh?" Lochlainn said with an Irish brogue, seeing his pit bulls lying on their sides in the darkness. "You had no reason to hurt my dogs."

"Shut up." I forced Lochlainn and his girl to the ground, face down, alongside his gang. McKee handcuffed everyone's hands behind their backs. Then he confiscated their wallets, checked for IDs.

"Okay, goggles off," I said.

We pulled them off.

McKee turned on the lights.

Although the gang had basically trashed the suite, I saw lots of dark woodwork and old mahogany furniture, coffered ceilings and a period chandelier.

"You're dead men," a gang member said.

"Shut up, Rat," Lochlainn said.

My rockers searched the suite. Looked under and behind furniture and bedding, in closets and cupboards, behind pictures and light fixtures.

"Money?" Lochlainn said. "You want money?"

Serria and McKee pushed some furniture aside, rolled up carpets, looking for loose floorboards. They found several and used knives to pry up the boards. Out came several packs of a white lightweight material packed in an olive-drab Mylar film container.

"Give that here," Kohlman said.

McKee handed a pack over.

The former Marine examined it. "M112 block demolition charges," Kohlman said. "1.25-pounds of Composition C4 plastic explosive. Enough to blow up a city block."

"What the hell these guys into?" McKee whispered.

"How 'bout it, Lochlainn?" I said.

"It's for personal use," Rat cracked wise.

"I told you to shut the fuck up," Lochlainn said. "Look, I'll pay you to let us go, eh? How much?"

Kohlman placed the C-4 in his pockets.

Serria confiscated a dozen handguns and two Uzis he found in a canvas sea bag in the bedroom.

"We've got a locked safe," Destiny said, pointing into a closet. "It's bolted to the floor."

"The combination, Lochlainn," I said.

"You have no idea who you're fucking with," Lochlainn said.

"The combination," I said.

"Go fuck your mother," Lochlainn said.

I couldn't help but laugh a little. I pressed the shotgun barrel to Lochlainn's neck. "I won't ask again."

"Don't tell him," Rat said.

"I'll count to three," I said. "One. Two—".

"Wait!" Lochlainn said.

I eased off. "Well?"

Lochlainn took a deep breath. "They'll kill me."

"Not our problem," I said.

"Look at it this way," Destiny said reasonably. "You tell us, we let you go and you can leave town."

"And go where?" Lochlainn said. "For Christ's sake, they'll find me no matter where I go."

"Good," I said.

Lochlainn snapped around to glare at me, his eyes fighting to pierce my mask. "I know you?"

I placed the shotgun barrel to his cheek. "The combination."

"How do we know you'll keep your word?" the freckled gang girl said. "That you'll release us?"

"Only one way to find out," Destiny said.

"They're fulla shit," Rat said.

"Fuck it." I repositioned the shotgun against Lochlainn's head. "Say goodbye, scumbag."

"Twenty-three left," Lochlainn screamed. "Nine right. Thirteen left."

Destiny dialed the combination, opened the safe.

"Bingo." She pulled out and thumbed through stacks of bills. "Looks like around twenty-five thousand, give or take."

McKee high-fived Serria.

"Take it all," Lochlainn said. "Just let us go."

Destiny reached into the safe and lifted out a canvass satchel. "What do we have we here?" She looked inside. "A white powdery substance."

"Give it here," I said.

Destiny handed it over.

"Hold this." I handed my shotgun to Kohlman, took the

satchel to the street side of the suite, dumped its contents—a large plastic bag filled with white powder—onto a coffee table. I cut the plastic bag open with a knife, opened a window, and poured the powder into the blowing wind.

"Are you crazy!" Lochlainn screamed like a man possessed. He struggled against his cuffs, banged his forehead against the floor until he bled.

"Okay," I said, reclaimed my shotgun from Kohlman. "Let's wrap it up."

McKee and Serria roughed the gang up as they pulled them to their feet, un-cuffed them, handed them back their IDs and allowed them to dress. We gathered what remained of the gang's personal belongings and chucked them out the window onto the street.

"Everyone out," I ordered.

"I want my dogs," Lochlainn said, dabbing at the blood that was coagulating on his forehead above his right eyebrow.

"Take 'em," I said.

Lochlainn and Rat picked up the limp dogs. We marched the belligerent-to-the-end Belfast Boys down the stairs and out onto the sidewalk.

94th Street was completely deserted.

"Consider yourself evicted," I gave Lochlainn a hard shove. "You or your gang ever come back, or go near the Schultzes again, you die. Understand?"

"The Schultzes?" Rat said.

Lochlainn scowled, sucked in a breath, spat in my face.

I saw red. Lunged. Slashed the barrel of my shotgun across Lochlainn's face opening the flesh to the bone. The gang leader let out a short, sharp cry, and dropped his dog as he hit the icy pavement.

I stood over Lochlainn.

"What're you waiting for," Kohlman said. "Kill him."

"Do it," Serria said.

"Yeah, kill the scumbag," McKee said.

"No!" Freckles screamed.

McKee grabbed her, shoved her into the gang.

"Don't. Please don't," Lochlainn blubbered, his hand to his bleeding face. "I beg you. Don't kill me, huh? I'll pay anything."

"Get it over with," Serria said.

"Shut up!" Destiny said. She grabbed my arm. "What the fuck you think you're doing?"

"Get back." I shrugged her away.

"Kill him," Kohlman said, "for Shannon."

For Shannon.

"Michael?" Destiny said, thoroughly alarmed. "Don't."

I pressed the shotgun barrel to Lochlainn's forehead.

"Do it!" Serria shouted.

"No," Destiny said.

"Yes!" Kohlman said.

"Don't!" Freckles screamed.

"This is for Shannon," I said.

And pulled the trigger.

CHAPTER 30

MY SHOTGUN CLICKED on an empty chamber.

Lochlainn let out a howl and shit his pants.

McKee, Serria, and Kohlman burst into whooping laughter and slapped each other high fives.

"Hey." Destiny pushed me away from Lochlainn. "That's enough fun and games."

I looked at my old partner. She was serious.

"You." I addressed Rat. "Get this punk the fuck away from me before I really do kill him."

Rat, Freckles and the others helped Lochlainn to his feet, picked up his dog, and hurried away. I kept my weapon trained on them until they made it to the corner and turned north out of sight.

Movement in the German Hotel. A glint of light caught my attention. Someone in the Schultz apartment was watching.

"We're outta here," I said.

We piled into the van. Serria started the engine, dropped it into gear and sped off.

"Did you see Lochlainn's face?" McKee laughed.

"That was perfect," Kohlman chuckled.

"You won't see that scumbag back again," Serria said.

"You're sick, the bunch of you," Destiny said.

"Relax, Destiny," Kohlman said. "No harm, no foul."

"Yeah." I pulled off my green hood and smiled at Kohlman. "Good thing you remembered to remove the round. Would've been one messy slip-up."

"Yeah: Kaboom! Oops," Kohlman said and guffawed.

"You're a bunch of adolescents," Destiny said.

"We are not," McKee said.

"We are too," Serria said.

"Are not," Kohlman said.

"Are too," McKee said.

"Enough!" Destiny said. "You guys give me a fucking headache."

Serria drove several blocks, made a series of quick turns, checking to see if we were being followed. He ran a couple of red lights, turned onto East 79th Street and raced toward the southbound entrance of the FDR Drive.

"Exactly how much money was in the safe?" McKee said

"I dunno." I looked to Destiny.

She pulled the money from a satchel and counted.

Kohlman was examining the confiscated weapons. "Here's a Smith & Wesson .357 magnum with the serial number filed off; untraceable. Hey, a disposable cell phone." He held them up for everyone to see. "Anyone?"

"Give `em here." I accepted the phone and weapon—you never knew when you needed a disposable cell phone and an untraceable, throwaway gun.

Serria blew another red light, drove a block, turned south and merged into the sparse FDR Drive traffic.

"Twenty-seven thousand, seven hundred sixty," Destiny said.

"Hand it out," I said.

Destiny divided the cash into five stacks totaling $5,552 each, handed them out, kept one for herself.

"What'll we do with it?" McKee said.

"Anything you want," I said.

"Get a hooker," Serria said. "Get drunk."

"What're you doing with yours, Kraut?" McKee said.

Kohlman finished counting his share, stuffed it behind his bulletproof vest. "My son's medical bills."

I glanced at the faint outline of boat traffic that was struggling mightily against the outgoing East River tide. The sky to the east showed the first glow of sunrise—I decided that my money problems could wait. "Here." I handed Kohlman my share. "I wanna make a donation."

A momentary silence in the van.

Serria handed Kohlman his money. "I'm in."

"I'm with the spic." McKee tossed his to Kohlman.

"Thank you," Kohlman said. "But you've all got your own problems. You don't have to—".

"Yes," I said, "we do."

McKee looked at Destiny. "Well?"

"There a question in there somewhere?" Destiny said.

"What're you gonna do with your share?" McKee said.

"Get a boob job, fuck face." Destiny pocketed her loot.

The van approached the East 63rd Street exit.

"Pull off here a minute," I said. "Park up on First Avenue." Serria flipped his right-turn signal, steered the van off at the exit and parked at the curb.

"We'll be right back," I said.

Kohlman and I exited the van carrying the C-4 and the sea bag full of guns. We climbed up the 63rd Street overpass, crossed over the drive, and took a bicycle ramp down the other side to the edge of the East River.

"C-4. That's some serious shit," Kohlman said as he threw the explosive into the fast-moving water. "We gotta alert the Terrorism Task Force without getting ourselves jammed up."

"I'll take care of it," I said.

"Use the disposable cell phone," Kohlman said.

I heaved the sea bag of guns over the rail and watched it sink below the surface. Then I pulled out the disposable cell phone, disguised my voice as best I could, and left a detailed message regarding the Belfast Boys at the Terrorism Task Force's hot line.

I dropped the phone into the East River.

"Who gets out first?" Serria said as Kohlman and I got back into the van.

"Anyone hungry?" Kohlman said.

"Is the pope Catholic?" McKee wheezed.

"Your place is closest, Beckett," Serria said.

"Yeah, but Solana's sleeping."

"Speaking of hot women," Serria said. "The babelicious blonde at the German Hotel?"

"Enia," I said.

"She blows dead mice," Destiny said.

"So?" Serria said. "I'd like to use her ass as a hat."

"You're disgusting," Destiny said.

"Thank you," Serria said.

McKee high-fived Serria.

"So, we'll be quiet," Kohlman said. "We won't wake Solana."

"Yeah," McKee said. "What's the big deal?"

I thought it over. Truth was, this *would* be a good opportunity to prove to Solana that I was telling the truth, that I'd worked with a team in which Destiny was merely a member. I checked the time. Solana would have to get up for work soon anyway.

"All right," I said. "My place it is."

We stopped at a twenty-four hour Korean deli, purchased breakfast fixings, parked in my building's underground garage and took the elevator to the fourteenth floor. I picked up my delivered copy of the *New York Times*, had to hush up everyone as we entered the quiet, dark apartment. I switched on the lights.

"Make yourselves at home," I said.

Destiny looked in my refrigerator, made a face. McKee and Serria located a tin of Yuban, some filters, and made a pot of coffee.

Destiny took eggs, cheese, mushrooms and bacon out of the shopping bag. She fried the bacon, cracked and scrambled eggs, put together and served omelets while we men sat around the apartment, drank coffee, and embellished old war stories.

Serria and McKee related the time they collared a gang of armed female robbers; Serria wound up marrying one and having a child; the ensuing bitter divorce left him full custody of his junkie offspring.

I repeated the yarn about the "major" drug bust Destiny and I had made—we screwed-up by arresting several undercover DEA agents and blowing their three-year sting operation.

The men and women in our pasts were all somehow more desirable, and we had, in retrospect, morphed from what we actually were—over-the-hill cops to Hollywood-handsome heroes.

I heard the bedside alarm clock go off. Within moments the bedroom door opened. Solana trudged in wearing one of my starched dress shirts, wiping the sleep from her eyes. To her credit, she didn't react negatively to the room full of unexpected visitors. She waved to everyone, walked across the carpet and gave me a kiss. She smelled of mouthwash.

"Morning, honey," I said.

Solana moved into the living room and greeted Serria, McKee, and Kohlman warmly.

"Hey, Solana," Destiny said.

"Oh, it's you," Solana said curtly and turned her back.

The room went silent.

"Can I get anyone anything?" Solana said to the guys.

"I've gotta be going," Destiny said, picking up her coat.

"Me too," Kohlman said.

"I promised to help the spic paint his apartment," McKee said, getting up from the table.

"The stupid donkey works for beer," Serria said, and everyone laughed. The rockers pulled on their coats and filed out the door.

I said my goodbyes, locked up after them, and turned to Solana. "I don't appreciate you being rude to Destiny."

"I wasn't rude." Solana walked into the bathroom.

"What do *you* call it, then?"

"You guys woke me up." She turned on the shower. "I was half asleep. What do you expect?"

Solana was stonewalling me. But, once again, I didn't feel like arguing the point. "Sorry we woke you," I said simply.

Solana dropped my shirt and stepped into the shower. After a moment she said, "How'd your job go?"

I had no intention of telling her what a rush it had been: charging into the building, busting into the Belfast Boy's suite, surprising Lochlainn, evicting him and his gang, watching Lochlainn beg for his life and shit his pants.

"It was fun," I said.

"Fun? That's it?"

"Yeah. Working with the old gang was really fun."

CHAPTER 31

"CORNED BEEF ON rye, extra lean, and a seltzer," Alex Schultz told an octogenarian waiter at Katz's Deli, on Manhattan's Lower East Side.

"Nothing for me," I said.

The waiter looked at me with a practiced Katz's Deli scowl, shook his head in feigned disgust, and departed.

It was mid-afternoon and I had managed to score an empty table in the back, against a wall covered with celebrity photos and other memorabilia, in the full service section. The deli had been open since 1888 and looked it. Although Katz's was, in my opinion, the best Jewish deli in the city, the dingy décor and cheap furnishings were more than showing their age. Even so, the place was still frequented by a "Who's Who" list of sport stars, entertainers and politicians.

I glanced around the sprawling, visually chaotic room and noticed that all two hundred and seventy seats were taken. The mayor and his entourage were sitting at a table across the room by the deli's long lunch counter. Reporters hovered, anxious for a sound bite—a misspoken word, a careless remark they could take out of context and use to invent a story. Over by the restrooms, Judge Judy Schindlin and her husband were being served a large plate of cold cuts.

Schultz leaned across our table toward me and spoke in hushed tones. "Enia and I don't know how to thank you." He handed me the envelope containing the $10,000. "You've given us our lives back."

I thought about telling him that he'd been sleeping a couple of floors below enough C-4 explosive to level 94th Street, decided it would serve no purpose—why freak the guy out? He had enough problems being married to Enia.

"You won't be seeing Lochlainn and his gang again. I guarantee it." I peered inside the envelope, thumbed through the ten grand, and slipped it into my blue blazer pocket. "If you wouldn't mind a bit of free advice: Be careful. Watch your back. Trust no one."

"You referring to Enia?"

This guy was no dummy. I shrugged.

"Look," Schultz said, "Enia told me all about you two."

"Did she?" I said skeptically, knowing that Enia's version of our relationship would greatly differ from mine.

"I'm not blind," Schultz said. "I know Enia's weak, self-absorbed. But I love her just the same."

"Lucky for Enia," I said, and meant it. The scary part being that if Enia hadn't run out on *me,* I could very well still be under her sexual spell.

"Enjoy your lunch." I started to get up.

"Wait," Schultz said. He checked the area, making sure the waiter and the swarm of political reporters were not close enough to overhear. "I know some other landlords, members of a building owners association that I belong to, who're having the same problems I did with other drug gangs. They're willing to pay whatever it takes to evict `em. If you want, I'll put you in touch."

I didn't know how to respond to Schultz mainly because I honestly hadn't given any serious thought to rocking again. "How many landlords?" I said.

"At least six, but there could be more."

"Lemme have their names, phone numbers," I said. "If I'm interested, I'll contact them."

Schultz took out a piece of paper that contained the building owners association's membership list. He used a pen to circle six names and handed it over.

I perused the list, folded it and put it in my pocket.

"It's a sad commentary, when you think about it," Schultz said. "Drugs are so prevalent, no one can stop 'em. Sometimes I get the feelin' that the law has given up. Maybe they should."

The waiter set down a can of Katz's seltzer, along with two small bowls overflowing with kosher pickles and coleslaw, and walked away.

"Legalize drugs?" I said. "Never."

"Why not? Society tolerates alcohol. Why not crystal meth, or cocaine, or OxyContin?"

"You don't know what the fuck you're talking about."

"Don't I?" Schultz said. "Look, we've lost the war on drugs, hands down," Schultz said. "Why not spend the drug enforcement billions on education? Sell drugs in hardware stores next to the paint thinner. People wanna kill themselves, let 'em. It's the Lord's way of thinning the herd."

I couldn't believe what I was hearing. "Anyone close to you ever die from drugs?"

A flicker of doubt crossed Schultz's face. "No."

"I didn't think so."

The waiter set down the corned beef sandwich. It was large enough to feed three average-sized adults. "Mazel tov," the waiter said and disappeared.

"You want half?" Schultz said. "No way I'll finish it."

"Take it home." I pushed back from the table, stood, picked up my coat. "Now you can do me a favor."

"Sure, if I can."

"Lose my phone number."

"I do something to offend you?" Schultz said.

"No, you haven't. Just don't call me, or email me. Don't stop by my apartment. I don't want to hear from you or your wife ever again."

CHAPTER 32

"WHEN YOU FIGURE what the landlords will pay," I said. "Add that to what we appropriated in the Schultz raid. Use that as an average. We stand to take in four or five grand apiece for each assignment."

My rockers were huddled in Elaine's, at the window section of the bar where we had a clear view of the entire restaurant as well as snow-swept Second Avenue—a desirable cop's view of who was coming and going. Destiny was half listening, her eyes unfocused, her mind somewhere else.

The normal dinner crowd had not materialized that evening. A neighborhood newlywed couple were drinking champagne at the other end of the bar. Only two or three tables were occupied, allowing my bartender pal Vernon ample time to over-serve us. Tony Bennett crooned "I Wanna Be Around" over the sound system.

"I had a blast," Kohlman said, all smiles. "Made me feel like a kid again. I'm in."

"Count me in too," Serria said.

"I'm with the spic." McKee wheezed, coughed.

"I need the money," Destiny said.

All eyes turned to me.

I let the silence build, knowing that, deep down, they were

saying what I wanted to hear. I'd helped Schultz because I wanted to get at Lochlainn. But what I hadn't counted on was how that experience would affect me: I felt empowered and keenly alive. I was doing something useful for the first time since being dumped in the Building Maintenance Division—I was protecting the weak against predators. And yes, rousting drug dealers might be a way to bring closure to my sister's death.

"Then we're all agreed," I said. "No bullshit jobs." I lifted my beer in a toast. "We check out every assignment before we accept it."

"Yeah," Destiny said dryly. "Don't wanna screw up another DEA sting operation. God forbid."

"Or get duped into being bouncers for greedy landlords," McKee said.

"We rock only violent predators," I said. "Agreed?"

Everyone lifted their glasses.

"Death to predators," Serria said.

Everyone clinked glasses and drank.

"Another round?" Vernon said. "On the house."

"Club soda for me." Kohlman checked his wristwatch. "I gotta get back to Langlois's place."

"Me too," I said. "Club soda."

"We're gonna grab a smoke," McKee said. He and Serria excused themselves and stepped outside.

"Hey," Destiny said. "Isn't that Mark Tesser sitting in the back? Look. The corner table?"

Tesser was indeed having dinner at the rear of the restaurant with two guys I recognized as his rockers. He caught me looking. Nodded a greeting.

"Yeah," I sneered, unable to keep the contempt out of my voice. "That's Tesser."

"Haven't seen him in years." Kohlman pushed back from the bar. "I'm gonna go say hello."

"Do me a favor," I said to Kohlman. "Don't tell Tesser our business."

"Give me a little credit, why don't you," Kohlman said.

I watched Kohlman head to the rear of the restaurant, shake hands with Tesser and his men, then sit at their table.

"What's with you and Tesser?" Destiny said. "Last time I saw you two, you were all buddy-buddy, buying each other drinks."

I glanced back at Tesser's table. "The guy's bad news."

"Always was," Destiny said. "Don't you remember? He was cozy, too cozy in my opinion, with a couple of drug dealers."

"My sistah." Vernon handed Destiny her rum and coke, set down the other drinks.

Destiny opened her purse, shook a couple of Vicodins from a prescription bottle and swallowed them with a sip of her rum and coke.

"You shouldn't drink with painkillers," I pointed out.

She recapped the prescription bottle and placed it back in her purse. "Thanks, Dad."

"How're the headaches?"

"I'm popping pain killers like candy. What do you think?"

I started to speak, then stopped. Destiny had always been, unlike most women I'd known, emotionally poker-faced. Be it a gruesome accident, bloody crime scene, altercation with a crazed civilian—and my sister's Shannon's death—she was strong, unflappable, cool. But I knew that being cool had a price. And I knew that Destiny felt guilty about killing Gregory Sonny McFarland, the Key Food robber. Add to that her impending divorce. All that stress was taking a toll, maybe even causing her headaches. Or perhaps it was just the female hormone thing, or a combination of both.

"I know, I'm being a bitch." Destiny sipped more of her drink. "I'm sorry, Michael."

I shrugged it off. "No sweat, sugar britches."

Destiny stuck a manicured finger in my face. "You call me that again, I swear, I'll shoot you where you stand."

I smiled. "That's my girl."

McKee and Serria walked back into Elaine's, shivering from the cold and reclaimed their stools.

"Yo, check it out," Serria flicked his head across the street. "We're being watched."

I stole a furtive glance. The fat jerk with the red, road-kill toupee was directly across the avenue, hovering in the doorway of Rathbones Bar.

"Him again?" Destiny said.

"Know him?" Serria said.

"He smacked his wife right here, in front of the whole restaurant," Destiny said. "Beckett roughed him up a little."

"Saw him again the other day," I said, "stalking his wife."

Destiny looked around. "She's not here."

"She shows up, there could be fireworks," I said. "He carries a gun."

Everyone looked at me.

"I saw it," I said.

"Vernon," Destiny said. "C'mere."

"Yes, my sistah," he said sweetly.

"The guy across the street?"

Vernon looked. "I see him."

"Remember his wife?" Destiny said.

"Yeah, I do."

"She have a reservation?"

Vernon stepped down to the end of the bar and checked the reservations book. "Dinner for two at eight."

I checked the time: 7:35 P.M. "She leave a contact number, home or cell?"

"Yeah, she did."

"Call her," I said. "Tell her not to come, her husband's waiting outside. He may be armed."

Vernon picked up the phone, dialed the number, shook his head. "Goes straight to her voice mail."

"That fucker starts shooting," McKee said. "He could hit one of us."

"I'll call 911," Destiny said. "Let the sector car handle it."

"Don't bother." I got off my barstool, slipped on my coat, thinking an off-duty gun collar might help propel me out of Building fucking Maintenance. "I'll take him."

"I'm in," Serria said, liking the idea.

McKee zipped up his coat. "Let's go."

The three of us stepped out onto Second Avenue.

Road-kill saw me coming. Recognition registered on his face. He hustled to the corner. Saw that Serria and McKee were also heading his way. He bolted east on 88th Street.

I jogged across Second Avenue, feet fighting for purchase on the snow-covered asphalt. I leapt over a parked car onto the sidewalk. Made the turn onto 88th Street just in time to see Road-kill dash up a set of tenement steps, enter the building and disappear from sight.

We followed him down the street, up the steps. I pushed open the front door but was halted by a locked vestibule door. Road-kill must've had a key. I considered kicking the door in, then thought better of it. If Road-kill had a key to the vestibule door, he was probably barricaded in an apartment by now. Then again, he might've run over the roof to an adjoining building. Or he could've simply high-tailed it out the back door.

"Slippery bastard," McKee said, huffing and puffing.

"We'll get him next time," I said.

"You think there'll be a next time?" Serria said.

"Oh, yeah," I said. "There'll be a next time."

CHAPTER 33

"GO FUCK YOURSELF," Don Langlois said.

"You go fuck *yourself*," Claudia Langlois shot back.

"How original," Langlois said. "Dumb cow."

"Prick!"

Mario the Asshole closed the front door as soon as the fighting Langloises and Kohlman crossed the threshold, then scurried inside the security office out of sight.

I was sitting at my post at the bottom of the sweeping staircase, watching the now familiar scene unfold. I figured that this was Langlois's cue to feign exasperation once again, dash out of the townhouse and into the arms of one of his paramours.

"And you," Langlois said to Kohlman, "you gotta be the dumbest, most incompetent white man I know."

I looked up from the desk.

"Mr. Langlois," Kohlman said, "the entire city is on lockdown when the president of the United States is in town. The Secret Service controls everything. The presidential motorcade has precedence wherever it goes. You know that."

Langlois glowered. "Then how come Trump's nigger driver had his limo at the front of the hotel?"

"I don't know," Kohlman said.

"Well, next time my car is not in front of a place *before* Trump's nigger, you're fired. Understand?"

Kohlman hung his head. "I can't control the movements of the president, or the Secret Service."

"You can't?" Claudia shrieked. "What the hell are we paying you for?"

"To expedite your movements, guard your lives."

Without warning, Langlois threw his cellular phone. It struck Kohlman on the forehead, shattered.

Kohlman yelped, grabbing at his forehead in pain.

I shot to my feet, ready to back up the old cop. But I stood my ground, waiting for Kohlman to give me a sign, make his move.

"Don't you ever argue with my wife," Langlois said. "And I mean *ever.*"

There were tears of frustration in Kohlman's eyes.

"You got that?" Langlois said.

I thought for a moment that Kohlman was gonna lose it and pummel the little twerp, Langlois. I smiled inwardly at the prospect. But Kohlman just stood there in humiliated silence, his eyes on the floor.

"Yes, Mr. Langlois," he said.

Langlois mumbled something to Claudia about firing Kohlman, the impertinent sonofabitch. He took her arm and they walked past me, into the elevator and rode up to the second floor.

Kohlman, face flushed with embarrassment, used a handkerchief to dab at the blood trickling from a small cut on his head. "You believe this shit?"

"Well, tell me you're gonna press charges for assault," I said. "Sue his short fat ass. Mario and I will be your witnesses. Right, Mario?"

"Hey." Mario the asshole stuck his head out of the security office. "Leave me out of it."

"Can't press charges," Kohlman said, scowling. "The Langloises're above the law. They know it. They know I know it. Thanks just the same, Beckett."

"Then quit." I lowered my voice so Mario couldn't hear. "You don't need this anymore."

"You're wrong," Kohlman said. "This is steady work."

I sat back down at the desk. "But the rocker raids—".

"Are good for extra money," Kohlman said. "But there's no guarantees, and I need guaranteed income."

I understood what Kohlman meant: The NYPD retiree medical insurance was not all it was cracked up to be and his son needed extraordinary care. Kohlman would have to cover a good portion of that care, over and above what the insurance paid.

"Well, guess I'm out of here." Kohlman buttoned up his overcoat, turned and headed to the exit. "Goodnight."

"Straight home," I said and watched Kohlman shuffle dejectedly out the front door.

I yelled to Mario. "You're a real standup guy."

"I take care of number one," Mario yelled back.

The switchboard phone rang. I looked at the blinking light, it was the Langloises' kitchen line. I let it ring; fuck the Langloises.

"Hey!" Mario stuck his head out of the security office, alarm in his voice. "You gonna get that?"

I answered on the sixth ring.

"Langlois residence. Beckett speaking."

"Put Kohlman on." It was Don Langlois himself.

"He left," I said.

"Make a note: Notify Chief Vogt that Kohlman is terminated effective immediately. Got that?"

I wanted to tell Langlois to go fuck himself, but stopped myself; Gunder *was* paying me. "Yes, sir, Mr. Langlois."

Langlois hung up in my ear.

CHAPTER 34

"HELLO, DESTINY. MARCUS Ian calling."

"Well, hello," Destiny whispered in the early morning light. She sat up in bed, checked the bedside clock: 7:00 A.M.

"I'm not calling too early?" Dr. Ian said.

"Not at all." Destiny looked at her sleeping husband. Fernando was supposed to be up, getting ready to take the train to the city, look for a job.

"Hold on a minute." Destiny rolled from bed and hurried into the bathroom. She looked at herself in the mirror and executed a neck-whipping double take; there were bags and dark circles under her eyes. "What's up, Marcus?"

"How're you feeling?" Dr. Ian said.

Now that you've called, Marcus Ian, I'm feeling energized, amorous, gloriously sexy. "A little tired. I was out carousing last night."

Destiny left the bathroom, tip-toed into the living room and closed the door quietly behind her. "I wanna thank you for setting up the neurologist's appointment for me, Marcus."

"That's what I'm calling about. This isn't a social call, Destiny. I just spoke to Dr. Goldsamp."

Destiny felt a spark of apprehension. "Oh?"

"The results of your CAT Scan were inconclusive. He wants to perform an MRI."

Destiny took in a sharp breath. "An MRI?" She sat down hard on a chair. "When?"

"Soon as possible. It's urgent, Destiny."

"You're scaring me."

"I'm sorry."

Destiny leaned back, massaged the bridge of her nose. She didn't know what to think, what questions to ask. "Level with me, Marcus. What am I looking at here?"

"When you set up the MRI, Dr. Goldsamp will discuss everything with you."

"*C'mon*, Marcus," Destiny said, trying to keep her voice down. "Tell me."

"I shouldn't...." Marcus hesitated. "The CAT scan revealed a brain mass."

Destiny shot up from the chair, crossed the living room to the picture window that overlooked the Hudson River. The morning sun illuminated the New Jersey Palisades. "This can't be happening."

"Don't panic," Dr. Ian said. "Nothing's definite."

Destiny's skin prickled to goose flesh. She wrapped her arms around herself. "What kind of brain mass?"

"There are over one hundred and twenty different types of tumors," Dr. Ian said. "The vast majority are treatable."

"Is mine treatable?"

"If I had to guess, I'd say yes."

Destiny started a caged lion pace. "I'm scared, Marcus."

"Look," Dr. Ian said. "Scared is normal. It's okay to be scared. The odds are that you're looking at a glioma: a low-grade astrocytoma or grade I or II astrocytoma."

"English, please."

"Astrocytomas are the most common form of tumor. They

grow rather slowly and may sometimes be completely removed. However, even well-differentiated low-grade astrocytomas can be life threatening if they're neglected or inaccessible, which is why we have to get you an MRI."

"Are you saying my tumor could be inaccessible?"

"No," Dr. Ian said. "I didn't mean to… Look, Dr. Goldsamp is more qualified than I to discuss all that with you."

"Please, Marcus," Destiny said, her voice catching. "Please, help me out here."

Dr. Ian took a moment. "Look, most tumors are accessible and therefore treatable with surgery, radiation therapy and chemo-therapy. But because brain tumors are located at the control center for thought, emotion and movement, some are inoperable."

"Okay, I'm gonna think positive here." Destiny walked back into her kitchen. "Let's say the MRI reveals that the tumor is acces-sible. Then what?"

"A biopsy will determine what type of tumor you're dealing with. Low or high grade."

Destiny shivered; a biopsy meant a needle in the brain. "What's a high-grade tumor?"

"A type IV astrocytomas glioblastoma multiforme." His voice was flat, professional, cold. "GBMs."

"C'mon, Marcus. E-n-g-l-i-s-h."

"GBMs grow rapidly, invade nearby tissue and contain cells that are malignant."

"How malignant?" Destiny said.

"They're devastating primary brain tumors."

Destiny heard a noise and startled.

"What's going on?" Fernando said, grumpily. He was standing in the kitchen doorway rubbing sleep from his eyes. His PJs were rumpled, his thick black hair askew.

"Thank you, Marcus," she said. "I'll follow up as soon as pos-sible." She hung up the phone.

"Who's Marcus?"

Destiny tried to sound nonchalant. "A doctor."

"A fertility doctor?" Fernando said with an edge to his voice. Coming into the kitchen he picked up a coffee pot, saw that it was empty, made a face. "What, no coffee?"

"What, you crippled?" Destiny snatched the pot from Fernando, put it in the sink, let the water run into it.

"You're in some mood." Fernando located a coffee filter and a tin of coffee and handed them over. "I asked you, what kinda doctor?" He opened the refrigerator and poured himself a glass of orange juice.

"He works the Metropolitan Hospital ICU," Destiny said. "He was taking care of the guy I shot."

"Yeah?" Fernando seemed puzzled. "I heard you say something was 'high grade.' 'Malignant?' What's going on?"

Destiny placed a filter in the coffee maker and began to measure out the coffee. She thought about how much to tell Fernando. Since he would undoubtedly look upon her dilemma in terms of how it would affect him, he would only add to her problems; she didn't need that kind of pressure. Then again, there was a part of her that wanted to tell him the truth, wanted to believe that he'd be there for her; for once in his life be a selfless and compassionate spouse.

"You know the headaches I've been getting. Well, they ran some tests, found some sort of growth, maybe a tumor."

"A tumor?" Fernando said, horror on his face.

"Marcus—the doctor—said, the odds are it's nothing too serious." Destiny proceeded to pour the water into the coffee maker's reservoir. "But they wanna run more tests."

"Oh." Fernando finished his OJ, put the glass in the sink. "You going to work today?"

Destiny nodded. "Another boring tour at the hospital emergency room."

"Yeah? Well, maybe Marcus will keep you company."

Destiny placed the coffee pot on the brewer's hot plate, flicked the on button. "What's that supposed to mean?"

Fernando let out a loud OJ belch. "If it's OK with you, I'm gonna take a shower first." He turned his back and walked out of the room.

CHAPTER 35

I MET JULIE Gunder at 3:00 P.M. at the Oak Room Bar. The wood-paneled baroque room was busy as usual with loud, boorish tourists and a smattering of well-heeled regulars sitting at tables overlooking snow-covered Central Park.

"She called you what?" Gunder was sitting on a bar stool in a tent-sized dress, sipping a cosmopolitan, stuffing her face with bar cashews.

"A prick. A moron," I said. "And my personal favorite: a motherfucker."

"Not to worry." Gunder said. "She always gives the new hires a hard time. It's a sort of a hazing, an initiation." She stuffed more cashews in her mouth. "I'll speak to her, smooth things out."

"I don't want you to smooth things out. I want out. I quit."

She gave me a sharp look. "You haven't even worked off your retainer yet."

"What difference does it make? You asked me to do a job. The job's done." I handed Gunder a bound report. "That's a detailed description of the townhouse's security system, staff, setup, and recommendations for implementing improvements. Plus a log of the Langloises' visitors."

Gunder glanced at the report. "Tell me about the visitors."

Something in her tone put me on guard. "All the visitors are business associates, or personal trainers, or massage therapists," I said. "The phone calls are, from what I can tell, all business related."

"What about the alarm system?"

"The alarm system's a joke—it's all in the report."

"I'd like a verbal. And please be specific," Gunder said, flipping through the report.

I took a swallow of beer. I supposed she deserved extra for the money she was paying. "The roof sensors are set off by falling leaves, blowing twigs, any kind of debris. So security turns them off. Claudia wants the rear of the house checked every fifteen minutes. But that means security has to shut down the system beforehand or the interior rear motion detectors will go off. So they keep those sensors off too."

"Easy access for a thief." Gunder took out a pad and scribbled some notes. "Solutions?"

"No quick fix. They need a whole new alarm system."

Gunder kept writing. "And the men?"

"Langlois fired the best man he had," I said. "Hans Kohlman was a first-rate supervisor. The other men are good. Regardless, I think the rank and file would be ineffective in an emergency situation."

"How is that possible? How could good men be ineffective in an emergency situation?

"They hate the Langloises."

Gunder raised an eyebrow. "Not surprising."

"The security pay is low and they get what they pay for: zilch. Know what we do all night instead of watching security monitors and patrolling the house? Sleep. That is, when the Langloises aren't fighting and Claudia isn't purposely tripping the alarm, running security's asses all over the house. In short, the inmates are running the asylum."

"So," she said, "if anyone made an attempt on the Langloises' lives——?"

"No one's gonna risk their lives to save the Langloises."

Gunder took more notes.

"From what I've observed and from what the men tell me, the Langloises are lonely, paranoid people. They're insolent, treat all their employees with contempt."

"That's true," she said, nodding. "I've experienced it myself."

"They fraternize only with business associates and the occasional minion who turns up every now and then. It's like their money has made them crazy. They're prisoners of their own wealth."

"You sound like you feel sorry for them."

I thought about that. "I wouldn't trade places with them, even with their billions." I'd been watching that bowl of cashews for a while now. I pulled it away from Gunder and claimed the last nut.

"That brings me to another subject," I said. "You privy to Langlois's investments? He into bearer bonds, precious metals, stones?"

"I haven't the faintest. Why?"

I chewed the cashew, swallowed. "There's a formidable vault in Langlois's safe room on the second floor. A thief could be interested in the contents."

"I'm aware of the safe. Anything's possible."

"That's about it."

Gunder signaled the bartender. "We'll have more cashews."

"So, now what?" I said. "You handle my resignation, or do I tell Chief Vogt I quit?"

"Don't resign yet. Finish out the week."

"Why? You have your report."

"Vogt will get suspicious if you suddenly quit."

I didn't see why that would matter. "He's the one warned me about Claudia. Besides, I can't take the Langloises anymore."

The cashews came. Gunder grabbed a handful, stuffed them

in her face. "Tell you what: I'll pay you a bonus of five-hundred if you finish out the week."

I drank some more beer. Thought about how much I disliked the Langloises. How much self-control it took for me to stop from pimp-slapping both Ron and Claudia, not to mention giving my shift partner Mario the Asshole a punch in the mouth. But I didn't wanna make things tough on Gunder. She might give me more work down the line.

"All right," I said. "But I'm done at the end of the week."

CHAPTER 36

"THERE HE IS," Serria said. He picked a potato chip out of a small bag, tossed it in his mouth, and pointed through falling snow. "The clocker."

It was 10:00 P.M. My rockers and I were seated in Serria's van—Vermont plates this time—on Houston Street on the Lower East Side, a full block west of a tenement that was overrun by a drug gang. Serria had the wipers on low. Between swipes large snowflakes collected on the windshield.

I had spent the last few days contacting the landlords that Schultz recommended. The owner of the Houston Street tenement had told me that members of a drug gang had traveled to her home in lower Westchester. "They killed our dog," the landlord told me. "Threatened my family's lives if we proceeded with a court-ordered eviction."

"Way it works," Serria said, "the buyer approaches the clocker, tells him what he wants, gives him the money. The clocker phones the target tenement down the street where they keep the stash. A runner shows up with the drugs a few minutes later, makes the exchange."

"So, he's the clocker?" Destiny said, indicating a fidgety, thin youth in running shoes and hooded sweats.

Serria nodded, munched another potato chip. He pointed out another youth. "He's a lookout."

"The lookout looks stoned," Destiny said, squinting at him.

"Good for us," I said.

"What next?" Kohlman said impatiently. "I mean, we got a plan, or what?"

We all looked at him.

Since being fired from Langlois's, Kohlman was becoming uncharacteristically irritable. Although he hadn't spoken to me, or any of us, about the incident, I figured he was worried about earning enough money to pay for his son's medical care. And I think he regarded the termination as an embarrassment. It had damaged Kohlman's pride.

"Can't do what we did last time," Serria said. "They have steel bars on the fire escape window. No way in or out. The apartment front door is steel framed."

"I know where I can get my hands on a door-buster," Kohlman said, referring to a gun-like tool that uses the force from firing a blank .22-caliber cartridge to thrust forward a chisel to break heavy door locks. "It'll take a day or two."

"Door-busters aren't reliable enough," Destiny commented. "Besides, it makes too much noise."

"How 'bout we grab one of his runners?" I said.

"Then what?" McKee said.

I grinned. "Persuade him to cooperate."

A late model car pulled to the curb. The clocker in the sweats stepped from a doorway and approached the car.

We all watched as the car window powered down. After some tribal handshakes and a brief conversation, money was exchanged. The clocker pulled out his cell phone, speed dialed, and spoke into the phone, presumably placing the order.

"Pull down the street," I said.

Serria slid the van in gear, tapped the gas, and rolled to a stop several doors beyond the target tenement.

Within minutes, a runner came rushing out of the building. He hot-footed up the street toward the clocker and handed off the drugs. The clocker handed the drugs to the buyer and the buyer drove off.

I unfolded and studied a detailed diagram that Serria and McKee had constructed during their surveillance. It showed the locations of all the lookouts within eyesight, a sketch of the tenement with all entrances and exits, as well as a Google Earth-type, bird's-eye view of the entire block and surrounding tenements—my team had done a first-class job.

"We'll hit the place day after tomorrow, 4:30 A.M." I said. "Serria, McKee, you guys will come in from the next block, down the alley, in the rear door. Kohlman will enter another building down the block and come over the rooftops. Destiny and me will go through the front door, grab a runner."

"Let's hit it now," Kohlman said.

"Yeah," Serria said. "We're ready."

"That we are," McKee said.

I looked at Destiny.

"What're you looking at?" Destiny said testily.

I shrugged. "What do you think?"

Destiny glanced up and down Houston Street. "The street's quiet, thanks to the snow—let's do it."

"All right." I folded the map, put it away. "Let's suit up."

McKee handed out bulletproof vests. Kohlman issued the weapons. Rounds were racked into chambers. It was a challenge getting ready in the van's tight quarters, but we managed. Pre-combat adrenaline was pumping.

"Gimme the chip bag," I said to Serria.

Serria emptied what was left of the potato chips into his hand, shoved them in his mouth, and handed me the empty bag.

"You play drunk," I said to Destiny as I folded and stuffed one of my gloves into the empty chip bag and then resealed it.

"*No problemo.*" Destiny pulled her coat on over her vest and buttoned up.

Within moments a buyer's car pulled to the curb down the street. The clocker approached, money was exchanged, and the clocker used his cell phone.

I stepped out of the van. "Easy, baby," I said in a loud voice so the lookouts could hear. Destiny lurched from the van.

"This your building, baby?" I said.

"Goddamned right," Destiny slurred, "it's my building."

The van pulled away.

Destiny and I were on our own.

Destiny slipped on the snow, into my arms, giggled, and sang some Aretha Franklin. "R-e-s-p-e-c-t, don't know what it means to me. R-e-s-p-e-c-t, blah, blah, blah," Destiny sang and guffawed.

I guided her toward the tenement, my right hand in my pocket, on the grip of my 9mm—expecting the unexpected: a gang of stray skells, or hopped-up meth freaks who might venture to jump us, attempt to rip us off.

I was half carrying Destiny as we pitched laughing and singing through the tenement front door into a urine-stenched vestibule.

A guy in his twenties, big as an NFL fullback, came thumping down the stairs—just my luck. The runners we'd seen outside were beanpole adolescents. Waylaying this goon would not be easy.

The goon spotted us and froze.

I smiled and waved. "Hey, can you get the door for us?"

The goon didn't bother to respond.

"C'mon, big man," I said. "I've got my hands full here."

At first I thought the guy would bolt back up the stairs. But he leaned on a railing, stood there watching us, acting like he was in no hurry. He took a cell phone out, started to dial, then stopped.

He glanced up the stairs, then looked to the street—I could almost see his thoughts move across his face.

"Ah is drunk, baby," Destiny said, slipping into her best Stepin Fetchit. "I be a member ob de Church of God. Savin' souls is mah bidness—praise the Lord." Then she let out a groan and slithered to the filthy tile floor.

"C'mon, baby, get up." I dragged Destiny to her feet and struggled to keep her upright. "Tell me what apartment you live in, baby." I shook her. "What apartment?"

The goon came off the stairs, opened the vestibule door; his mass filled the doorway. "You in the wrong building," he said.

"No shit?" I let go of Destiny, lunged, grabbed the runner by his coat, and shoved. Twisting away, the runner grabbed me by the arms, bounced me off a wall. Then threw me against the stairs. I felt my head strike the steps and I saw stars.

"Police." Destiny stuck her gun and shield in the guy's face. "Let him up." The goon's eyes found the gun. He backed off. I shook the cobwebs from my head and got painfully to my feet.

"Keep your mouth shut." Destiny's gun was pressed to the goon's temple. "Understand?"

The goon nodded.

I grabbed the punk, twisted him around, face against a wall. Spread-eagled him, frisked him, and found a quarter-ounce of cocaine. "What's this?" I held it up to his face. "Know what this kinda weight will get you?"

"Nothing," the goon snarled. "It ain't mine."

"Oh, no?" I pulled the chip bag from my coat pocket and dropped it in his pocket. "That's two ounces of coke. Add that to attempted murder of a police officer and you're looking at twenty-five to life."

"Muthafucka, that ain't right," the goon said, outraged.

"Hey," Destiny glared at me, easing into our well-worn good-cop bad-cop routine. "You can't do that."

"I can," I said, "and I will."

"You're just doing this cause he's black," Destiny said.

"Word, sistah," the goon said, earnestly. "And you ain't gonna get away with it, muthafucka. I got a nigga lawyer lives for racist cops. Makes the ACLU look like the mutherfuckin' Taliban."

"That's it." I feigned a burst of rage, pointed my gun. "Any last words, black boy?"

"No!" Destiny stepped between us. "Don't shoot. Please."

"Get the fuck out of my way."

"Look," Destiny said. "Give him a chance. Let me talk to him, see if he can help us out."

"He's too stupid to help himself," I snarled. "He sure as shit is too stupid to help us."

"Please," Destiny said. "I'm begging you. Just let me talk to him. I mean, he's just a boy."

"Yeah, muthafucka, I'm just a boy."

I glared murderously at the goon, then lowered my weapon and reluctantly backed off. "You got three minutes."

"All right. Thank you. Three minutes is all I need." Destiny pulled the goon aside and said quietly, "Now look here, young man, this guy is a racist. He's practically Ku Klux Klan."

"Yeah, I got that," the goon said, his eye fixed on me. "But this ain't right."

"What's right?" Destiny scowled. "You're selling drugs."

"Everyone `round here sells drugs," he protested.

"I don't wanna hear that," Destiny said.

The goon shuffled his feet, his eyes everywhere.

I had to bite my tongue to keep from smiling as I watched Destiny do her thing: morph from tough street cop to siren—the goon didn't have a chance. In a few minutes, he'd lie down, roll over, and bark if she asked him to.

I became alert at a distant noise. I cocked an ear, tightened my grip on the Browning. I looked out to the street—the clocker would soon be wondering what happened to this goon and his drugs.

"You help us get into the apartment," Destiny pointed up the stairs, "and we'll cut you lose."

"I help you, they'll kill me!"

"You don't," Destiny gestured to me, "he'll kill you."

"That muthafucka's gonna kill me anyway."

I was eye-raking the goon, grumbling, gritting my teeth, hitting him with Hollywood death looks.

"Trust me." Destiny said. "You help us, I won't let the honky hurt you."

"Shiiit." The guy's eyes found the floor. He clucked his tongue, shuffled his feet. "You promise you'll cut me loose, no arrest, no jail time?"

"I promise," Destiny said.

The goon took a moment. "Awright."

I took out my radio. "Everyone in place?"

"We're out back," Serria said.

"I'm on the roof," Kohlman said.

"Do it," I said.

Serria and McKee filed in through the back door, ski masks in place, weapons at the ready.

I grabbed the goon. "You try to warn them—". I stuck my gun in the guy's face. "I'll blow your fucking brains out." I slipped on my kelly green hood. Destiny slipped on hers.

We moved as a group, silently, cautiously up the stairs.

Kohlman was waiting for us on the third floor.

I signaled for everyone to take up positions on either side of the target apartment door. I whispered instructions in the goon's ear. Then backed off.

The goon knocked. A peephole opened and a voice from the other side said, "What?"

"Hey, yo, it's me."

Locks clicked. The door swung open. I shoved the goon in and my rockers rushed in behind me.

The heavily armed Hispanic occupants were caught completely off guard. Several made futile attempts to grab their weapons. But shouts of "Freeze!" and the sound of guns cocking stopped them in their tracks.

The apartment was a dump that smelled of cigarette smoke, sweat and spoiled food. The rickety kitchen table was piled high with white powder, scales, bagging equipment, pipes and other drug paraphernalia.

"What the fuck is going on?" a dealer demanded.

"You're being evicted," I said. "That's all."

Serria ordered the dealers to lie face down on the floor. McKee frisked and began to handcuff them. That's when one of the gang made his play.

A heavyset Hispanic male pulled up a pant leg and moved for the gun that he had tucked away in an ankle holster.

Kohlman caught the movement off to his right. Using his shotgun like a bat he took a mighty swing and shattered the Hispanic guy's hand. The guy screamed and writhed in pain.

"Frisk `em again!" I said.

McKee re-frisked the gang while Serria finished handcuffing them. The rest of us spread out.

I searched the kitchen area, looked inside, under and behind the refrigerator, cupboards, under the sink. I found a stack of bills in a box of laundry detergent. "Looks like around 18K," I said.

Destiny and Kohlman rummaged around the remainder of the one-bedroom apartment. Under a row of twin beds they found an assortment of weapons.

A large trash bag of packaged crystal meth was stuffed in the stove. I pulled the junk out, carried it, along with the pile of coke that was on the rickety kitchen table, into the bathroom, and flushed it all down the toilet.

"Get 'em up," I ordered.

Serria and McKee pulled the drug gang to their feet.

We allowed the gang members to gather their coats, then marched them out of the apartment, down the stairs, onto the street.

"Consider yourselves evicted," I said to the gang. "Get the fuck outta here. And don't come back."

Still stunned by what had just transpired, the gang skulked away without even a hint of protest.

I heard a commotion, turned and saw Kohlman in McKee's face.

"Where'd you learn to do a frisk," Kohlman said, "at a fuckin' titty bar?"

"You're right," McKee said, hands raised in surrender. "My fault."

"Your carelessness could've gotten one of us shot."

"Hey, I apologized," McKee said. "What more do you want?"

"What I *don't* want is you doing any more frisks," Kohlman said, growing angrier by the minute.

"Get off his back," Serria said, defending his former partner. "He screwed up. It happens."

"Tell that to the guy whose hand I broke," Kohlman fumed.

"He's drug dealer," McKee said. "Who gives a shit?"

"I do," Kohlman said.

"Cool it," I said. "Let's get the hell outta here."

CHAPTER 37

Raised voices.

D ESTINY WAS SITTING at the desk at her Metropolitan Hospital emergency room post, flipping absently though magazines, agonizing over her medical condition. She checked the time: 5:00 P.M.

She had planned to drive back to the stationhouse at 5:45, sign out at 6:00, then hurry into the city to the Park Avenue Radiology clinic for her 7:00 o'clock MRI appointment.

Calls for help.

Destiny got to her feet, hurried into the ER proper and saw two Hispanic men carrying a third, bloodied male and yelling for a doctor.

A nursed rushed to check the victim, called instructions to a nurse at the desk, and instructed the men to lay the injured man on a gurney. All at once a trauma team assembled and started attending to the wounded man.

Destiny corralled the two men who'd carried the injured man in. "What happened?"

"I was showing my friends an old gun I found," the thinner of the two said in heavily accented English. "It went off. My friend got shot. It was an accident."

Groan.

Since she'd scheduled her MRI appointment today, the last thing she wanted to do was make an arrest. But since the idiot perp had just admitted that he shot his friend, Destiny would be forced to take police action—-unless.

"Where's the gun?" Destiny said, hoping it was not in his possession. But the thin guy pointed at an old black car in the hospital parking lot. "En mi Chevy."

"*Ay carumba.*" Destiny asked a couple of the low paid, unarmed hospital cops to do her a favor and guard the three men while she went out to the Chevy to retrieve the gun.

Big mistake.

Destiny was in the front seat of the guy's jalopy, rummaging around for the weapon, muttering about the fact that she *really, really* didn't want to miss her MRI appointment when, much to her surprise, the thin guy opened the rear door and reached under the seat.

What the hell? Destiny stepped out of the car.

"You want to see my gun?" the thin guy said. He pointed the rusty automatic at her.

With lightning quickness, Destiny knocked the gun aside and field-goal kicked the man in the groin. He let out a yelp as his feet came off the pavement. He hit the ground hard and lay groaning, in the fetal position.

"Hey, Dead Eye." Two vaguely familiar plainclothes cops alighted from an unmarked police car, guns drawn. "Why the hell didn't you shoot the prick?" the fatter of the two said.

"Yeah," his partner said, looking down at the gunman. "The fucker deserved it." He picked up the guy's weapon and inspected it. "This is an antique."

"An 'attempted murder of a police officer' collar," the fat cop said with outright envy. "You'll get another medal for this, Dead Eye."

"How'd you like the collar?" Destiny said.

The two cops exchanged glances: stupid question. Attempted murder of a police officer collars were much sought after and hard to come by. "You serious?" the fat cop said.

"As a brain tumor," Destiny said.

That went over real well at the stationhouse.

"Hey, Destiny. Where the fuck do you get off giving an attempted murder of a police officer collar away?" Sergeant Hill said. "And to cops from another command?"

It was 6:00 P.M. and Destiny was in the middle of a long line of frenzied, raucous cops, anxious to sign out and go home.

"What's the big deal?" Destiny said, talking above the din. Since giving arrests away to other cops who wanted overtime or department recognition was routine, she didn't know what Hill's problem was. She reached over another cop's shoulder and scribbled her initials on the sign-out sheet. "I didn't want the collar."

"They said you froze," Hill said.

"Who?"

"The cops you gave the collar to. They said the scumbag pointed a gun at you and you froze."

"Bullshit." Destiny shook her head at their treachery. "I disarmed him."

"Not shooting that skell when you had the opportunity jeopardized your life, maybe even theirs."

Destiny noticed that several cops had stopped to listen.

"What, you gonna write me up for *not* shooting a suspect?" She threw her hands up. "I don't believe I'm hearing this."

"Don't be a wise ass. What I'm saying is, it was your felony collar. Had you arrested the asshole, you could've gotten another medal."

"I'm not interested in medals."

The sergeant was getting exasperated. "Life ain't always about you," Hill said. "Look, Destiny, department recognition is good for the command. You know that."

"Fuck the command," Destiny shot back, regretting the words the instant she said them.

All at once the room fell silent.

"All right." Hill raised an unforgiving eyebrow. "I'll remember you said that."

CHAPTER 38

ANOTHER NIGHT AT the Langloises'.

It was my turn to stay up, watch the switchboard, listen for alarms, check the rear of the house. Mario the Asshole was downstairs in the movie theater sleeping. The Langloises were upstairs, doing whatever the Langloises did when they got along, which wasn't often.

Feeling restless, I tossed aside a newspaper I'd been reading, sat back and considered the predicament I found myself in: Even though I'd toiled in some of the poorest, most depressing, crime-ridden neighborhoods of the city, I'd never worked in a more pernicious atmosphere. The Langloises were spoiled, insecure, mean-spirited adolescents. Their twenty-million-dollar townhouse was as cold and devoid of warmth and humanity as they were. And Mario the Asshole? He was an aberration, something out of a bad reality TV show.

I despised Don Langlois for firing Kohlman. Hated the little twit for causing my old friend, and his family, so much anxiety. *I should just quit*, I told myself. Walk out the door without saying a word to Mario, or telling anyone. Any emergency phone calls would go unanswered. More importantly, Langlois's precious newspapers would not be sent up in the morning. Langlois would go absolutely ballistic. Mario would himself be called on the carpet, fired.

But Julie Gunder had paid me a $500 bonus to finish out the week, and I'd said I would. Besides, I'd be done with the Langloises for good in a few days. Loathing them, trying to understand what made them tick was a waste of my time and energy.

I couldn't stifle a yawn. Got to my feet and stretched. I stepped out from behind the desk, strolled into Claudia's darkened office and over to the forbidden couch.

Sure looked comfortable.

I sat on the couch, tested it for comfort and recalled what Mario had told me: "*If you sit on Claudia's couch she'll know it—don't ask me how—and you're fired.*"

I decided that Mario was as paranoid as the Langloises. Long as I straightened the couch, fluffed the pillows, there was no way anyone would know I'd slept there. I lay back and put my feet up, closed my eyes and felt myself drift off.

Noise.

I startled awake.

I bolted upright on the sofa, my heart pounding. Looked around the dimly lit room. "Mario?" I said.

I leaned on an elbow, cocked an ear and my eyes swept over an antique rosewood desk, a computer, a high-back chair, a coffee table dominoed with family pictures. I checked my watch. It was 3:02 A.M.

I heard movement close by, outside at the rear of the townhouse: the sharp crack of splintering glass. I rolled to a sitting position, felt a blast of frigid air and knew that the beveled glass doors in the next room had opened and closed.

Someone had broken into the Langlois residence.

I saw the shadow of an intruder flit past the entrance to the formal dining room.

I executed a Dali-clock slide from the sofa, crawled under

the coffee table, across the thick-pile carpet to the dining room entrance and stopped. I pulled my gun, held my breath. Listened for a sound that would pinpoint the location of the intruder.

Suddenly a form cloaked from head to toe in ninja black glided past me and into the office. When I turned, my ankle joint cracked, giving my position away. The intruder responded with a vicious kick to my solar plexus—I felt like I'd been shot. My breath roared out. I dropped my gun. Collapsed hard to my knees and could no longer feel sensation in my arms or hands. The next blow struck me somewhere on the side of the head or face. I wasn't sure. All I knew was that the room spun away.

Slowly I regained consciousness. I had the presence of mind not to move in case the assailant was near. I forced my mind to explore my body to determine the extent of my injuries. My head was throbbing but I could feel sensation in my hands and feet. Good. The attacker had not broken my neck.

I heard the tapping of computer keys. I opened one eye and saw a dark, hooded figure sitting at Claudia's computer a few feet in front of me. I scanned for my gun as best I could without moving. It was nowhere in sight.

I knew it would be impossible for me to move without the intruder seeing. And I had no way of knowing if my body would even respond if I did move, or how much damage had been done by the assault. I had no choice but to lie there, playing possum.

I heard the elevator and alarms went off in my head—the infant's nurse must be sending the elevator down for the daily newspapers, as she did each morning. But the intruder apparently did not know that. Because he switched off the computer and moved swiftly across the office, ducked behind a heavy floor-to-ceiling window curtain.

I rolled clumsily to my feet and limped to Claudia's desk. Picking up a heavy paperweight, I lurched across the room and struck the bulge head-high behind the window curtain. The intruder let out a grunt and crumbled to the floor.

I dragged the limp body out from behind the curtain, disarmed him and found my own gun in the intruder's waistband.

I handcuffed his hands behind his back and left him on his stomach. I pulled out my cell phone and dialed Julie Gunder. She answered on the first ring.

"It's Michael Beckett." I flexed my sore neck, rubbed my aching solar plexus. I was in definite pain and having some difficulty breathing. "Sorry to bother you."

"No, it's all right," Gunder said groggily.

"Look, a guy broke in. Came through the back."

"What?" Gunder sounded instantly alert.

"Don't worry, I got him cuffed. He broke the beveled glass on the rear door. Went straight for the computer. I'll call 911."

"No," Gunder said. "Don't call anyone."

"The guy might need medical attention."

"*Don't call anyone*," Gunder repeated. "I'll be right there," she said and hung up.

"Bullshit." I put my phone away. No matter what Gunder said, if the blow with the paperweight did any real damage, I was calling for an ambulance. I bent down to examine the intruder. Turned him over. Pulled off his hood.

The intruder was male, white, mid-thirties, had a military haircut and looked to be in excellent physical shape. I inspected the guy's head. I tested his neck flexibility, then felt swelling. The blow had landed just below the skull on the side of the neck. Nothing was broken far as I could tell. The intruder was in no immediate danger.

I searched the guy's pockets and found a flash drive. I looked for some ID, but there was none. The intruder groaned and his eyes fluttered. He was awake.

"Who sent you?" I said.

The intruder reacted to my voice. His bleary eyes found me.

"I asked you a question."

"Fuck you," the intruder said.

I left him lying on the floor, sat on Claudia's couch. "Who do you work for?"

"Your mother."

"Who hired you?" I said.

"Suck my dick."

"How much they paying you?"

I thought about beating the information out of him, then thought better of it—there was nothing personal about any of this. My cell phone rang. "Yes?"

"I'm outside," Julie Gunder said.

I opened the service entrance door and led Gunder and two men—a thick, scary-looking, bald brute dressed in black leather, and a glazier carrying a pane of beveled glass and tools—to Claudia's office.

The intruder lay face up on the carpet.

"Know him?"

Gunder took a close look at the intruder. "No."

"Fuck you, too," the intruder said.

I pointed the glazier to the next room, to the door with the broken pane. Then I handed Gunder the intruder's gun.

".22 Beretta," Gunder said.

"He was carrying this." I handed her the flash drive.

"So you were after the computer information?" Gunder said to the intruder. He looked away and did not respond.

"He was at Claudia's computer," I said.

Gunder motioned to the bald guy. "Take him out to the car."

With little effort, the bald guy lifted the intruder off the floor and walked him out of the house.

"Where're you taking him?" I said.

"You don't wanna know."

"Yeah," I said. "I do."

She scowled at my persistence. "He's being taken to a safe house for interrogation."

Gunder walked behind Claudia's desk, flipped though some files. Apparently found nothing of interest. "I want you to back up Claudia's documents," Gunder said. "I want to see what the thief was after." She tossed me the flash drive.

"I'm not copying someone's personal files," I said.

"Look, Beckett, I work for the Langloises," she said levelly. "There may be sensitive information in that computer I should be aware of."

I shook my head. "Clear it with Claudia."

"I'll pay you an extra thousand dollars—no, make it two thousand." Gunder reached in her bag and took out a checkbook. "Copy her documents onto that flash drive tonight. Bring it to me at the Oak Room Wednesday afternoon."

I considered the offer and what it meant.

As I had suspected from the beginning, Gunder had a hidden agenda—the $2,000 incentive proved that. Not that I cared. Gunder was paying me, Langlois was paying her. And it would be an absolute pleasure to participate in something that might upset the Langloises' lives.

The glazier interrupted. "Done."

Gunder told him to wait outside. The glazier picked up his gear and left.

"We have a deal?" Gunder said.

"Make it twenty-five hundred," I said.

Gunder smiled, wrote out the check, handed it over.

"Thanks." I escorted her out the service entrance and locked the door behind her. I returned to Claudia's office, sat at her desk. I flicked the computer's power switch to on. And as I waited for the system to boot up, I wondered if Gunder was planning to tell the

Langloises about the break-in. Would she report it to the police, or even tell Chief Vogt?—Christ, I'd forgotten all about the old chief.

I took out my cell phone and hit the speed dial.

"It's me," I said.

"You know what time it is?" Destiny whispered.

"I know, sorry. Tell me about Chief Vogt."

"Hold on."

I waited.

"What do you want to know?" Destiny said, her voice no longer a whisper.

"Gunder's trying to involve me in something not kosher," I said. "Would Vogt go along with it?"

Destiny took a moment. "Not a chance."

"Be specific."

"He might be a sleaze, but he's honest, a cop's cop. Got himself in hot water with the mayor and police commissioner a couple of times by taking the side of cops in hot-potato shooting incidents."

That's all I needed to know. "Thanks, partner," I said. "Get some sleep. Kiss your future ex-husband for me."

"Kiss my ass," she said and hung up.

Anytime.

I dialed Chief Vogt's office, left a message on his voice mail, asked that he return my call ASAP. Then I did what Gunder had asked, copied Claudia Langlois's files onto the flash drive.

CHAPTER 39

"TEAM LEADER," HANS Kohlman whispered over the radio.

It was 4:30 A.M. and Kohlman had spent the last five minutes peering in a West 125th Street tenement's fire escape window. He was freezing his ass off, watching a group of dreadlocked Jamaican drug dealers who were sitting around a kitchen table playing cards, listening to some catchy reggae, smoking ganja—the sweet smell was unmistakable.

Serria and McKee's surveillance had alerted us to the fact that this particular gang sold drugs directly out of their apartment to a more-or-less regular clientele. There were no drive-by customers, lookouts, or runners for us to utilize or be concerned with. And the door was reinforced, steel framed; no way we could kick it in, or force it open with a hand-held battering ram.

"Go ahead," I told Kohlman.

"Now I count six, I repeat, six armed men," Kohlman said. "Awake, stoned but awake. I don't like the look of this. I think we should abort. Come back another day."

"Abort, my ass," Serria said.

"Serria's right," McKee said. "Kohlman's turning into a pussy in his old age."

"Stand by," I said.

We were stationed in a fetid tenement stairwell, lounging against a graffiti-covered wall, weapons at the ready, waiting for a random drug customer to arrive so we could rush the apartment.

"Destiny?" I said. "What do you think?"

"We're here," she said irritably, "aren't we?"

I trusted Kohlman's judgment implicitly. But I also trusted my team's ability to take the apartment occupants by complete surprise. I keyed the portable radio. "How stoned?"

"Ganja stoned," Kohlman said.

"Ask about weapons," Serria said.

"Weapons?" I said into the radio.

"Side-arms," Kohlman said. "Looks like five automatics, one revolver. I don't see anything heavier."

I turned to my team. "Well, you heard what I heard."

"They're fucking stoned," Serria said, dismissively.

"We go in fast, they won't know what hit `em," McKee said.

"Yeah, but how do we *get* in," Destiny said. "You see any buyers knocking on the door?"

"Those guys are staying up this late for a reason," Serria said. "They're expecting customers."

"Let's force the issue," McKee said. "One of us knocks on the door, asks to buy drugs—long as they're safe behind a steel door, worse they'll do is tell us to go fuck ourselves."

"Sounds good to me," McKee said.

"Worth a try," Destiny said. "Who's gonna go?"

"I'll go." I keyed the radio. "Kohlman. We're going in."

"10-4." Kohlman sounded reluctant. "Use extreme caution."

I reached into my pocket, took out my reading glasses, slipped them on. I handed my portable radio to Destiny, pulled my weapon and placed it in the small of my back. I stepped out of the stairwell, walked down the hall, and knocked on the dealers' door. A peephole opened.

"Fuck you want, whitey?" a voice said from the other side.

"Blow," I said.

"Let's see your money."

I held a wad of cash up.

The door opened and a gun was pointed at my face.

"Whoa." I raised my hands. "Look, I don't want any trouble."

"Shut the fuck up," the furious face behind the gun said. He looked down the hallway, patted my waist, scowled. "I don't know you. Who the fuck sent you?"

"Hector."

"Hector hangs out on 127th Street?"

"No." I sniffled, coke-wiped my nose with the back of my hand. "The one hangs out over by Sylvia's restaurant."

"Don't know him," The dealer snapped. I flinched as he cocked the gun hammer.

Oh, shit.

"Sure you do," I said, fighting hard to keep the panic from my voice. "He's got a glass eye, harelip, walks with a limp." I scrunched up my face, circle-limped, and spoke through the side of my mouth. "Tauks wike dis."

The dealer broke into a grin, lowered his gun. "Good one. Let's have the money, funny man."

"Thanks, pal." I held the cash out and, when the dealer went to take it, I grabbed the guy's hand, yanked, and slammed his face against the doorframe.

Kohlman crashed in from the fire escape.

McKee, Serria, and Destiny came racing out of the stairwell and we all barreled into the apartment.

The five Jamaicans grabbed their guns. Pointed them at us.

We pointed our guns at them.

Standoff.

Kohlman racked a round into his shotgun, underscoring the fact that the Jamaicans were outgunned and in a no-win crossfire.

The Jamaicans exchanged glances, gauging their chances.

They were not good.

"If we wanted you dead," Destiny said reasonably, "you'd be dead already."

"You cops?" the one who had been at the front door said, using his shirt to deal with a free-flowing bloody nose.

I shook my head. "We're here to evict you."

"You mean, kick us out of the apartment?" Bloody Nose said.

"That's right," I said.

"Well fuck, you better be ready to use those guns, mutha-fucka, cause we ain't going anywhere."

Kohlman stepped forward. With a whip-like swing he cracked Bloody Nose with the butt of the shotgun. The guy's head split. Blood gushed. He crumbled to the ground.

Fingers went tight on triggers.

"Easy," I said. "Take it easy, everyone."

"We'll leave the premises, mon," a Jamaican with the longest dreadlocks said. "But we taking our stash and cash with us."

"No," I said. "You're not."

"Then we got ourselves a problem, mon."

"You walk out the door," I said. "it's over,"

"No, it ain't, mon," dreadlocks said. "People we answer to ain't gonna accept us getting robbed."

I honed my gun in on Dreadlocks.

Serria, McKee, Kohlman and Destiny locked on their targets.

The Jamaicans stood their ground.

No one breathed.

"Tell you what," I said after a moment, lowering my weapon slightly, easing the tension a notch. "You can keep the money. But you're leaving the drugs."

Dreadlocks thought it over, lowered his gun. "Deal," he said, a little too quickly. "Drugs're in the bag." He pointed to a large, brown paper shopping bag that was set alongside a rusty, folding dinner tray table.

Guns steady, fingers on triggers, we watched as the Jamaicans picked up their cash, backed out of the apartment, then bolted for the stairs.

McKee picked up the brown paper shopping bag, looked inside. "No wonder." He looked at me in disgust. "There's less than a grand worth of shit."

"Flush it," I said.

"I told you to abort, Beckett," Kohlman said, angrily, yanking off his hood. "You almost got us fucking killed, and for what?"

"It was his call," Destiny said. "He's running things."

"Yeah," Kohlman growled. "Well, maybe he shouldn't be running things anymore."

"Hey, fuck you," Serria said to Kohlman. "Don't you even think about taking over."

For once his ex-partner didn't agree. "Kohlman's right," McKee said.

"What? You voted to go in," Serria said. "You donkey motherfucker."

"Fuck you, spic," McKee said.

"Hey! A little less testosterone," Destiny said, "for Christ's sake."

"Look," I said. "Kohlman's right. I should've listened to him." I holstered my weapon. "I fucked up. Won't happen again."

"It better not," Kohlman said.

CHAPTER 40

"IT'S A BLIZZARD out there," I said to Julie Gunder as I walked into the Plaza's Oak Room Bar. I slipped off my coat, shook off the snow, draped it across the back of a vacant stool and ordered a beer.

Gunder was hunched over the bar, working on a humongous turkey club sandwich. Sides of coleslaw, French fries and pickles circled her plate.

"You hungry?" She stuffed a sandwich wedge in her mouth. The muscles in her jaws flexed and popped as she chewed. "Help yourself."

"Thanks." I plucked a French fry from her plate and dabbed it into a side of ketchup. As I tossed it in my mouth, I noticed that the Oak Room was unusually empty—compliments of the bad weather, no doubt. But the tide of after-work regulars would soon flood the place, regardless.

"How did it go," Gunder said, "at the Langloises'?"

"Went well," I said absently.

"So, you have the files?"

I ate another fry. "Been studying Claudia's data," I said. "Makes for interesting reading."

Gunder stopped mid-chew, glared at me for a moment, then

resumed eating. "I told you to copy Claudia's files," Gunder said. "Not peruse the data."

The bartender served my beer.

"Had to know what I was getting into." I reached into my suit jacket pocket, pulled out the $2,500 check Gunder had written me and placed it on the bar in front of her, between the French fries and pickles.

"Deal's off," I said.

Gunder put her sandwich down, pushed away the plates, and looked at the check. "What are you trying to pull?"

"Going into business for myself."

"You son of a bitch."

"Relax," I said. "I'm planning on cutting you in."

"Cutting *me* in?"

"I mean," I placed my elbows on the bar. "It was your idea originally—stealing the data, selling the information; operative word being *was*."

Gunder wiped her large, livery lips with a napkin. "You have no idea who, or what you're dealing with here."

"Traitors, turncoats, informants, I get the picture."

"This is way over your head."

"Give me a little credit," I said. "Will you?"

"Look, there are those who are ready, willing and able to pay a small fortune for the names of Claudia's confidential sources."

"No shit."

"I've already identified the interested parties," Gunder said. "Had meetings with them, struck deals."

"Good girl. Which is why I'm cutting you in. You'll save me time and energy."

"Fuck you." Gunder bunched up her napkin, threw it down.

"Now, be nice." I plucked another French fry off her plate. "Here's the deal: I'm taking seventy-five percent."

"No, you're not," Gunder said.

I chuckled. "I don't need you, Julie. I can take the data to any-one I want, make my own deals. Remember that."

"I'll retrieve the information on my own."

"You don't have the access. Of course, you could try to con that ghoul Mario into doing your dirty work for you. But I don't think you will. 'Cause if there were anyone in Langlois' organiza-tion you trusted, you wouldn't have hired me."

Gunder tapped her finger on the table. "Understand, the peo-ple interested in Claudia's sources, they're not 'nice' people. If I tell them you're killing the deal—".

"I'll tell them I'm not killing the deal. Just taking a piece of the action. You're the one causing the problems."

Gunder sat back, studied me. She picked up a sandwich wedge and took a bite. "Fifty, fifty."

"I'm not negotiating."

"Sixty, forty."

"Forget it."

"You greedy prick!"

"Me?" I slammed down my beer glass. "You think I'm stupid? This whole thing was a setup from the get-go. You deny it?"

"I don't know what you're talking about."

"You used me to find the best way into Langlois' house. *You* hired the intruder."

"You can't prove that."

"You endangered my life, Julie," I said harshly. "For that you're gonna pay."

Gunder sucked on her teeth and didn't say a word.

"You'll take twenty-five percent or nothing."

Gunder stared at her food. Her head down, jaws tight.

"What's it gonna be?" I said.

"I'll let you know."

"You do that." I gulped down my beer, stood and shrugged into my coat. "If I don't hear from you by midnight, I'll assume you're not interested and make my own deals." I buttoned my coat. "Oh, and thanks for the beer."

I walked out of the bar through the lobby and out onto Central Park South. I buried my head in the collar of my coat as the snow swirled around me. I walked to the corner, crossed the street and knocked on the driver's side window of a parked, black four-door sedan. Slowly, the window powered down.

"How'd it go?" Chief Vogt said.

I reached into my inside suit pocket, took out a tape recorder, and handed it over. Vogt briefly rewound the tape, then clicked 'Play'. The voices were loud and clear:

"This is way over your head."

"Give me a little credit, will you?"

"Look, there are those who are ready, willing, and able to pay a small fortune for the names of Claudia's confidential sources."

"No shit."

"I've already identified the interested parties, had meetings with them, struck deals."

"Good girl. Which is why I'm cutting you in. You'll save me time and energy."

"Fuck you."

The chief stopped the tape. "Good work."

I didn't feel like I'd done good work. Looking back toward the hotel, I spotted Gunder hurrying out of the 59th Street entrance and into the back of a waiting limo. The limo headed south and disappeared behind a veil of snow.

"Now what?" I said.

"We'll let her have her head for a while. See who else is mixed up in this."

"You planning on prosecuting her?" I said.

"I dunno. I don't think Langlois would want the publicity. But she'll never work in the security industry again."

"Fair enough," I said.

"Get in." The chief unlocked the sedan's doors. "I'll give you a lift."

I thought about it. The snow stung my face and clung to my coat. "No, thanks, chief. Think I'll take a walk."

"See you around, Beckett. Say hi to Destiny for me."

"Will do." I turned away and trudged north into the winter no-man's land called Central Park.

CHAPTER 41

"I'M SORRY," DR. Goldsamp said.

"No problem." Destiny waved off the apology as she stepped into the doctor's office, sat in the usual chair. "I didn't mind waiting. I'm in no hurry for once in my life."

"I wasn't apologizing for the wait," he said.

Destiny made eye contact. "What're you saying?"

"May I come in?" a voice said.

Dr. Marcus Ian appeared in the doorway, his winter coat unbuttoned, colorful wool scarf fashionably askew.

"Marcus," Destiny said with a slight, tentative smile.

Dr. Ian stepped into the office and kissed Destiny on the cheek. His full lips were cold against Destiny's warm skin.

"I hope you don't mind." Dr. Ian slipped off his coat, hung it on a hook behind the door. "I wanted to be here."

"Not at all," Destiny said. *Wanted to be here for what?*

The doctors shook hands and griped about the frigid weather. Dr. Ian pulled up a chair and sat alongside Destiny.

"Can I get anyone anything?" Goldsamp said. "Coffee—high test and decaf. Tea. Soda. Bottled water?"

Destiny and Dr. Ian said no, thanks.

"Let's get started then." Goldsamp took his glasses off and sat back in his chair. "There's no easy way to say this. The results of the MRI are conclusive. You have a brain tumor."

"Oh." Destiny looked off into space, letting the news sink in, fighting an emotional free fall. She thought she'd prepared herself for a worst case scenario, now she wasn't so sure. She sucked in a deep breath, let it out. "Now what?"

"We could try a combination of radiation therapy and chemotherapy to slow it down. Steroids and anti-convulsants can help. But in the end…."

"Slow it down?" Destiny said. "Can't you stop it?"

"Doubtful," Goldsamp said.

Destiny stared expressionless at the neurologist: What was he telling her? "I don't understand."

"I'll show you." Goldsamp reached for a flat-panel computer screen situated on his desk and spun it around so Destiny and Marcus had a clear view. Using a mouse, Goldsamp clicked on several icons. An image of a skull appeared on the screen.

"This case is more advanced than yours. See, everything appears normal from this view." Goldsamp spun the three dimensional MRI image with the mouse and then stopped. "Here." He used a pen to point at a dark patch on the brain stem. "Malignant tumors grow the way a plant does, with 'roots' invading various tissues. See how it extends into the deep areas of gray matter and down the spine?" He pointed to a series of root systems.

"Now, here's your MRI." He clicked the mouse and another skull, Destiny's, appeared on the screen. "As you can see, your tumor is not as developed." Goldsamp pointed at a dark patch on Destiny's brain stem. "But the location is, well, critical."

"What about surgery?" Destiny said, swallowing hard.

Goldsamp took off his eyeglasses. "Absolutely," he said. "But there's a risk of damaging critical neurological functions."

"So, you're saying, if the surgery didn't go right—".

"You could lose the ability to think, see, speak," Goldsamp said. "Or even move."

"I'd be a vegetable?"

"It's possible," Goldsamp said.

"What if I choose not to have surgery?"

"If you're lucky," Goldsamp said, "about twenty-five percent of females survive for five years following the diagnosis of a primary or malignant brain tumor."

Destiny hung her head. She took another deep, shaky breath. "Be honest with me. I'm not gonna be one of the lucky twenty-five percent, am I?"

"I doubt it." Goldsamp shook his head. "I'm very sorry."

Dr. Ian reached out and took Destiny's hand. She looked away, fought back tears.

"Are you sure I can't get you anything?" Goldsamp said.

"I don't believe this," Destiny said, weakly. "Really, I don't." She addressed Dr. Ian. "There's no cancer in my family of any kind. Certainly no brain tumors."

"Heredity is not always a factor," Goldsamp said.

"But why?" Destiny said, sounding pathetic even to herself. "Why me?"

"Destiny," Dr. Ian said, "I assure you that Dr. Goldsamp will make every effort to treat and relieve your pain and other symptoms. He will not abandon you."

But Destiny had already started thinking along other lines. "I killed a man," she said almost to herself. "God's punishing me."

The two doctors exchanged worried glances.

"How about other opinions?" Dr. Ian said.

"Of course," Goldsamp said. "I can recommend several highly qualified specialists. He handed Dr. Ian a typed list of doctors. "And there's a hospice I'd like to refer you to, Destiny: Calvary, a truly wonderful organization."

"Hospice?" Destiny forced a laugh. She wasn't going that

route. "That won't be necessary, Doctor." She stood abruptly and shouldered her purse. "Thank you for your candidness." She turned and practically ran out the door.

"Go after her, Marcus," Goldsamp said.

Dr. Ian caught up with Destiny just outside the clinic. She was leaning against a car, staring down at the pavement, breathing heavily.

"Destiny?" He approached cautiously, took a position alongside her. They stood silently as several laughing men in tuxedos walked by.

"I'll get a second opinion," Destiny finally said.

Dr. Ian handed her the list of specialists that Goldsamp had given him. "That's always a good idea."

Destiny turned to look at Dr. Ian: tall, handsome, educated, a caring gentleman. They would have wound up as lovers, she was certain of it. But now there was no reason. There was no hope.

"A second opinion won't do me any good, will it?"

"No," Dr. Ian said. "I don't think it will."

Destiny and Dr. Ian walked slowly down Fifth Avenue through the wintry air, past the Pierre Hotel, across East 59th Street. Walked until Destiny paused outside the garage where she'd parked her VW.

"Thank you for your kindness, Marcus." She extended her hand. "We won't be seeing each other again." Before Dr. Ian could speak, Destiny turned, walked down the garage ramp and disappeared from sight.

CHAPTER 42

DESTINY DROVE HOME in a daze. She unlocked her front door, walked into the apartment and knew immediately that something was wrong. She looked around: A rectangular white spot was left where a picture once hung. A TV, lamp, and some other furniture were missing. Papers were scattered everywhere—old bank books and deposit slips, charge card receipts. At first she thought she'd been burglarized until she checked and saw that Fernando's personal belongings were gone. She looked for his suitcases. His toothbrush and shaver. Not there.

Fernando had left her.

Destiny checked her clothes closet. Her dresses, jeans, shoes were undisturbed. Fernando had left a couple of music CDs on a high shelf, the ones he did not like. She walked into the kitchen and gazed at the one knife, one fork, one spoon, one cup, one saucer, one plate, one glass Fernando had left on the counter.

"I can't believe this." Destiny found an unopened bottle of rum in a cupboard, broke the seal, sat at the kitchen table, poured herself a shot and swallowed it in one gulp, poured another and swallowed that too. The booze hit bottom and she felt a sickening emptiness in the pit of her stomach. Her world, what was left of it, was coming apart.

Although Fernando had given her no warning, Destiny knew the reason he was gone. His inability to hold a job, coupled with his pathological lying, stealing, and gambling addiction had caused her to become more warden than wife. And Fernando would want no part of a sick wife.

Destiny poured another shot and tried to find some solace in the fact that she was planning on divorcing Fernando anyway, although that was not really the issue.

He dumped *her*. And that hurt.

Destiny reached for the phone and dialed Michael Beckett's cell. She left a message on his voicemail, then dialed his home.

"Hello," Solana said.

Destiny almost hung up. "Hey, Solana. It's Destiny. Michael there?"

Silence. Then: "No."

"Would you ask him to call me when you see him?"

Solana hung up.

"Bitch." Destiny placed the phone back on the charger.

She needed someone to talk to.

That someone had always been Beckett. But from the first time they met, Solana had made it crystal clear that she believed Beckett and she were more than friends. Not that Destiny blamed her. Beckett and she shared a chemistry that many misunderstood.

Destiny's doorbell rang. Her heart skipped: Maybe Beckett had stopped by. She hurried across the room, threw the door open and was greeted by a middle-aged man in a somber blue suit.

"Destiny Jones?" the man said.

"Yes."

"I'm serving process." He handed Destiny a folded legal document. "Sorry," he said and walked away.

Puzzled, Destiny looked after the man for a brief moment, then closed the door. She walked back into the kitchen, found her reading glasses, and perused the document: divorce papers.

Fernando was accusing her of "constructive abandonment," whatever the hell that was.

Destiny tossed the document aside. It sailed off the kitchen counter and onto the linoleum floor, landing on a pile of, what had to be, Fernando's discarded personal papers.

Destiny spied something of interest.

She plucked it from the pile; the personal check Fernando had stolen from her checkbook—he'd made it out for $1000, forged her signature but had not cashed it. And there was a pawn ticket receipt. Fernando had received $1,800 for her watch and diamond earrings.

Feeling a slow burning sensation in the pit of her stomach, Destiny continued to scan the remaining papers. She stopped when she came upon an old, dog-eared doctor's brochure. Destiny opened it up, found a receipt with Fernando's name on it. She perused the paperwork, read and then re-read the date. According to the receipts, Fernando had had a successful vasectomy procedure performed three months before they were married.

Son of a bitch.

Feeling overwhelmed, Destiny dropped onto a chair. She closed her eyes, felt suddenly numb. And for the first time in her life she contemplated suicide.

CHAPTER 43

I HADN'T BEEN able to get the last rocker raid out of my mind. My rash decision had almost gotten my team killed. I was losing sleep. Had nightmarish dreams of the raid turning deadly: of my rockers and me being ambushed. Shot. Killed.

Solana felt the pressure too. She'd lie awake at night and watch my fitful sleep, hear me talk in my dreams. My body would glisten with sweat, thrash in spasms. One night I yelled, "No!" and bolted out of bed, my heart pounding and fists clenched.

"We have to talk, Michael," Solana said early one morning on her way to work. I watched lasciviously as she sat on our bed, pulled silk stockings on her long shapely legs and affixed them to a black lace garter belt—I'd never seen her wear a garter belt before.

"Talk about what?"

She slipped on a pair of four-inch high heel shoes—another first—pulled a form-fitting sweater over her head, fluffed her thick hair, checked herself in a mirror.

"Us," she said.

"Okay," I said.

Here it comes.

Solana followed me into the living room. She sat on the arm

of an easy chair. "I don't know the right way to say this so I'm just going to blurt it out, tell you how I feel."

I nodded, waited for her to get to it.

"This—". Solana stopped. "I mean, we; I mean us; we're not working anymore."

Wow. Just like that. I sat on the couch, tried to compose myself, think of what to say. "This about Destiny again?"

"It's about a lot of things." Solana yanked her sweater sleeves up. "Our relationship has become too hard, Michael."

"I don't understand."

"You're not the same man I fell in love with."

"I'm not?"

"You blame yourself for your sister's death. You're sick with guilt, obsessed with assigning blame. Revenge. You brood. Drink too much. Have nightmares."

"Everyone has nightmares."

"You're moonlighting at something you don't want me to know about, aren't you? Something dangerous. Something to do with Shannon."

I sat there dumbfounded, mystified by her keen insight.

"So you're moving out?" I said.

"Yes, I'm moving out."

"Great. Typical female," I said. "Things get tough, you bolt for greener pastures."

"I didn't expect you to understand."

"There's someone else, isn't there?"

Solana stood, signaling that the conversation was over.

"Why the high heels, the garter belt?"

She picked up her house keys and purse.

"You're not going to answer me?"

"I've hired a mover," Solana said. "I'll be gone day after tomorrow." She headed to the door, opened it and stopped. "Oh, by the way—." She turned and looked at me. "Who's Enia?"

Now, that caught me off guard. "Enia?"

"You called to her in your sleep last night."

I was taken aback by that revelation. I didn't remember dreaming about Enia. Yet, come to think about it, there was some vague memory. Yes, now I recalled. I had indeed dreamt about Enia: I had her bent over my bed, thrusting deeper and deeper inside her. Enia saying, "Michael, treat me like a dirty girl, treat me like a dirty girl," over and over again.

"Enia is someone from my past."

"Didn't sound that way to me," Solana said. She walked out of our apartment and closed the door behind her.

CHAPTER 44

AN ICY WIND blasted Woodlawn Cemetery in the Bronx. I knelt on the frozen ground and said prayers over my parents' graves, apologized for never having visited. I thanked them for being who they were: hardworking, solid, loving in that standoff and remote Irish way. Then I advanced to Shannon's tombstone and began struggling with my emotions. I looked toward a line of stately mausoleums beyond. The likes of F. W. Woolworth, Jay Gould, and J. C. Penney were interred in those mausoleums.

"I'm doing my best, Shannon," I said, my words hollow. "I ran off Lochlainn O'Brian, but the drugs are everywhere. I don't know if I can ever stop them." I glanced north toward Woodlawn, a community in the north Bronx where Shannon was born and we were both raised. A neighborhood populated by mostly "off the boat" Irish.

"I knew you'd be here," Destiny said.

Startled, I turned and regarded my friend. Her cheeks and nose were discolored from the cold. She looked tired, no, haggard.

"How could you know?" I said.

"You told Vernon."

Destiny blessed herself, knelt on the frozen grass, and said a prayer over Shannon's grave. "C'mon," she said when she'd finished. "Let's get warm."

We retreated to her car. She started the engine, turned the heat to high. "You're not answering your cell phone," she said. "There a reason?"

I pulled off my gloves, held my hands up to the heating vents. "Solana's gone."

"Gone. What's that mean?"

"We broke up."

"You broke up with her, or she with you?"

"I got dumped."

"Figures." Destiny scrunched her face, shook her head.

I smiled slightly at that crack. "I take it you're assuming it was my fault?"

"Duh?"

We were silent for a long moment.

"I'm thinking I should be more upset about this breakup," I said, "but I'm not."

"How do you feel?"

I thought a moment. We hadn't been a couple for quite a while. We were leading separate lives. And I wouldn't miss dealing with her constant depression. "Relieved. I guess."

Destiny stared off through the windshield. "I came home last night. Fernando was gone. Took all his things. No note. No message of any kind. Looks like he's not coming back."

I allowed the news to settle in. My first instinct was to say, Congratulations. Good riddance. You're better off. I mean, she was planning on divorcing him anyway.

"It's just as well." Her lips quivered. "Our life together was one big lie." She used her coat sleeve to wipe tears from her eyes. "Remember when having a family was the most important thing in his life? It's all he ever talked about?"

"How could I forget."

"The lying prick had a vasectomy *before* we got married."

"He what? I don't believe it."

"Believe it."

"But why? Why would he make you think he wanted children?"

"Because he's a fucking narcissistic, lying, thieving, deceitful, lazy-assed deadbeat."

"Oh," I said. "Is that all?"

Destiny squinted at me.

I smiled. "Aren't we a couple of losers."

She looked off again. "Got that right."

"If there's anything I can do... I mean, you want me to shoot Fernando?"

Destiny couldn't stop herself from laughing. "There is something," she said. "A favor."

"Name it."

Destiny reached into a brown paper bag, pulled out a bottle of black rum, took a slug.

"You need a drink for courage?" I said.

"You have no idea." Destiny offered me the bottle. I took a generous swallow, handed the bottle back, and waited for her to get to it.

"Let me ask you a question," Destiny said. "Say a cop dies from natural causes. How much money would her heirs get?"

"I dunno." I shrugged. "I never thought about it."

"Well, think about it."

I gazed absently out the VW window. A group of gravediggers were having a tough time cutting into the frozen earth with a back hoe.

"If a cop had twenty years in," I said, "his pension; half pay before taxes. There'd be insurance."

"How about a cop like me with less than ten?"

I shook my head. "Not much. You could vest, I think. I guess you could take a lump-sum pension payout, depending on exact time in, rank. Why're you asking?"

"Just bear with me—what if a cop with less than ten died in the line of duty?"

This bizarre line of questioning started to bother me. "Where's this going, Destiny?"

"Just answer me: how much?"

"Lots," I replied, thinking about it. "It'd be like hitting the lottery."

"That's my point," Destiny said.

"What is?"

"The favor."

"You've lost me."

Destiny took a deep breath. "I need to die in the line of duty, Michael." She took hold of both my hands, looked me straight in the eye. "I want you to kill me."

CHAPTER 45

"SAY WHAT?"

"I want you to kill me," Destiny said.

"I repeat: Say what?"

Destiny went on to tell me about the severity of her headaches, the Hastings on Hudson rooftop blackout. Her visits to the neurologist, the battery of tests; the fact that the conclusive result of an MRI was that she had what amounted to an inoperable brain tumor, and only a short time to live.

"Are you sure?" I said, feeling an icicle pierce my heart. "There's no chance?"

"No chance I'm willing to take."

I could feel my mind glaze over, my tongue go dry, and my stomach turn to acid. I didn't know what to say, how to console my friend—her predicament amounted to a death sentence, a living, breathing nightmare.

"Never mind the fact that I'm facing a slow, agonizing death. If that was all, I'd eat my gun."

"Christ." I couldn't take anymore. I popped open the door and got out of the car.

Destiny followed close behind.

We strolled silently along a cemetery path. Took seats on a

marble bench that overlooked the stately Neo-Egyptian Woolworth mausoleum. The wind had died down. A light snow began to fall.

"I want my death to benefit someone," Destiny said almost inaudibly. "My parents are having a hard time of it, you know that. Dad lost his pension; they're both in failing health. They can barely afford to eat, what with the cost of doctors and prescription drugs. Last few months they've had to choose between food and their medications."

I didn't realize things were that bad.

"When I die," she continued, "they'll lose their only child. But I die in the line of duty, at least they'll be financially set for life, or whatever's left of their lives. I mean, I'm gonna die soon anyway." Destiny drank more rum. "I know this is a lot to ask, Michael, but I've got a plan."

"I was afraid of that."

She pivoted on the bench and faced me. "I'll get myself assigned to a Second Avenue foot post, up by Key Food. There're some old German ladies who walk their dogs same time every night by Elaine's."

"Elaine's?" I was incredulous. "You crazy?"

"There'll be plenty of first-rate eyewitnesses at Elaine's: network news anchors, gossip columnists, print and media reporters. We get lucky, maybe even an NYPD deputy commissioner or two."

She looked at me for approval but I slumped over.

"Don't stop now," I said miserably.

"I want you to steal a car, double-park it across the street from Elaine's. I'll be talking to the old ladies when you pull up. I'll comment on the fact that your car looks suspicious. The old ladies will be watching when I approach you on the driver's side. I'll knock on the car window. You roll it down. I ask for your license and registration. That's when you *do it*."

I flinched in horror at her words. "'Do it,' I said. "Just like that: 'Do it?'" I forced a brittle laugh. "Gotta admit, it's a good plan. Only problem is, you're out of your fucking mind."

"You're angry."

"Goddamned right I'm angry. You come to my family's grave site, ask me to fucking kill you. Kill you?!" I threw my hands up. "I can't do it. I won't do it."

"You've shot people before."

"In self-defense, like you," I said. "But I'm not capable of shooting anyone in cold blood."

"What about Lochlainn O'Brian?"

I started to speak, then stopped.

"You'd have killed Lochlainn if the opportunity had presented itself. I know it; you know it. Now, don't bother to deny it."

I didn't.

"That's how I got the idea," Destiny said. "When I saw you with Lochlainn. When you had him on his knees. I saw that look in your eyes. I knew you were capable."

"It's personal with Lochlainn."

"And my situation isn't?"

"That's not what I'm saying."

"What are you saying?"

I drew in a deep, exasperated breath, got to my feet, paced up one side of the cemetery path, down the other. "What if we got caught? Huh? Have you considered that? You'd be DOA. I'd face murder charges—hell, maybe even the death penalty."

"We plan right, we won't get caught."

"Yeah," I said. "Right."

Destiny took another swig of rum, handed me the bottle. I took a huge swallow, handed it back.

"So," she said, changing the subject. "We still on for the rocker raid tomorrow?"

"Why? You're not planning on going? I mean, in your condition."

"My condition is why I have to. I'm not letting my parents inherit my debts."

"Look, Destiny," I stopped and placed both my hands on either side of her. "I don't want you on the rocker raid. You're my best friend. I love you, but—".

Her expression cleared. "You love me, Michael?"

"What? Yes, of course I love you."

"No." Destiny shook her head. "You know what I mean. Do you love me, *really* love me?"

"C'mon, Destiny." I let my hands fall from her arms. "What's that got to do with anything?"

Destiny moved close, picked some lint from my coat, lowered her voice. "You love me, you'll do this for me."

"Aw, that's bullshit, and you know it."

"Is it?" Destiny put her arms around me, buried her face in my chest and held me tight. "You're my best friend, Michael, the only one I can ask. The only person in the world I trust. Please, I want my death to have meaning."

I eased her away and held her at arms' length. "No," I said, looking her in the eyes. "Not a chance."

"All right," Destiny said, defeated. "I understand." She pulled away from me, headed back to her car.

I watched from a distance as she reached into the VW back seat and took out a bouquet of flowers. She stepped over to my sister's grave and laid the flowers at the base of her tombstone.

CHAPTER 46

" I DON'T GET this." I was perusing McKee and Serria's latest rocker's surveillance report, checking out the target tenement's schematics: alleyways, exits and entrances, fire escapes. "You're saying this gang is comprised of kids?"

"Central casting geeks," Serria said. "Nerds."

"But the landlord is terrified," I said. "I mean run-and-hide terrified."

"They're Columbia University students," Serria said. "English and political science majors. A couple are pre-law."

"From rich families," McKee said.

"Spoiled punks," Serria said.

"Doesn't make sense," I said, scratching my head.

"Obviously." McKee stretched a rubber band, aimed and zapped a roach off a wall. "The landlord scares easily."

It was 4:30 A.M. My rockers and I were sequestered in a crumbling, yet blessedly warm, unoccupied tenement apartment across the hall from the target. The physical setup was similar to the last rocker raid: There were no street dealers or runners to contend with. The dealers were selling out of a vacant West 106th Street tenement to a regular clientele. Yet this job had a few new twists. The landlord had informed me that the drug gang had, without his permission, installed a steel-framed door—breaking in was nearly impossible. They'd also secured the fire escape windows with heavy-duty steel gates and painted the glass black so that no one could look inside.

And so we were waiting for a buyer to show so we could rush the apartment, catch the drug dealers off guard. But an hour-long wait was causing my people to become edgy, increasingly restless. Adding to the pressure was the fact that no one had actually *seen* the drug dealers that morning. We had no idea who, what, or how many awaited us.

McKee aimed another rubber band, popped a fat roach off a windowsill. "That was five." He took aim at number six.

I was tired, fighting sleep, sitting on a filthy, splintered bare wood floor alongside Destiny. She was staring across the room at a pitted wall, a morose expression on her face—it struck me then that s*he was dying right in front of my eyes.*

After losing Shannon, both my parents, and Solana, the idea of losing Destiny was almost too much for me to contemplate. She was my best friend, closest confidant, an ally and cop I trusted more than anyone. I tried to envision life without her. I couldn't.

Serria yawned. He was at the front door peephole acting as lookout, doing his best to pass the time and ease the tension by cracking wise.

"McKee told his doctor he swallowed a bottle of sleeping pills," Serria said. "His doctor told him to have a few drinks and get some rest."

"Very funny. You idiot." McKee zapped Serria.

Serria grinned and tried another joke. "A hooker once told Beckett she had a headache."

"Your mama," I said.

"Kohlman's so broke, he goes to KFC and licks other people's fingers."

"Keep it up," Kohlman said, in yet another foul mood, "and I'm gonna shoot you."

"Kohlman's so broke he and his wife got married for the rice," Serria said, pressing his luck. "Kohlman's so broke, the bank asked him for their calendar back."

Kohlman lunged at Serria.

"Hey!" I shot to my feet.

McKee and I got between the two grappling men.

"Cut it out," I said, restraining Kohlman.

"Tell him to keep his fucking mouth shut," Kohlman said.

McKee held Serria back. "He was only joking," he said.

"Yeah," Serria said. "Fuck's your problem, Kraut?" Serria broke free of McKee and stalked to the other side of the room, sat on a chipped, dusty windowsill and brooded.

"You OK?" I said.

"No, I'm not," Kohlman said. "Look, I'm getting tired of waiting. We gonna do this or not?"

"Soon as a buyer shows."

"That's not good enough," Kohlman said. "Either we force the issue, or we come back another day."

He was right. I mean, for all I knew, the target apartment could very well be empty. The college boy dealers could be out somewhere partying. No one had come to the door since we'd arrived. I looked at McKee and Serria. "Best guess: What're we dealing with here?"

"Already told you." Serria lit a smoke, took a drag. "College punks. Geeks."

"Risks?" I said.

"Minimal," Serria said.

"This job's a piece of cake." McKee said.

Piece of cake. Yeah, right. That was what Mark Tesser told me before my first disastrous rocker raid.

"All right," I said. "Let's force the issue. I'll knock on the door, play buyer. It worked once before."

"They could be sleeping," Destiny said. "If they're not expecting a customer, waking them up would ruin any surprise. Like last time; remember what happened with the Jamaicans."

"She's right," Kohlman said.

"Anyone else have an idea?" I said.

"Yeah," Destiny said. "Didn't you tell us the floors above are vacant? That the landlord was planning on gutting the entire building, renovate so he could charge market rate?"

"Yeah," I said. "So?"

"We could try flooding them out," Destiny said.

We all looked at her.

"Have Serria and McKee break into the apartment directly above," she said. "Stuff the drains, run the water. They'll think it's some sort of major water leak. Happens a lot in these rat traps. They'll open the door eventually."

"Works for me," Serria said.

"I'm with the spic," McKee said.

"Then it's a go," I said.

Serria and McKee moved stealthily out the front door, edged down the hall, and climbed the stairs.

"This works," I said. "We won't have to forcibly evict anyone. The place floods the way I think it will, they'll leave on their own—job done."

"What about the drug money?" Kohlman said. "There's been drug money in every raid."

"Kohlman's right," Destiny said.

Serria and McKee came back into the apartment a few minutes later snickering mischievously.

"Well?" I said.

"We stuffed the sinks and bathtub," McKee said. "Ripped the guts from a toilet tank. Turned the water on full blast."

"Let's roll," I said.

We pulled on our masks, exited the surveillance apartment and took offensive positions on either side of the target apartment door.

It took about five minutes for the hallway ceiling to darken with moisture. A few minutes later water ran down the walls. The ancient ceiling would soon begin to flake, then fall.

All at once I heard movement inside the target apartment. Young men's voices, low at first, grew increasingly loud, frantic.

"Here they come." I readied my weapon.

The drug dealers unlocked their door, opened up.

"Freeze," I shouted.

The college boys, five clean cut adolescents, stopped in their tracks. They were completely surprised, sleepy eyed, half dressed, carrying two bulging black leather satchels—money and drugs? It was as if we'd happened upon a campsite and awakened a troop of Boy Scouts.

I lowered my weapon, felt foolish with our over-the-top show of force. These frightened kids would be no trouble.

"All right," I said. "Hand over the satchels."

"Fuck you, asshole," a guy with thick bifocal eyeglasses said. He threw a right cross. Struck me on the jaw. I grabbed him by the hair. Bounced his head off the steel doorframe.

Then *more* college boys came charging out of the apartment— what the hell? All at once the gang of punks was attacking us. Throwing punches. Executing karate kicks. Swinging baseball bats. It was as if we'd disturbed a hornet's nest.

McKee hit the ground with four guys on top of him. Serria was using his shotgun like a club, fending off the angry pack. Kohlman cold-cocked one guy with his shotgun butt. Knocked another one's teeth out.

I fired my shotgun. Shot into the floor. Walls. Shot into the ceiling. Wet plaster rained. The college boys, screaming obscenities, backed off momentarily.

"Hey!" someone shouted.

A slender, pasty-faced young man was holding a handgun to Destiny's head.

CHAPTER 47

"EASY, PAL," I said guardedly.

"Drop your weapons," Pasty Face said.

"Just take it easy," I said.

"I'll kill her."

"This ain't the movies, kid," I said. "We're not dropping our guns. You shoot her, and I'll blow your fucking brains out—it's that simple."

But Pasty Face didn't flinch.

"We represent the landlord." I said. "You're dealing drugs out of the building, he wants you evicted—nothing more."

Water was running down the grimy walls. The ceiling was sagging precariously.

"This place in uninhabitable now anyway," I said. "Just hand over the satchels before you go."

"Fuck you," Pasty Face said.

I held my tongue—he had the advantage.

"Out," Pasty Face told his gang. "I'll cover you." He kept his gun pressed hard to Destiny's head as his gang filed past my rockers, out the door, carrying the satchels.

"OK, now let her go."

"No way," Pasty Face said. "She's coming with me, just in case you get any ideas."

"No," I said. "She's not."

"I swear I'll kill her," Pasty Face screamed, clearly losing it. "I will."

Destiny threw out her legs and dropped to the floor giving me a clear shot. I fired.

Pasty Face was blown back. Crashed hard into a wall. He toppled over and lay face down on the soggy floor.

I helped Destiny to her feet.

Kohlman hurried to Pasty Face. "His shoulder's torn off." He shot me a dark look.

"Let the scumbag die," McKee said.

"Leave `im," I turned to McKee and Serria. "Get upstairs. Turn the water off." Then to Kohlman. "Call an ambulance."

Kohlman pulled out a cell phone, dialed 911.

"This was my last rocker raid," Serria announced as we hurried out of the tenement to the sound of an approaching siren. "I've had it."

"Me too," McKee said, as we piled into the van, massaging an injured arm. "Guess I gotta face it, I ain't a kid anymore."

"What's that?" Kohlman said, strapping on his seatbelt. "You're both quitting?"

"That's what we said," Serria started the engine, hit the gas.

"Well, I'm not," Kohlman said. "This raid was a bust. All we're gonna get is a measly twenty-five hundred from the landlord. Destiny? What do you say?"

Destiny pulled off her mask. "It's only a matter of time till someone gets killed."

"Majority rules," I said, quietly.

Gotta admit, I was actually relieved that my rockers were calling it quits. I don't think I ever could. To me, quitting would be tantamount to letting Shannon down—even though the stark reality was this: We'd routed some vicious gangs, made some money, but we hadn't made a dent in the drug trade.

And we'd done little to bring closure to my sister's death.

"That was our last rocker raid," I said.

"Yours maybe," Kohlman said. "Not mine."

CHAPTER 48

I TOOK SOME time off from the NYPD. Started with four weeks' vacation. Had more accumulated time in the bank in case I needed it.

Destiny continued to work at the 19th Precinct, Metropolitan Hospital emergency room post every day. Sometimes we'd meet at Elaine's afterward to visit Vernon, who'd fill us in on all the neighborhood gossip—Enia, sans husband, had been frequenting the bar. But then simple chores like driving her VW became a challenge and Destiny lost interest in socializing.

Mornings I'd travel to her Hastings on Hudson apartment and drive her to work. Afterward I'd pick her up and drive her to her doctor's appointments. (I became well acquainted with her neurologist, a very capable and caring doctor named Goldsamp). Then I'd drive her home. At times I'd sleep on her couch.

Although I tried to stay focused on Destiny's needs as much as possible, I couldn't escape the fact that watching her fade was breaking my heart. In an attempt to deal with my emotions, I exercised every chance I got, cut down on my drinking. I had trouble sleeping and dreaded each new day. But I hid my angst as best I could.

Destiny experienced mild depression and exhaustion after her chemotherapy sessions. Thanks to a medication Dr. Goldsamp gave her, the headache lessened, became almost bearable, but her prognosis did not change.

Destiny never complained.

I was humbled by her courage.

"I'm more afraid of the process of dying than of death itself," Destiny said one evening. We were sitting on the couch in front of her TV, watching a *Cheers* rerun—Diane had slept with Sam for the first time—and eating a sausage and pepperoni pizza. I opened my second beer; I was becoming adept at being a good listener and not commenting on Destiny's ruminations.

"You believe in heaven and hell, Michael?"

"I'm not sure what I believe," I said, adding a generous amount of crushed hot red pepper to my slice. "But I believe in something, a supreme being of some sort."

"I haven't been in a church in years," Destiny said.

"Same here." I folded the temperature-hot slice in half and took a small, cautious bite. "Even as a kid in Catholic schools, I couldn't relate—the virgin birth thing. Jesus rising from the dead never made any sense. Makes even less sense now."

Destiny put her slice down and looked off, deep in thought. "I wonder if I'll be forgiven for killing McFarland."

I finished chewing and swallowed. "There's nothing to be forgiven for." I cooled my burning tongue with a large gulp of cold beer. "It was you or him."

"That might not make a difference."

"Damned right it makes a difference," I said. "Morally, you have the right to protect your own life."

"There are those who would disagree."

"Yeah? Well, they're assholes."

Destiny smiled a little. "Must be nice to be so sure of yourself."

I stopped eating. Picking up the TV remote, I muted *Cheers*. "Look, you used necessary physical force. You were cleared by the

NYPD who, I might add, would've hung your pretty little ass out to dry if they saw the slightest opportunity. Stop beating yourself up over it."

Destiny nodded but I could tell I hadn't made the slightest difference in how she felt. She took the TV remote from me, turned up the sound.

"Wish I didn't have to go to work tomorrow," she said.

"Go on sick report. What's the difference?"

"I'm not going on sick report," Destiny said. "I'm gonna keep going to work. Get off the emergency room fixer. Get back to walking a foot post."

This was the first I'd heard about this plan. "You can't. Doctor Goldsamp said—."

"I know what the doctor said."

Goldsamp told her that, since she'd ruled out surgery, the end could come suddenly and soon. Destiny would lose motor functions: control of her speech, eyesight, hearing. She would experience quick, progressive physiological breakdowns.

"Are you ever telling your parents about your condition?"

"No," Destiny said. "They have their own problems to deal with."

"So, you're gonna keep going to work and—what?" I said in a hard voice. "Put yourself in harm's way, try to get killed in the line of duty?"

Her reply was just as tough. "Something like that, since you won't help me."

I ignored that remark.

"It's almost nine o'clock," Destiny said.

"Yeah?"

"My prescriptions are supposed to be ready."

"I'll go." I finished my slice. Slipped my coat on. Decided it was a beautiful night for a walk. And I needed to clear my head. Needed to get away from Destiny for a while.

I did not encounter a single soul as I hiked the hilly, tree-lined half-mile to the pharmacy. I breathed in the cold, fresh air. I was feeling bone-tired.

I needed to come to terms with the fact that, watching Destiny deteriorate day by day, was causing me intense psychological pain. I didn't know how much more I could take.

Being honest with myself, I didn't know whether or not I was capable of sticking with my best friend to the bitter end. I mean, there were alternatives: I could contact her parents, arrange for them to fly in and take care of their daughter. And Dr. Goldsamp was urging me to insist that Destiny consider a hospice; let the professionals handle things. That might be the best way to go, for both of us.

I had to wait an additional ten minutes for Destiny's prescriptions to be filled. I spent the time reading the Hastings on Hudson village bulletin board; lost dog and cat notices, homespun commercial services advertisements, a memorial service for a local fireman who died in the line of duty.

"Prescriptions for Destiny Jones," a pharmacist called out.

"That's me," I said.

"Got insurance?" the pharmacist said.

"No." I had to sign for the controlled substances and used my American Express card to pay the over $200 bill.

"Michael," a voice said as I was about to reenter Destiny's building. It took a moment for me to make out who was standing in the shadows. "Oh, great. How the hell you find me?"

Enia stepped into the light.

"No," I said irritably. "Don't tell me—Vernon."

Enia was wearing a full-length mink. The heels on her boots were six inches high.

"What the hell do you want?" I said.

Enia reached into her coast, took out an envelope and handed it to me. I looked inside; it was the money she owed me.

"I'd say thanks," I said as I pocketed the loot. "But I know you didn't drive all the way up here just to pay me."

Enia leaned against her idling car. "Last night Lochlainn O'Brian and his gang moved back into our hotel. They kicked in the lobby door. Came looking for us. Fortunately, we were out. We're lucky to be alive."

"Go to the 19th Precinct," I said.

"You said they wouldn't come back."

"Obviously, I was wrong.

"Alex will double your pay," Enia said. "And if Lochlainn dies, there's an extra five thousand."

Warning bells went off; could she be wearing a wire? "I don't know what you're talking about."

"It's your fault," Enia said. "If you'd killed him like Alex asked, we wouldn't be in this position."

I heard what sounded like an oceangoing ship's horn and looked off toward the Hudson River. "Like I said, I don't know what you're talking about."

Enia relaxed her posture and her coat fell open, revealing a short, tight black mini and boob-baring leather vest. I couldn't stop myself from leering.

"Remember how good we were together, Michael?" Enia's eyes slipped to half-mast, her grin was utterly self-assured. "We couldn't get enough of each other."

"I remember," I said reluctantly.

"I want you, Michael."

"What about your husband?"

Enia's smile was alluring, downright evil. "What about him?"

Enia offered her hand and I took it. She came off the car into my arms and I let my hands wander, caress, searching for a wire; she was clean. I caught her scent, looked deep into her baby blues, felt myself roused. Enia pressed her warm, moist lips to mine and the memories came rushing back—not erotic memories but vivid recollections of the pain and humiliation she'd caused me: her ridiculous, self-serving versions of the truth.

I broke the embrace. "No."

Enia stepped back as if she'd been slapped. "No?" She glared at me in disbelief. "You know you want me."

"No." I used the back of my hand to wipe her red lipstick from my mouth. "I don't."

Enia glared hatefully. "All right." She covered up, buttoned her fur. "If you won't help us, what about your men?"

I shook my head. "They won't be interested."

Her lips firmed into a tight line. "Please."

It killed her to have to say that.

I regarded Enia, the way she was looking at me with that familiar, feline aloofness. If ever I wanted to strike a woman, haul off and punch her fucking lights out, it was then and there.

"I'll pay you for the referral."

"You mean your husband will." I attempted a sardonic smile. "It was always about money with you, wasn't it?"

She smiled in turn. "What else is there?"

"Nothing, for you." I caught myself. It was useless trying to understand or reason with Enia.

"We're desperate," Enia said. "Help me; help us, or recommend someone else, and I promise you'll never hear from me again."

That caught my attention. "You swear?" I said. "You'll stay out of my life? Never bother me again? You swear?"

"I swear," Enia said.

I had to admit, it sounded too good to be true. But I said, "I know an ex-cop, but he's bloodthirsty, totally out of control."

Her face brightened with interest. "What's his name?"

"I'm just warning you. He's trouble."

"I'll take the chance," Enia said eagerly.

"On second thought, maybe you and he would be good for one another." I took out my cell phone, found Tesser's number.

"His name's Mark Tesser." Enia took out a pen and paper, wrote the number down.

"Thank you." Enia said.

I walked away without saying a word.

The elevator opened and I heard a loud argument.

Destiny's front door was ajar.

"Get out!" Destiny screamed.

I rushed into the apartment.

Destiny was on the floor. Fernando was straddling her.

"Fucking bitch!" Fernando grabbed Destiny by the hair and slapped her, hard. "Gimme the money."

Fernando never knew what hit him.

I dashed across the room, smashed him on the side of the face. Threw him across the room into a wall. Pictures flew as Fernando bounced off the wall with a sickening thud, and crashed to the ground.

"Michael," Destiny cried.

I kicked Fernando once, square in the face, then rushed to Destiny, pulled her off the floor, sat her on the couch. "You all right?"

"Yeah," Destiny said, breathless. Her face, a mixture of anger and fright, was beginning to swell. "Just get him the fuck outta here."

"Not a chance." I walked over to Destiny's closet and located a pair of handcuffs. I kicked Fernando onto his stomach and hand-cuffed his hands behind his back. I searched his pockets, found a glassine envelope with methamphetamine residue. I picked up Destiny's phone and dialed 911.

Two Hastings on Hudson cops arrived in minutes.

Destiny was too upset to speak to them.

I identified myself, handled the interview. "She's pressing charges." I handed the cops the glassine envelope. "I found that in his pocket. He's got priors, not sure how many, or for what."

"Don't do this, Destiny," Fernando pleaded as he squirmed

against the handcuffs. "I'm sorry. I love you. Don't do this to me, Destiny. Please."

The two cops roughly dragged Fernando to his feet and out of the apartment. I locked the door after them.

"Well," I said, "I could sure use a drink."

Destiny rushed to me and fell into my arms sobbing. I could feel her warm breath on my neck and face. I placed my finger on her chin, lifted her face to mine.

"It's over," I said softly. "He won't bother you again."

"I've been in love with you for a very long time," Destiny said.

I couldn't move, breathe, or think. Time seemed to stand still. I looked deep into her eyes, saw that she was serious—and felt something akin to fire corkscrew into my heart. I realized at that instant that I'd been a fool: involving myself in a string of dead-end romances when the woman of my dreams, the woman who understood me, the woman I loved, was my former partner and best friend.

"And I've loved you." I could feel my heart thumping. "We've wasted a lot of valuable time."

"There's no more to waste," Destiny said.

CHAPTER 49

I N THE FRIGID, pre-dawn hours a nondescript gray van roared south on snowy Second Avenue, made a left at 94th Street and came to a skidding stop half a block west of the German Hotel.

Mark Tesser shifted to park, then slipped an old mug shot of Lochlainn O'Brian out of a manila envelope. He handed it to Alex Schultz in the passenger seat, who handed it back to Hans Kohlman.

"I already know the punk." Kohlman passed the photo to the man sitting beside him. "I was part of the first raid."

Tesser turned to look at him. "Anything we should know?"

Kohlman thought about telling Tesser about the C-4 he and Beckett's rockers had found. Then thought better of it; he couldn't afford for the raid to be called off. His son's crushing medical bills were piling up. Besides, they had removed the Belfast Boys' stockpile. C-4 was expensive and hard to obtain. Even if the gang managed to acquire more, it would be packed away, hidden from view—unless the Belfast Boys were expecting them. "No."

Kohlman unbuckled his seatbelt, fiddled with his shotgun, preparing himself for what lay ahead. For this was not a normal rocker raid. This was an assassination. Alex Schultz was offering a bonus of $5,000 cash to whoever killed Lochlainn O'Brian; thus the mug shot. And every man there, including Kohlman, intended to collect.

"Let's get ready," Tesser said.

Tesser's rockers checked their weapons, readied their ski masks, adjusted their bulletproof vests.

"You know Michael Beckett well?" Schultz said to Tesser.

Kohlman cocked an ear.

"Well enough," Tesser said. "We worked in the same precinct. Why?"

"Was wondering," Schultz said. "What kind of guy is he?"

Tesser grinned. "'Cause he dated your wife?"

Schultz looked surprised.

"I keep tabs on Beckett," Tesser said. "We were never friends but I felt bad about what happened to him."

"What did happen?"

"Drugs were found in his car."

"Really," Schultz said. "Beckett a drug dealer?"

"Hell no," Tesser said. "Beckett's a fuckin' Boy Scout."

"But you said drugs were found in his car."

"He made underworld enemies," Tesser said. "A drug dealer hired someone to plant the drugs, then tipped the Internal Affairs cops."

"You know that for a fact?" Schultz said.

"I do."

Kohlman watched Schulz's reaction.

"Then how come you didn't go to the authorities?" Schultz said. "Back Beckett up? Don't cops stick together?"

Tesser smiled self-importantly. "I said I felt bad about what happened. I didn't say it shouldn't have happened."

"I don't get it," Schultz said.

"You're not supposed to."

Schultz did a double take. "You mean you *know* who planted the drugs?"

Kohlman and the rest of the rockers stopped to look at Tesser. Most of them were not fans of Michael Beckett's, but they were, after all, cops.

"I don't know shit," Tesser said a little too forcibly; the obvious lie was left hanging in the air. He pulled on his ski mask. "You're sure you wanna come along?" he said to Schultz, changing the subject. "Things could get hinky fast."

"I'm sure." Schultz slipped on a ski mask that Tesser had given him. "I wanna see Lochlainn O'Brian dead."

Tesser shrugged indifferently. "You're paying the bills." He pulled out a revolver and offered it to Schultz.

Schultz waved it off. "You're the experts."

Tesser put the revolver away, shifted to drive, tapped the gas. "Here we go."

"They're here," Rat said to Lochlainn O'Brian over the cell phone. Rat was sequestered in the Schultz's first floor apartment, watching the street.

Lochlainn threw back a generous slug of twelve-year-old Irish whiskey, took his arm from around his girlfriend, Freckles, and checked the time: 4:21 A.M. "Where?"

"They just pulled up," Rat said. *"One got out, went around back. The rest're just sitting there."*

Lochlainn smiled. So the phone call was not a hoax.

A woman had phoned Lochlainn, left a message saying that Schultz had once again hired the masked men to evict his gang from the German Hotel. Said that this time Schultz himself would participate. Freckles had recognized the woman's accent. She swore the caller was Schultz's wife, Enia.

"Everyone ready?" Lochlainn said.

"Ready," Rat said.

Lochlainn ended the call.

What, he wondered, would prompt a woman to betray her

man? Money, he concluded, had to be. With women it was always about the money.

Lochlainn rose and his two pit bulls scampered to their feet. He picked up a 9mm automatic, checked that it was loaded.

"Go in the bedroom, Freckles. Lock the door. Watch TV or something. This'll be over soon."

Freckles did as told without comment, went into the front bedroom, closed and locked the door, switched on the TV.

Lochlainn heard a noise at the rear of the suite and the dogs charged into the rear bedroom. He was glad that he'd thought to string razor wire on the fire escape and paint the glass black. It would be difficult for anyone to get in, impossible to see in.

"No," Lochlainn said. The dogs at once settled down.

Lochlainn opened the door to the suite, stepped into the hall. Half a dozen heavily armed Belfast Boys were milling about.

"Let 'em come to me, eh?" Lochlainn said. "Remember, stay out of sight. No one fires until I do."

The gang indicated that they understood.

"Kill the lights," Lochlainn said.

The gang spread out, used guns to break the hallway lights, leaving it in total darkness. Then they split up as planned, filed into several empty suites, closed and locked the doors behind them.

Lochlainn's cell phone vibrated. "Yeah?"

"Five guys in ski masks heading our way." Rat said. *"They got shotguns, automatic weapons."*

"Get up here, quick." Lochlainn put the cell phone away. He walked back into the main suite, lit a cigarette, took a long drag, and exhaled.

Lochlainn heard Rat rush up the stairs and thump down the hall. Entering the suite, he went straight for the Irish whisky. He poured himself a shot, drank it down.

"Look, lad," Lochlainn said. "I'm sorry about this."

"Sorry?" Rat looked puzzled. "About what?"

Lochlainn drew his weapon and cracked Rat hard on the head. The pit bulls reacted to the violence, pacing fretfully as Lochlainn squatted alongside the prone, unconscious man. He removed Rat's wallet, took out his own wallet, and switched them.

"See you in hell, lad."

Lochlainn heard the men enter the building below. Slow, muted footfalls hit the stairs; the masked men were in no hurry. Lochlainn signaled for his dogs to follow. He opened the suite door, set a trip wire. Backed out and closed the door ever so gently behind him.

Alex Schultz led Tesser's rockers up to the pitch-dark fourth floor landing. They stopped, switched on flashlights, listened.

"Son of a bitch," Schultz said, examining the shattered hallway light fixtures. "Know what these fixtures cost me?"

"Which suite?" Tesser whispered.

"Fourteen," Schultz said. "End of the hall, on the right."

Tesser's rockers tried the doors to several other suites—-they were all locked—as Tesser moved down the hall. He came abreast of suite fourteen, placed his ear to the suite's door, listened. A TV was playing.

Tesser keyed his radio. "Talk to me."

"Can't get near the window," the rocker on the fire escape said. *"There's razor wire everywhere."*

"10-4," Tesser said.

"Now what?" one of Tesser's men said. "We don't know how many are in there, if they're awake; they could've seen us pull up and be ready for us."

"We're going in," Tesser said. He took several steps back, preparing to kick the door in.

"I wouldn't do that," Kohlman said from down the hall.

But Tesser didn't hear him, wouldn't have stopped if he had. He took a step back, lunged forward and kicked the door open.

Lochlainn O'Brian, sitting down the street from the German Hotel in a stolen car, saw the flash of light, followed by a loud, flat boom. The pit bulls freaked as the German Hotel's fourth floor windows blew out. Slivers of glass, splinters of wood, and chunks of brick pierced the morning air. A dozen car alarms went off in unison.

A second, even more powerful explosion rocked the neighborhood. Everything above the hotel's first floor was obliterated. The building was swiftly engulfed in flames.

One by one, apartment lights flicked on up and down the block. Terrified neighbors opened their windows, stuck their sleep-tousled heads out into the cold, gaping at the inferno. Within minutes the German Hotel buckled and then collapsed in on itself as flames shot to sky. Thick black smoke roiled.

"Quiet!" Lochlainn screamed at the dogs. As the sound of sirens filled the air, he tossed a cigarette butt out the window, put the car in gear and drove slowly away.

CHAPTER 50

I SPOTTED THE perfect car in the long-term parking lot at LaGuardia Airport: American made, a plain-looking late model with tinted windows and a kick-ass V8. I waited until an ex-cop I knew relieved the steady parking lot security guard for dinner. Then I slipped on leather gloves, climbed the hurricane fence, hot-wired the vehicle and headed to the exit.

"When're you back in the booth?" I said, noting that the parking lot security camera was pointed to the ground. It would be repositioned soon as I left.

"Eleven," the ex-cop said.

"See you then." I hit the gas, pulled onto the Grand Central Parkway and headed to the westbound Long Island Expressway and the Queensboro Bridge. There were no tolls or EZ-pass scanners or cameras that might allow authorities to trace the stolen car's movements.

I took the bridge's upper roadway, rolled into Manhattan. Turning north on Third Avenue, I slowed to check out a few of the singles bars I frequented. Every place seemed to be doing a brisk business. The frigid temperatures obviously did little to dissuade the barflies, the lonely, and the lovelorn.

I made a right on East 96th Street, a right on Second Avenue and marveled at the clutter of police and fire department vehicles; there were network and local news vans and trucks, their satellite disks extended into the sky.

I steered to the far left lane and slowed as I passed the street on which sat the remains of the German Hotel. The entire block was sealed off with barricades and yellow crime-scene tape. Teams of investigators from the NYPD, FDNY, FBI, and ATF scurried about. In front of me, a car pulled out. I parked between two news vans.

I walked around fire trucks, groups of on-air TV reporters and camera men rolling tape and approached a 19th Precinct cop who was standing by a police barricade smoking a cigarette.

"Hey, Beckett," the cop said. "Sorry about Kohlman."

"Yeah. Anything new?"

He shrugged. "Eight bodies, so far."

"Any females?"

"Possibly. But I don't think they can tell."

I looked down the street. If there were a female body it had to be Enia's. Hated to admit that, deep down inside, I hoped it wasn't.

"They have a cause yet?" I said.

"Gas leak," he sneered.

A reporter stuck a microphone in our faces. "What're federal investigators doing at a common residential gas explosion?"

The 19th Precinct cop shrugged. "Fuck should I know."

I walked away, took a serpentine path down the busy block around fire fighters, investigators, official vans and trucks and stopped in front of what was left of the German Hotel. I watched as a recovery team dragged two black body bags from the ruins and placed them into the rear of a New York City Medical Examiner's mobile morgue wagon; I wondered who the dead were.

I gaped at the pile of smoldering rubble—total devastation—and saw that the tenements on either side of the hotel were severely damaged, their brick walls buckling and residents long evacuated.

This was no gas leak.

Lochlainn O'Brian had obviously gotten his hands on more military grade C-4 explosive. But C-4 couldn't go off by itself. So what had happened here? Were the Belfast Boys building a bomb that was detonated by accident? If so, who or what was the intended target?

I walked over to the morgue wagon, said hello to an attendant I knew—a ghoulish stub of a man—and asked to see a list of the dead.

"The bodies are in pieces," the attendant said. "Can't even determine the sex until we autopsy. We found ID on some of them, but we're still waiting for dental record verification." He handed me a clipboard.

I said thanks and scanned the list of the tentatively identified: Alex Schultz. Lochlainn O'Brian. Mark Tesser. And my friend, Hans Kohlman.

So Enia had given Tesser's contact information to her husband. He'd hired Tesser's rockers of which Kohlman had become a member—I was afraid that might be the case. Here was yet another death I'd spend my life feeling guilty about.

I wondered what Kohlman's wife Helga would do now about her son's medical bills. Had Hans had the foresight to provide for them? I vowed to call Helga ASAP, see if there was anything I could do.

An NYPD mobile command center truck's rear door opened and a uniformed cop tipped his hat as a dozen federal and local investigators rushed to help a leggy woman in six-inch catch-me-fuck-me shoes step down from the vehicle; Enia was dressed in a sexy, sophisticated business suit.

An ESU bomb squad detective came up behind me. "That's

one lucky broad." The tall, potbellied cop reeked of fire and his blue NYPD coveralls were covered with soot and mud.

"She just lost her husband," I said.

"She wasn't in the building when it exploded."

"Okay. So she *was* lucky," I said.

"Since when you start believing in coincidences?"

I looked at the bomb squad detective, searched his face. "What are you saying?"

The detective smirked. "She's the sole beneficiary of a five million dollar life insurance policy."

Holy shit.

My eyes found the widow Schultz. Enia's eyes were red from crying. She was acting appropriately bereaved.

I knew from experience that she was utterly amoral. But could she have been somehow involved in the hotel explosion? Was Enia that cunning, that diabolical? I was confident that the NYPD Major Case detectives would find out.

My cell phone rang. I checked the caller ID but didn't recognize the number. "Beckett speaking."

A man's voice said, *"I own a building that's overrun with drug dealers. I need help."*

My response was hostile. "How'd you get this number?"

"I need rockers."

"I dunno what you're talking about." I heard a shout from the hotel rubble. They'd apparently found yet another body. "You've got the wrong guy, mister."

"Look," the landlord pleaded, *"they're dealing drugs to my daughter. She's only sixteen years old. It's only a matter of time until—".*

I stopped listening and forced myself to breathe.

It was then that I realized that my sister's role in my life had changed. The remorse I felt over her death had defined my life ever since. I hadn't been rocking for the love of my sister, I'd been driven by a need for revenge.

And guilt.

I'd been a lousy big brother. Truth was, I'd ignored Shannon, never wanted her around. And, yes, I'd felt guilty about all that when she died. But I now knew that vengeance was no cure for guilt. Rousting drug dealers wouldn't change a thing. I'd loved Shannon in my own way and I could only pray that she had known it. With that realization I felt my guilt lessen. For the first time since she died, I felt a sense of closure.

"Go to the police," I told the landlord.

"I did. They did shit. I need rockers."

"Look," I said. "Everyone knows rockers are a myth."

"That's not true," the landlord said. *"I know other building owners who hired them."*

"You're being bullshitted," I said. "There's no such thing as rockers."

I ended the call and checked the time. I waved thanks to the ESU cop as I walked back to the "borrowed" car.

I had a date with destiny.

CHAPTER 51

I PULLED THE car to the curb at 89th Street and left the motor running. I reached into a gym bag on the seat beside me. Out came my kelly green ski mask and the untraceable, .357-magnum revolver that Kohlman—God rest his soul—had given me after our first rocker raid at the German Hotel.

As fate would have it, the day of the German Hotel explosion happened to be the same day that Destiny was taken off the Metropolitan Hospital emergency room fixer and put back on full duty. She'd made certain that she was assigned to the Second Avenue foot post, across the street from where I was sitting, by Elaine's.

I inspected the .357, checked that it was loaded with hollow points, placed it on the seat beside me. I couldn't believe that I'd allowed Destiny to talk me into this.

Destiny had begged me to assassinate her last night while we lay in bed. Basically, she took up where she'd left off at Shannon's grave in Woodlawn Cemetery. Her headaches, she told me, were becoming unbearable. Her hearing, eyesight, and ability to walk were being affected.

"You're not just doing this for me," she said. "You're saving my parents. The money will free them from poverty. You're the only person in the world I trust. The only one capable."

I told her no. She persisted. I got angry. She burst into tears and told me she loved me. That if I loved her I'd do as she asked. She had been in such pain, so desperate, the end was so near, that I had agreed. I think I would have agreed to anything to ease her deepening despair.

Her plan was for me to double park in front of Rathbones bar, across from Elaine's on Second and 88th Street. Destiny would approach me in the illegally parked car, make an issue of asking for my license and registration. I was supposed to roll down the window, shoot her at point-blank range, dead center chest and roar off.

I looked at the murder weapon—the .357 lying there, black, shiny, deadly—and the enormity of what I was about to do came crashing down on me. I thought about what a single hollow-point round would do to the body of my ex-partner, best friend; the woman I loved. It would blow a hole in her the size of a fist, pulverize her heart and lungs, sever her spinal cord.

"I can't do it," I said aloud in the car. "I'm sorry, I just can't." I snatched up the gun, stuffed it, along with my kelly green ski mask, back in the gym bag, zipped it up.

I drove down Second, found a legal spot on 85th. Stepping out of the car, I walked north, into the wind, to the proposed crime scene.

The streets were teeming with the twenty-something set. Attractive young women were forced to tolerate lurid comments from a clot of drunken, cigarette-smoking sports geeks who wore their baseball caps backwards. Several wore Bermuda shorts. It was twenty-eight degrees, the wind chill made it feel like 18, and these chuckleheads were wearing shorts.

I glanced through Rathbones' plate glass windows—it was fairly crowded—and spotted someone familiar. I repositioned myself to get a better look. Road-kill was standing at the bar.

I slipped into Rathbones and bought a bottle of beer. Fading into the crowd, I stood where I could keep a clandestine eye on the toupee-wearing wife-stalker.

Road-kill was drinking a martini and seemed to be engrossed with the football game on the bar's TV. He did not appear to be drunk, brooding, or watching Elaine's; just another neighborhood guy stopped in for a drink at his local saloon.

I watched a bit of the football game, finished my beer and decided that Road-kill was not a threat, not tonight anyway. I paid for the beer, left Rathbones and took a position in a doorway next to the bar.

Destiny would soon walk south on her foot post and spot me standing in the doorway. She'd see that I was on foot, unmasked, and know immediately that I'd punked out.

She'd be angry at first, would not speak to me. Wouldn't take my calls. But I'd persist in calling and showing up at her door. Once she forgave me, I'd see her though her final days. I'd come to terms with the fact that, no matter the negative effects on me, I could not abandon Destiny. Ever.

I truly loved her.

I heard laughter and looked across the street. The familiar toothless panhandler was working Elaine's front door. Patrons were entering, others were filing out. The place was jumping as usual. The bar area appeared to be overcrowded.

I could see my friend Vernon glad-handing—I walked to the curb to get a closer look—of all people, Julie Gunder. The panhandler opened the door and Gunder stepped out, accompanied by none other than Mario the Asshole. Mario said something in harsh tones to the panhandler and shoved him aside. Then he and Gunder climbed into an idling black limo and drove away. A blue sedan squealed out from the curb and followed them—Bill Santic was driving. True to his word, Chief Vogt had Gunder under surveillance.

I glanced north and spotted Destiny standing under an

overhead street light on the west side of Second Avenue at 91st Street, right on schedule. She strolled south on Second, glanced into Ruppert Park, probably checking out the rodent population, in no hurry.

Destiny chased a double-parked car from in front of a fast-food store at 90th Street. She gestured to a motorist parked in a bus stop at 89th to move on. She stopped to say something to a couple of old women who were walking dogs. As she drew closer I couldn't help but be saddened by her startling weight loss. Gone were her womanly curves. Her uniform coat hung on her. Even her cap looked too big.

Destiny glanced across Second in my direction. But the Rathbones cigarette-smoking sports geeks blocked her vision. She didn't spot me lurking in the shadows. Instead she seemed to focus on a series of double-parked cars in front of the noisy bar. She must have thought I was in one of those cars.

Elaine's door flew open, and laughter and light spilled out onto the street. I saw two vaguely familiar middle-aged revelers stagger out, a tall gray-haired man and a frumpy albeit attractive older woman—Road-kill's wife and her boyfriend. The boyfriend tipped the panhandler, who dashed into the street and attempted to hail them a yellow cab.

Gunfire.

I flinched. Ducked. Spun.

Road-kill was at the curb, twenty paces to my right, firing at his wife and her boyfriend, using the roof of a car to steady his weapon. Pedestrians screamed, ran for cover.

"Freeze! Police!" Destiny was suddenly there, standing in the middle of Second Avenue.

Road-kill pivoted. Pumped out five quick shots.

Destiny lurched back. Staggered forward. Dropped to her knees. Fell face down onto the cold pavement.

"No!" I screamed. Pulled my .38. Shot Road-kill once in the

head. Grabbed his gun and ran blindly into the street—a taxi slammed on the brakes to avoid hitting me. I leapt back; that's when I saw the monster garbage truck barreling down Second Avenue heading straight for Destiny—the driver couldn't have seen her.

I vaulted over the taxi hood, raced across the street, stood over Destiny's body frantically waved my arms.

The garbage truck's driver hit his brakes; the truck went into a tail spin. It crashed into the row of double parked cars, was jolted back on course, skidded for what seemed like a fucking eternity, and stopped just inches before striking me and crushing Destiny.

I knelt beside Destiny. Rolled her over.

Her weapon was still holstered.

The bullets had stuck her in the arm, shoulder, and neck. Blood spurted from the neck wound.

"Destiny!" I pressed my hand against the wound, applied all the pressure I could in an effort to stop the bleeding.

Destiny pushed my hand away.

"Let me go, my love," she whispered weakly.

I didn't have the chance to acknowledge her dying request.

Her eyes rolled back, her breath seeped out.

And Destiny went still.

CHAPTER 52

A 19TH PRECINCT RMP screeched to a stop. Moynihan and his partner rushed out, guns in hand. I reached under Destiny, picked her up; she couldn't have weighed more than ninety pounds.

"Beckett!" Moynihan said. "What happened?"

"He shot her." I indicated Road-kill as I ran to Moynihan's RMP. Moynihan opened the rear door, dashed to the driver's seat. I placed Destiny in back, leapt in beside her, cradled her in my arms. "Go, go!"

Moynihan hit the gas, leaving his partner behind to deal with Road-kill and the aftermath of the shooting. He tore across Second Avenue, made a careening left onto 88th Street, a left on First Avenue. He grabbed the radio.

"Central, 19 Peter. We're transporting a shot officer to Metropolitan Hospital. Tell them to have a trauma team ready."

"10-4," Central said.

I kept my fingers pressed to Destiny's neck; she was bleeding all over me. "Stay with us, Destiny," I urged her but knew that I was wasting my breath.

My best friend, the love of my life, was dead.

The RMP raced into the hospital emergency room entrance

and skidded to a stop. I threw the rear door open and carried Destiny in.

"Trauma team!" I yelled. "Where's the fucking trauma team?!" I saw an unoccupied gurney and gently laid Destiny on it. That was when the trauma team converged. They pushed me out of their way, and proceeded to take Destiny's vitals.

"What happened?" a young, square-jawed doctor said to me. His nametag read Doctor Marcus Ian.

"She's been shot," I said.

"No pulse!" a trauma team member yelled.

"Area G," Dr. Ian barked. "Stat."

I watched helplessly as the trauma team propelled Destiny down the hall to Area G—the same place where Shannon had died.

I sat on a chair against a wall, not sure what to do, how to feel or act. I glanced around the emergency room, saw that every patient and hospital employee was staring at me.

I looked down at my bloody hands, they were shaking, tremors were causing my whole body to shudder; I knew I was in shock.

"I'm with you," Moynihan said, his hand on my shoulder. "The whole department is with you."

He was right. Within minutes the emergency room was flooded with cops of every rank offering to give blood and their support.

TV news crews and newspaper reporters tried to gain access to the hospital but were ordered out of the building and off the property. They and their vans lined up along the sidewalk.

"Make way for a cop killer," I heard someone say.

Road-kill was handcuffed to the stretcher that they wheeled him in on. An oxygen mask covered his face, blood stained the white pillow under his head—he had to be brain dead but still alive. Gone was the ridiculous toupee. I thought for a moment about pulling my weapon and shooting Road-kill in the brain one more time, finish him off; would have if I thought for a moment I could get away with it.

A couple of homicide detectives showed up and took me into what used to be Destiny's emergency room security office. I told them the basics: I was standing in front of Rathbones' bar, waiting for my ex-partner so we could have dinner on her meal hour. That I saw Road-kill shoot at his wife and her lover. That Destiny ordered him to drop his weapon and Road-kill shot her. I handed over Road-kill's gun.

"That's when I shot him. Once. In the head."

"You ID yourself?" the homicide detective said.

"Fuck no," I said.

"Just asking."

"Destiny married?" another detective said. "We need to notify her next of kin."

"Her parents…." There was a choke in my voice. I cleared my throat, tried again. "Her parents are her next of kin," I said. "I'll notify them personally."

Ten minutes later, a police department chaplain arrived, followed by the commanding officer of the 19th Precinct, the borough chief, the police commissioner, and the mayor of the City of New York. A few minutes later we got the official word: Road-kill was pronounced DOA.

My former commanding officer, the 19th Precinct CO, shook my hand as did the borough chief, the police commissioner, and the mayor. The very men who'd once persecuted me were now treating me like some sort of hero.

"You can choose any assignment you want," the borough chief said. "Any command. You name it." How ironic could it get? Destiny's life was the price of me escaping the fucking Building Maintenance Division.

McKee and Serria arrived about an hour later; they'd heard about the shooting on the news.

"There's a car parked down on Second and 85th." I gave them the plate number. "I don't have keys. It's gotta be back at Kennedy Airport long-term parking just after 11:00 P.M. And there's a gym bag on the passenger seat," I said. "Hold onto it, will you?"

"Done," Serria said.

As the media frenzy subsided, the mayor, PC, and most of the department brass straggled away. A man I recognized as Destiny's neurosurgeon, Dr. Goldsamp, rushed into the emergency room; what was he doing here?

I hurried over and collared Goldsamp.

"Doc. You here for Destiny?"

"Yes." He took a moment to shake my hand. "I've been informed that a bullet entered the base of her brain."

"You mean, she's alive?"

"She was," Goldsamp said. "Twenty minutes ago." He pressed an elevator button, stepped in, the doors closed, and was gone.

I walked across the emergency, fell into a chair.

Destiny was alive.

The hospital crowd thinned as the night wore on.

When I finally checked the time, I realized that Destiny had been in surgery for more than six hours.

Serria and McKee dropped off the car at Kennedy Airport and returned with Italian deli sandwiches and coffees. As we sat around Destiny's old office, they kept telling me not to worry. Destiny would pull through. Everything would be all right.

Of course I knew better.

"Lemme ask you something," McKee said, mercifully changing the subject. "How'd the C-4 get detonated at the German Hotel? I mean, that kind of damage, it had to be C-4."

"My guess," Serria said. "Lochlainn O'Brian."

We looked at him.

"He's dead," I said.

Serria shook his head. "They recovered his wallet. Not his body."

"You sure?" I said.

"Positive. I got a contact at the ME's office. His dental records don't match."

We all thought a minute, considered the implications.

"So Lochlainn planted the wallet?" McKee said.

Serria shrugged. "Who else?"

"And booby trapped the hotel?" McKee said. "So he had to be expecting Tesser and his rockers."

"Sure," I said. "That makes perfect sense. He figured Schultz would try to forcibly evict him again. He was right."

"Yeah, but how would Lochlainn know when?" McKee said.

"Good question," I said, and recalled what the detective had told me about Enia inheriting her husband's five million dollar estate. Far as I knew, she was the only one who stood to gain from her husband's death, *and* who was in a position to tip off Lochlainn about Tesser. But had she? Was she really that evil?

"So, bottom line, Lochlainn killed Kohlman," McKee said.

"Yeah," I said. "He did."

Make that one more score I had to settle with Lochlainn.

"Officer Beckett." Dr. Goldsamp, the police chaplain, and Dr. Ian came into the security office. The two doctors wore green surgical scrubs that were soaked though with sweat.

I rose apprehensively from my seat, knowing that the news would not be good. "Give it to me straight, Doc."

"All right." Dr. Goldsamp smiled.

The Chaplin smiled.

Dr. Ian smiled.

I wondered what the fuck they were smiling about. "Well?"

"Destiny is fine," Dr. Ian said.

That news nearly bowled me over. Stunned, I looked at both doctors before I said, "Say that again."

"You heard correctly," Dr. Ian said.

"I don't get it," I said, trying to control the tremor in my voice. "How can she be fine?"

"The shoulder and face wounds were superficial, not life threatening. However the third bullet lodged in her neck; that was critical."

"You see," Dr. Goldsamp said. "the bullet invaded the base of her neck, at the site of the tumor."

"Tumor?" Serria and McKee said in unison. "What tumor?"

I shushed them up.

"While removing the bullet," Dr. Ian said, "Dr. Goldsamp had no choice but to remove the tumor; successfully I might add."

Dr. Goldsamp went on to say that Destiny was in recovery. That, when she was transferred to the ICU, they'd run tests.

"We don't expect any complications," Dr. Ian said.

"So, she's all right?" I said, starting to feel light all over. "I mean, really all right?"

"Well, we'll have to keep a close eye on her," Dr. Goldsamp said. "Make sure the cancer hasn't metastasized any further."

"But she's got a chance," I said. "A real chance?"

"Let's put it this way," Dr. Goldsamp said. "A short time ago I gave her a twenty-five percent probability of surviving five years—and that was wildly optimistic. Today I'd give her an even chance; fifty, fifty."

A sudden surge of emotion overwhelmed me. I fell back onto the chair, covered my face with my hands.

EPILOGUE

DESTINY MADE A full recovery and returned to work just long enough for the New York City Police Department to retire her on a three-quarters disability pension, and award her not one but two Combat Crosses—one for the Key Food shootout, the other for the Road-kill toupee shooting.

I was transferred from the Building Maintenance Division (finally!) back to the 19th Precinct. Assigned to a sector car with a young lunatic who reminds me of my deceased partner, Vinnie D'Amato. We are already leading the borough in felony arrests.

No link was ever established between Enia Schultz and the German Hotel explosion. Enia took her five million dollars and flew back to her hometown in Romania; I'd like to say never to be heard from again. But I know better.

Last week's *New York Post* reported that a man previously thought to have been killed in the German Hotel explosion, one Lochlainn O'Brian, was shot to death on a Hell's Kitchen street. Witnesses stated that, at around 4:00 A.M., the victim stepped out of an Irish pub, and a man wearing a kelly green ski mask fired a single shot into his brain.

"It looked like an execution to me," one eyewitness said.

An untraceable .357 Magnum was recovered at the scene.

Dear Reader:

If you enjoyed this book, kindly tell your friends about it. And please post a review at amazon.com and/or barnesandnoble.com, or Goodreads. Thoughtful and positive reviews encourage a writer. And they help sales. After all, writers have to live and eat, just like real human beings. ☺

TF

*Please keep reading for a sneak preview of Thomas Fitzsimmons'
new novel, "Confessions of a Celebrity Bodyguard".*

Six years earlier

Grammy Award–winning singing sensation and international sex
symbol Audra Gardner expired on September 15 at approximately
12:05 a.m. Her two bodyguards, a retired New York City police
lieutenant, Shamus Beckett, and his son, moonlighting off-duty
police officer Michael Beckett, discovered Audra naked in the bedroom of her lavish twenty-million-dollar Manhattan town house,
lying face down in a pool of her own vomit. A hypodermic needle containing heroin laced with fentanyl—a powerful opiate usually found in patches given to cancer patients—was still stuck in
her slender arm. The twenty-one-year old, multitalented superstar
who was adored by millions, had died utterly alone.

Although she had received thinly veiled death threats—e-
mails, texts, and phone calls—from a mysterious individual claiming to be a divine messenger calling himself the Angel of Death—
the police found no evidence of foul play. Besides the lack of real
motive or other physical evidence, tracing the source of the easily
available heroin had proven futile. And so the medical examiner
ruled, over the vehement objections of her dogged senior bodyguard, that Audra's passing was an "accidental combined drug-
intoxication overdose." The superstar's recent, well-publicized
booze- and drug-fueled public meltdowns, arrests, and stints in
various rehabilitation centers left them no choice.

Which was exactly what the Angel of Death had anticipated.

He had attended Audra's rain-soaked funeral at Westchester County's Sleepy Hollow Cemetery. Hidden under an umbrella in a sea of umbrellas at the back of the crowd, standing beside the famous New York socialite Brooke Astor's tomb. Watching as a cherubic-faced minster delivered a canned graveside eulogy while, off to his right, he overheard Shamus Beckett telling a skeptical journalist that Audra had been murdered by the Angel of Death. All of this took place while Shamus's son Michael—*A heroically handsome Irish-American possessed of quick fists and a .38- caliber temperament,* according to one gushing female crime reporter— lurked menacingly on the fringes of the interment, scrutinizing the attendees.

Although Shamus continued to investigate Audra's death for months, he died never knowing that her slaying was a divine act of His love. That the Angel of Death was, in actuality, an Angel of Mercy. For he had saved Audra from further earthly suffering and, most importantly, the loss of her immortal soul. Saved her from becoming just another sad, drug-addicted has-been, a faded star to be pitied and forgotten. The Angel of Death would not allow that to happen. In death, the world would always remember Audra as a great talent and beauty. In death, she'd be immortal.

That was the Angel of Death's gift to Audra Gardner.

His gift to them all…

ABOUT THE AUTHOR

Thomas Fitzsimmons worked 10-years as a New York City Police Officer in the precinct dramatized in Paul Newman's "Fort Apache-The Bronx." His is a Vietnam era Navy veteran, film/soap opera/TV commercial actor and the former co-host of the NBC-TV magazine-format talk show, "Now". An A-list celebrity bodyguard, private investigator and recognized security expert, he has appeared on shows such as "Good Morning America," "Geraldo Rivera" and "Montel Williams."

COMING SOON...

CONFESSIONS OF A CELEBRITY BODYGUARD

www.thomasfitzsimmons.com

www.ingramcontent.com/pod-product-compliance
Lightning Source LLC
Chambersburg PA
CBHW052018240626
47153CB00006B/1863